NOT WITHOUT ME

HOT TREE PUBLISHING

MARIA DEAN

For information, contact the publisher, Hot Tree Publishing.

WWW.HOTTREEPUBLISHING.COM

EDITING: HOT TREE EDITING

COVER DESIGNER: BOOKSSMITH DESIGN

E-BOOK ISBN: 978-1-922679-87-1

PAPERBACK ISBN: 978-1-922679-94-9

*To my sister, because its_all_about_the_books_*

ONE

ALEX

THERE ARE MOMENTS IN MY LIFE WHEN I COULD quite easily murder someone. Not often, but moments, all the same.

Slamming the phone down, my hand almost reverberates off the receiver. No matter how many years I've done this job, it never ceases to amaze me how normal, rational people turn into complete idiots when it comes to selling their houses.

"You okay there?" Donna asks, emerging from the staff room with a large cup of tea in her hand. The side of the mug reads: *This is what an awesome estate agent looks like.* Above the words, a black arrow points straight up at Donna's concerned face. In this case, it's true. At forty-three, she's been doing the job long enough to have dealt with all kinds of people and houses. With neat brown hair pinned in a low tidy bun, a dark blue blazer with a matching skirt, and flawless make-up, she looks more like an air hostess—she's only missing the neckerchief and a trolley.

"Just Mrs Wells," I huff.

"Ballantyne Road?" She can't associate a name without an address.

"Yup."

"She's a nutcase, that one." Donna sets the mug down on her desk.

"No shit. Must be the third phone call this week."

"What was it this time?"

"She demanded to know why she hasn't had any more viewings."

"When did her house go on the market?"

"Last week." I tut. "She can't understand why it hasn't sold yet."

"It probably has something to do with the hideous bathroom." Donna smirks as she settles behind her desk, propping her feet on the caster stems of her chair.

"Or the fact that she has four dogs and hasn't cleaned since they were puppies. The only person who is going to buy that house is someone who has no sense of smell."

We return to our computer screens as I hear the familiar clunk of the door opening at the front of the shop.

"This could be him." Donna's eyes widen as they leave her monitor.

Leaning over my desk, I try to see what's going on,

but our desks are at the rear of the shop and positioned behind a large freestanding board advertising a conveyancing firm strategically positioned to give us some privacy.

"The email said afternoon, and it's just after one." She tilts her head toward the large clock on the back wall.

"Should we carry on working or stand up or something?" I wonder aloud.

Donna shrugs. A little jolt of nerves sparks in my stomach even though I haven't given the new owner of Malcolm and Co. a second thought.

The sale had been announced months ago. George Malcolm was heading for retirement, and with no family heir to take over the business, it was only natural he would sell. The only worry had been if our rival agents, Bowling Sales, would make a bid for the company.

Mathew Bowling is a name most people in the locality know. He's a creature of habit, a dinosaur who's been in the business longer than any of us, a great salesman but certainly not a people person. I've had to deal with many a vendor who's been in tears on the phone because of something Mathew Bowling had said or done. He's a bully, a cut-throat businessman who doesn't see the houses as homes. Yet they are busy, as people are always putting their houses up for sale with them even though they have a reputation for being the Rottweilers of the housing market. It amazes me when I drive home from work and yet another Bowling For Sale sign has popped up in someone's garden.

But we've been told it's an outsider who's purchased the business. Someone from down south. A man with money. A man with ideas.

"It's him," Donna confirms, half standing, half sitting now as she begins to smooth her hands down the front of her skirt.

I've paid little attention to the emails. I don't care who I work for, and I'm sure he won't be hanging around long, as he has a few other shops dotted about the county. Today's visit is probably just to familiarise himself with the staff and the area. There aren't many businesses that can't be run via Zoom conferences and emails. At best, I guess we'll get a yearly visit around Christmas, just to show goodwill.

Ian's deep baritone voice booms from the front of the shop. Having worked here the longest, Ian is the natural leader of our small group of staff. He's asking about the guy's journey here, the standard polite topics of conversation when meeting someone new and important.

"I think we should stand," Donna decides as she shuffles out from behind her desk.

Letting out a sigh, I follow, slowly pushing my chair back and rising.

"I can see him now," she whispers, craning her

head around the advertisement poster. "Oh my." Her face drops.

"What?" I hiss. "What is it? It's not someone we know, is it? Or someone you went to high school with and had a fumble with behind the bike sheds? Oh my God, it's the man who was flirting with you at Coolio's bar last year, isn't it?"

"No." Donna shakes her head. "It's worse."

"Worse?" I'm confused.

"Much worse."

Stepping from behind my desk, I'm desperate now to get a look at the newcomer. "How can this guy be worse than that?"

"Trust me, this is much worse." Donna shoots me a look, her face like stone, her eyes wide with… something. Surprise, maybe? "He's good-looking, as in drop-dead bloody gorgeous. God, it's about time we had a little eye candy about the place." She rakes a stray hair back into her bun.

"I thought you were a happily married woman." I smile, watching my colleague preen herself like a bird grooming its feathers.

"Happily married women are allowed to window-shop, and besides, I'd trade Ed in for this guy. Can you sell your spouse on eBay?" Donna queries. "I'm not sure what I would put in the description though. Used—definitely. In good working order? Maybe not."

I laugh. "This guy can't be so good-looking that you're considering selling your husband."

"Oh, he is. Dark hair, tall, broad shoulders, strong hands. He looks angry, like he'd shove your face into the pillow and tell you to keep your mouth shut. I hope to God he doesn't turn around, because I don't think I'll be able to cope with those tight trousers."

"I need to see this." Taking a step forward, I feel the little tingling fizz of excitement. "What did you say his name is?"

"Callum something, I think, or Cody? No, I've forgotten. I'll have to look in the email." Leaning over her desk, Donna begins to scroll through her inbox.

"I'm sure you'd like to meet the rest of the team, if you'll follow me." Ian's voice carries from the front of the shop.

"They're coming," I whisper, standing up straight and pressing my lips together.

"I can't find his name." Donna panics, letting go of the mouse just as Ian appears.

"Ladies, I'd like you to meet Cade Westwood, our new owner."

And the whole world stops.

Time halts and the air freezes as I'm thrust back to when I was fifteen years old, and the first time I heard that name.

Then

"When you ask me what I think, are you saying my opinion will matter, or is it one of those situations where it's going to happen whether I like it or not?" My eyes remain on my phone, the heat from my mum's stare on my bare skin. She hadn't approved of the cut-off shorts when they were on the hanger, and she looks even more appalled now I'm wearing them.

"Hey, come on, Alex, don't be like that."

"I'm not being like anything. I just want to know if it's a done deal or whether I actually have a say."

My mum sighs the kind of sigh she makes when she wonders what happened to her compliant little girl and when exactly I was replaced with a smartarse.

"His landlord is selling the house. He's been given weeks to find somewhere else to live. We were thinking he could move in here until he finds a new place."

"So, it's not forever?"

"Well, we can give it a go and see what happens."

"So, it could be long-term if things work out?"

"I'm not saying one way or the other. What I am saying is that I've been on my own for a while. Now this situation has presented itself, and it seems like as good a time as any to see what happens. And you like Mark."

I wouldn't go as far as saying I like Mark. He just isn't as weird or as nerdy as some of the other guys she's dated.

"It's not me who's dating him."

Her eyes soften like a dog's who is trying to convince its owner to give it another treat. "I really want this to work."

"Okay." I exhale my answer as if I'm agreeing to having Coke instead of Pepsi—no big deal. I don't want her to think I'm bothered by it, as it's obviously a big deal for her.

She breathes out heavily through her nose, like she's just cleared the first hurdle, but there's a secondary intake of breath, as if she's preparing herself for one more jump.

"The thing is, it won't just be Mark," she reveals. "His son, Cade, will also be moving in with us."

I look up from my phone.

DAYS LATER, I'M LEANING ON THE DOORFRAME OF THE small room that, for the entire fifteen years of my existence, has served as the dumping ground for sports kits, wellington boots, and mismatched furniture, and I wonder how they're going to fit a seventeen-year-old in here.

The room is directly opposite my bedroom and is one of only two bedrooms and a small shower room in the attic space of our inner terraced house.

This has always been my floor of the house, and I'm not sure whether I'm ready to share it.

Over the past three days, Mum and Mark have cleared the spare room of all its refuse and "spruced it up," as my mum keeps referring to it.

I've never met Cade. My mum has barely mentioned him in the nine months she and Mark have been dating.

Mark is tall and lean. He's the manager of a supermarket, a job which I struggle to place him in. I've only met him in passing, nothing meaningful—a fleeting "Alex, this is Mark," and he had bowed his head and offered a short "Hi there."

But Mark is going to be here in my house at the weekend. He'll arrive with his razor and his manager's uniform. His bike will be wheeled into the hallway, his car will pull up outside, and his son will be unpacked along with his other belongings.

Cade.

I know nothing about Cade other than that he's seventeen and goes to a different high school. "He's nice," Mum said— meaning she knows as much about Cade as I do about Mark.

Is he a skater, a nerd, a gamer? I need a label to imagine what he might look like.

Staring at the small bed, the freshly painted walls, and the new set of drawers, I continue to wonder about the boy who'll fit into this room.

TWO

ALEX

A VORTEX OPENS AS CADE FRACTURES MY LINE OF sight. I sway, gripping the back of my chair as he glares at me like I have three heads. Donna and Ian are like spare parts, extras in the background who need no attention paid to them. The air becomes thick like thunderous clouds on a red-hot day as Cade and I regard each other.

It doesn't matter how hard I try to push away the thought of the last time I saw Cade. His contorted face flashes before me; the feral anger and the seething pain had made him unrecognisable. Now, he's taller, his frame filling the small shop, his features darker than I remember and his eyes just as intense. He always had a presence, one that never failed to grab my attention, his glare making me feel like I was the only person in the room. On that count, nothing has changed other than that the boy I used to know has been replaced with a man — one wholly fuckable man.

Donna had not exaggerated. He's aged well, matured into something brooding and dangerous, someone who could make you drop to your knees at the click of his fingers. He clearly hasn't lost the ability to command female attention, as Donna is already under his spell.

She isn't the only one. I recall my best friend Anna meeting Cade for the first time.

Then

"OMG, why didn't you tell me Cade is an absolute hunk?" Anna wails as soon as my bedroom door is closed.

"I didn't think it was important," I reply, casually pulling a pile of clothes from my bed so Anna can sit down.

"Why would that not be important?"

"Sorry, I guess I've been a little distracted," I lie.

"You should've told me as soon as he arrived."

"He only moved in on Friday night."

"But that was two days ago. I could've bagged him by now if you'd introduced us on Saturday." Ignoring the space I've cleared for her, Anna slumps on the floor. "I can't believe you didn't mention how hot he is. You should've texted me. How old is he?"

"Seventeen."

"Is he moving to our school?"

"No. My mum said he's halfway through sixth form at his old school, so it seemed pointless moving him."

Anna wraps her long blonde hair around her hand as if she's squeezing water from it before she flings it back over her shoulder.

Her beauty accompanies her everywhere and makes her one of the most popular girls in our year. She's dated several boys, and Luke Penthouse holds the title for claiming her virginity.

"There's something about an older guy that makes them seem hotter, don't you think?" Anna says.

"He's not that much older than us, and I don't think he's that hot," I argue, but even as I say the words, I can feel Cade's eyes on me when he'd first walked through the front door on Friday night.

The preconception of the geek and the nerd had been blown way out of the ballpark when Cade had stood before me, wearing a black T-shirt and dark jeans, his height filling the doorway, his presence consuming the air. With the yellow tinge of a fading black eye and a scar above his eyebrow, he might as well have written the words Bad Boy on his forehead.

He'd shifted a box on his hip and stared as I'd gawked, taking in his grey eyes and heavy brow. Geek I could've handled. Nerd I could've dealt with. But a bad boy?

The box was full of trophies. Could he be into boxing? Had I read this all wrong, and he was just a talented fighter in the confines of a controlled environment?

Maybe.

Anna drags me back to the present. "Why would the fact that your new brother is superhot not be important?"

"He's not my brother," I snap. "Let's get that clear."

"So, what is he, then?"

"He's the son of the guy my mum happens to be dating."

"But what if they marry?"

"Let's not get carried away. They've only been together a few months. I doubt it'll last."

Anna shifts her legs from underneath her and goes back to twisting her hair. "Really?"

"Yes, really."

She waits for me to elaborate, but I'm not about to share my fears with my friend.

"Well, I hope it lasts long enough for me to get my hands on Cade. He's so fit and not like any of the guys in our school." Anna's eyes roll back in her head as she falls backward onto the carpet, her hands clutched to her chest. "I think it's the dark hair," she says, pulling herself back up. "Dark hair always seems to do it for me. And did you see the jeans he had on? God, they were so tight. Does he work out?"

I stare at Anna, wondering if I should interrupt her daydream, but I'm also thinking about Cade's jeans.

"I like a guy who takes care of himself, takes pride in his appearance." Her eyebrow arches, and I know what she's about to say; it's been brewing in the air ever since she laid eyes on Cade. "You need to help get us together. You're my best friend, and what a perfect situation for you to be able to orchestrate him going out with me. Please?" She clasps her hands under her chin in prayer.

There's no surprise here. This isn't the first time I've had to play a part in helping Anna get together with some guy.

"I don't know. It feels a bit weird."

"Weird how?" Her face drops. "You just said it's not like he's your brother or anything."

"It's not that," I explain, quickly trying to think of why it's weird. "It's more the fact of him sleeping in the next room." I nod toward the door. "What if you guys got up to something in there, and I'd be in here." I shiver.

"Okay, I agree, that's weird. So, we say we don't do anything under your roof. We'll use my house instead. Problem solved." Anna smiles as if her fairy godmother has just waved her magic wand. I'm in awe of my friend's confidence.

She waits, looking expectantly at me.

"I still don't know."

"What's there to think about? We would make the perfect couple, and can you imagine what our kids would look like? I think it's meant to be, him arriving here and you being my best friend. It's written in the stars." Anna twirls her hands up to the ceiling as if she's trying to catch a falling star.

I smile, but it's weak.

"Unless," she begins, sensing my hesitation. "Unless you like him?"

"No! God, no, that would be —"

"Weird," Anna interrupts. "Now that would be weird." She forces a laugh, but I don't laugh with her.

"No, it's not that. I'm not sure what it is. Maybe it's just the whole thing of him and his dad moving in. And I know *nothing about Cade. He goes out a lot, so I haven't seen him much. He could be a complete jerk."*

"I get that it must be hard on you," she sympathises. "But can you imagine how cool it'll be when I'm dating him? And no one really cares if you're a jerk when you're that hot." She wiggles her eyebrows, and I can't help but smile. "So, it's agreed." She holds her hand out toward me, ready to shake on the deal. "You'll help me bag the man of my dreams."

She beams as I examine her waiting hand. We've been besties since the start of high school. We've never fallen out, not properly. So why do I feel like I'm betraying her when I place my hand in hers?

THREE
ALEX

"This is Donna Fewston." Ian tries to push the greeting forward, but Cade doesn't take his eyes off me.

"Nice to meet you." Donna beams.

"Likewise." Cade nods. His face is like slate, smooth and cold.

"And this is Alex Knowles." Ian extends his hand in my direction, but there's no need. Cade's focus is glued to me.

"Alex?" Cade raises an eyebrow.

"Yes, Alex," I confirm, the strength in my voice making both Ian and Donna take notice.

Cade looks like he's stepped into *The Twilight Zone*. I feel like I've stepped into a nightmare.

"I'm not sure if you guys have ever met before," Ian begins, his voice trailing off, waiting for either of us to explain what's going on here.

Donna's gaze is like a ball boy at a tennis match, her eyes batting between Cade and me.

"No, we haven't," I snap, my response too quick, too frantic.

For a second, I'm worried Cade will challenge this, but instead, he says, "Nice to meet you, Alex."

Alex. That name doesn't suit his mouth, doesn't sit right. He's never called me Alex. And I know he's pulling up the same memory I am as we stare at each other, my foreign name hanging between us, suspended in the past.

Then

"Hey." Cade's voice makes me jump as he appears from behind the fridge door I've just closed.

"Hey." I edge over to the toaster, acutely aware of my ruffled-bedhead-and-pyjama look compared to Cade's smart school uniform. Even in his black trousers and stiff blazer, there's an air of danger about him, one that makes me butter my toast a little quicker than normal.

"You're ready early," I say when the silence seems to stretch the full length of the kitchen.

"Either that or you're very late." Cade fills a glass of water.

I glance at the clock on the wall, in a sudden panic that I've lost track of the time. He leans back against the sink, clutching the glass to his chest.

"I'm not late." I put the butter back in the fridge.

"What time do you start school?"

"Not for another hour. My mum drops me off on her way to work. How about you?"

"I don't start for another hour either," Cade replies.

"Then why are you ready now?"

"I have a hell of a long walk."

"You walk to school?" The pitch of my voice rises on the word school as I envisage him trekking ten miles in hail, rain, and snow to his old school.

"My dad starts work at five, so he's not around to give me a lift." Cade takes another gulp of water before pouring the rest down the sink. He turns to me, still holding the glass. "Is it just me, or is this all a bit fucked-up?"

I flinch. I'm not some naive wallflower, as I hear this language all the time at school, but I've never heard it at this early hour in my kitchen. My mum doesn't swear—well, most of the time—and there's no way I'd be allowed to use such language.

"Oh my God, yes," I gush. "It feels weird."

"I didn't know if it was just because I feel like a lodger in your house, but I guess it must be just as strange for you." He eyes me as if this statement is more of a question.

"We've been on our own since my dad left when I was about one, so I don't remember him anyway, but yes, it's very odd suddenly having other people in the house."

Cade assesses my answer with a silence I want to prod. Where has he come from? What did his life look like before he came here? I'm thirsty to know all about him, eager to learn why he dresses in black all the time, why his hair is so long, and why he walks around with a hard look on his face.

"At least it's weird for both of us," I say.

"It's bad enough our parents are dating. That alone is just fucking weird."

"Is this the first relationship your dad has had?"

"He's always been a bit of a ladies' man, but nothing serious. Nothing like this."

"Do you think it's serious?"

"We're here, aren't we?"

"I guess." My toast has gone cold, the butter solidified on the surface.

"I don't want it to be weird," Cade says at last, pushing himself away from the sink.

"Me neither. Maybe we just need to get to know each other."

"Okay." He nods. "Every day, we should tell each other one thing about ourselves."

"Okay." I smile, my shoulders dropping. "You go first."

"Right. Let me see… erm… okay, I never eat breakfast." Cade holds out the empty glass as if it's evidence of his statement. "Now it's your turn."

"Let me think." I rack my brain, trying to find something interesting but not odd. "I hate my name."

He raises an eyebrow. "Is it short for something?"

"Alexandria." I say it as if my mouth is full of sour sweets.

"Wow." Cade whistles. "It's a beautiful name."

My heart stops for a second. The way his lips mould

around the word beautiful and the way he looks at me when it leaves his mouth is such a contrast to the scar above his eyebrow, the darkness in his gaze, and the hardness to his jaw.

"Thanks." Thanks? Is that all I can manage? "But I hate it."

"Why?"

"Well, when I was in junior school, there was this boy named Alex in my class, and he was such a jerk, even at the age of eight. And everyone used to say we were twins. They called us the two Alexes." I try my best to mimic my childhood friends' annoying voices. "I hated it, and I've always wished I was called something else, but Alexandria is too long. People can't be bothered to spend that long saying my name, and Andrea is just too middle-aged. So, I'm stuck being an Alex."

Cade's eyes narrow, something flittering behind the darkness as he stares at me.

"I'm not going to call you by a name you hate," he says at last.

"Then what are you going to call me?"

He licks his lips as if tasting an idea, moving the possible choices around his mouth to see if they feel right before he speaks. "Lexie. I'm going to call you Lexie."

Lexie. No one has ever called me Lexie.

"I like it."

"It suits you." Cade stares at me.

I look away, heat rising above my neck, flooding my face, which I'm sure now looks pink. I'm about to respond when my mum comes bustling into the kitchen.

"Hey, kids, we need to get a move on," she announces.

"Good morning, Cade. Are you needing a lift to school? Alex and I are setting off in half an hour. I can drop you off."

"It's fine, thank you. I can walk," he says whilst opening the cupboards one at a time and peering inside.

I pull the dishwasher open for him and he glances at me, a silent thank you coming from his gaze as he places the glass inside.

"Are you sure?"

"I'm sure. I like the exercise."

"Okay, but you're not walking when it's raining. That isn't up for debate." She gives Cade her firm look that I know means there's no arguing.

I stifle a laugh as he gives her a tiny salute.

"Good, I'm glad that's sorted," she replies, either ignoring his gesture or misconstruing it as compliance.

"I need to get going. See you later." Cade nods before heading out of the kitchen.

I watch him leave, memorising his movements, the way his head drops, the way he shoves his hands in his pockets.

"You need to get a move on, Alex. We don't have all morning," my mum barks as she scoops coffee into the machine.

But I don't hear her. I'm too busy playing my new name over and over in my head.

Lexie.

FOUR

ALEX

"I'm not sure what you'd like to look over first." Ian's voice pulls me back to the present, his attempt to break the uncomfortable silence now drifting in the air like a poisonous smog that's crept in with the new owner.

Cade responds quickly, his head snapping to attention like someone's just cracked a whip against his leg. "I'd like to look over some of the properties you have on your books. In particular, the ones you've had on for over four months."

"No problem." Ian fires into action. "If you'd like to follow me, we have a small office at the back of the shop we can use. I can get all the files for you, and we can go over them in there."

"Perfect," Cade says without a hint of a smile.

Ian leads him toward the office. Cade hesitates before following.

Donna immediately turns to me. "What the hell was that all about?" she demands. Her hands are on her hips, her face matching her stance.

"All what?" I sit down, my legs unable to hold me any longer. I try to remain composed, natural even, but Donna is no stranger to potential gossip.

"Don't give me that," she huffs. "What was all that between you and the new man? He was looking at you like he wanted to eat you, and you… well, I can't quite work out what's going through your head, but something isn't right."

"You're imagining it," I point out whilst tapping away on my keyboard. "I was just trying to weigh up how good-looking he is after the fuss you made."

"And?"

"And I can see where you're coming from, but he's not my type."

"Oh really? And who is your type?" Donna rolls her eyes. "Oh, I forgot about your mystery man. And what does he look like? You still haven't shared a bean about him."

"He's blond and boyish." I have to steer Donna off the topic of Cade. She can't find out.

No one can find out.

Staring at my screen, I pray Donna will get bored and do some work.

How the fuck has this happened? How has he found me? Did he know I work here? He looked as surprised as I did.

Shit.

This is bad.

Really fucking bad.

Mrs Wells is now the least of my problems.

Remembering I have a huge to-do list, I go back to the brochure I was working on for a new property we've just taken on and hope it'll take my mind off Cade Westwood.

Scrolling through the photos of the Victorian terraced house, I stop on the one of the kitchen, the cream shaker units in a classic L-shaped layout with an island in the centre of the room lined with bar stools. It could be a replica of the kitchen I grew up in, the one that came to be mine and Cade's meeting place.

Then

"I see you're ahead of schedule this morning," Cade observes as he enters the kitchen looking like a carbon copy of yesterday morning, whereas I'm a complete contrast, perched at the island in full uniform.

"I couldn't sleep," I say, placing a half-eaten slice of toast back on my plate.

He opens the cupboard, gets himself a glass, and fills it from the tap. I'd fought the urge to get the glass out for him, but I thought it might look odd. Besides, he'll be in the kitchen longer if he has to get his own drink.

"You're going to have some time to kill before your mum

sets off," Cade points out.

"I'm sure I'll think of something to do."

"You could walk to school."

I snigger. "My mum would never let me walk to school."

"Seriously?" His eyebrow arches, an expression I've already logged as one of my favourites.

"Seriously. I've never been allowed to walk to school."

"But it's only down the road, and you're what, fifteen?"

"I'm sixteen next month," I quickly add.

"So, why won't she let you walk to school?"

I sigh, letting out a pent-up breath that's come from years of arguing with my mum about this very topic. "She says it isn't safe."

Cade shifts his weight, the glass held casually in his hand. "In what way isn't it safe? Does she think you're going to get lost or a bit wet if it rains?"

I glare at him, unsure whether he's implying that I'm a baby. "I don't know what she thinks will happen—an earthquake or a tsunami, probably—but I know she'll never let me walk. I think she'll be driving me to work when I get a job." I roll my eyes.

"Well, as one of those who have to walk, I have to go." He places the glass in the dishwasher. "But before I do, you need to tell me something about yourself."

"Oh." I try to act as if I've forgotten this, when in fact it's the reason why I couldn't sleep. I hesitate, making it look like I'm thinking of what to say. "I'm allergic to peanuts."

"Really? Like properly allergic?"

"Properly allergic."

"So, what happens if you eat a peanut?"

"I get light-headed, disorientated, and then I can't breathe. It's quite scary."

"Jeez, that's proper allergic."

"Yeah, I have an EpiPen I have to carry around with me."

"A what?"

"It's a syringe in a plastic tube that injects adrenaline directly into my bloodstream. Here, let me show you." Leaning over, I open the kitchen drawer, pull out an EpiPen, and hand it to him.

He twirls the tube, inspecting it.

"We have several all over the house. Not that my mum would let a peanut get within an inch of me." I groan.

"So, what would happen if you didn't get this in time?" he asks.

"I could die." I shrug, trying to lighten the fact that a small nut could be fatal. It's something I've lived with for the majority of my life, so I don't know what it's like to not live with it. And I know my mum's overbearing parenting stems from the peanut allergy that nearly killed me as a child. "So, what about you?" I ask, not wanting to miss out on his fact of the day by blabbering on about myself.

"My interesting thing seems very boring compared to yours."

"I'm sure it isn't."

"Hm." Cade smirks.

It's the closest to a smile I've seen, and I don't miss the little tremor inside my stomach.

"This may shock you, but I have a fear of cats."

"Really? Now I am shocked!" My grin widens. "How can a big guy like you be scared of a fluffy little cat?"

"Hey, let me stop you right there." He takes a step forward, his face hardening. "They aren't all cute and cuddly. Some of them are downright vicious. And they have claws as well as sharp teeth. And when they hiss at you, they mean business."

I laugh, still bemused that a guy like Cade could be afraid of anything.

"I was attacked by my friend's cat when I was younger. Big ginger thing that scratched me right down the side of my face. It had nothing to do with the fact that I'd been trying to pick him up whilst he was sleeping."

"That makes a little more sense. I can see why you'd be scarred for life after an encounter like that."

"Hey, not just mentally," he adds. "I have physical scars. See here." He pads over to me and leans in. I hold my breath as he points at the side of his face.

I stare.

Breathing in slowly, I inhale the scent of his spicy cologne mixing with the smell of minty toothpaste. His skin is smooth, his hair still a little damp from the shower, his eyelashes heavy.

I'm meant to be looking at his scar.

"Wow, you're very brave to have survived."

"Lived to tell the tale." He remains close.

My eyes wander to the fading black eye. "And what about your eye?"

Cade shifts back. "Oh, that was nothing."

"Another cat attack?"

"God, no. Someone I had a disagreement with."

"A disagreement?"

"Just something a guy said that he shouldn't have." His eyes narrow, his head dipping toward mine, a severity in his voice that sends a little chill down my back. "Put it this way—he won't say it again." There's a depth to his voice that convinces me this other guy will never even speak again.

"I'm going to be late." He turns on his heels and heads for the door.

"Have a good day," I call in the hope he'll turn around.

He does.

FIVE

ALEX

THANKFULLY, DONNA FINDS SOME WORK TO DO, and although I try to concentrate on the new brochure for the Victorian terraced house on Summerly Road, my mind is in free fall, my thoughts spiralling like Alice down the rabbit hole. I've not allowed myself to have these thoughts in a long time, but now that they're back, I can't seem to hold them at bay. It's as if the gates to a forgotten city have been opened, and the residents are running through them, screaming.

Cade.

He's here.

In the flesh.

All six foot four of him.

Is this what reunions are supposed to feel like? Surely they're meant to be happy events where people forget their differences and grievances, age and maturity replacing the old squabbles that used to litter the conversation.

But Cade and I are different.

This is different.

And I'm not sure how I'm supposed to make it through the day, let alone the rest of my working days with him here, so close, so near.

Staring at the closed door to the back office, I wonder what he's thinking, whether he's even listening to Ian or reading the files. Because even though I'm at my desk, my workload goading me, fingers poised over the keyboard, I'm running through the gate, revisiting those precious moments, the good ones, the ones I usually don't allow myself to think about.

Then

Anna and I are in the kitchen after another boring day of school.

I can almost feel her energy, the excitement emitting from her like she's radioactive. This is "the introduction phase," as Anna has coined it, where I will introduce her and Cade, and, according to her forecast, they'll fall madly in love. Anna has been a jubilant bag of nerves all day, topping up her mascara and raising the hem of her skirt, whereas I feel a strange sense of foreboding, as if something has been niggling at me all day like a small stone in my shoe.

As her best friend, I should be happy for her. I'm usually on board with these things, like best friends are supposed to be, but I can't commit to this project. Cade lives under the same roof as me, and when it all goes wrong, which it eventually will, it'll be awkward to say the least.

Anna perches herself on one of the bar stools. "Do you think I should be sitting or standing when he arrives? I don't want him to think I'm too short. He is coming back here, isn't he?"

"He always comes back straight from school to get changed before going out again."

"Oh my God, just the thought of Cade taking his clothes off." Anna squeals as I tear open a large bag of sharing crisps. "Ooh, these are my favourite crisps."

"My mum is more than happy to buy anything that doesn't have peanuts in it," I joke, eager to move the conversation on from a naked Cade.

Anna and I became friends in high school after getting paired with each other in Miss Lamb's physics lessons. The first time she met my mum, she received a lecture about my peanut allergy. She'd practically run a full training course on the signs to look for if I was having a reaction and how to use the EpiPen. It'd scared Anna when my mum had started to tell her how severe my allergy was, and that as my best friend, she could be responsible for saving my life. But I've never reacted in front of Anna, and as we've got older, I sense that she thinks it's a bit of a myth.

We're halfway through the crisps when the front door opens. Anna shoots up from the bar stool, frantically wiping her hands down the front of her blazer before dusting the edges of her mouth for remnants of crisps whilst trying to look at her reflection in the mirrored oven door.

"Do I look okay?" she whispers loudly.

I nod as she shuffles back over to the bar stool. She climbs on and waits for the inevitable.

"Hey." Cade nods in my direction as he enters the kitchen. An atmosphere follows as if he's dragged it in off the street, something heavy and meaningful that weighs the air down, yet he seems oblivious to it.

"Hey." I can feel Anna's eyes upon me, waiting for me to wave my magic wand of love. But all I can see is Cade.

"Good day?" he asks, opening the fridge and peering inside.

"Okay, I suppose. You?"

"I've had worse." He pulls out a carton of orange juice.

I slide off the bar stool and get him a glass, saving him from my mum's wrath about not drinking from the carton.

"Thanks."

We stare at each other.

Anna clears her throat.

"Oh, this is my friend, Anna," I tell him.

We both look at Anna, who is now standing next to the island. She gives Cade a little wave as if her elbow has been glued to her waist.

"Hi." She smiles her winning smile, and I know it'll happen. Cade will see her blonde hair, her blue eyes, the make-up, and her perfect figure, and he'll be ensnared, phase one complete. I've yet to meet a guy who has been immune to Anna's many attributes.

"Hey." Cade nods in her direction before continuing to pour his drink.

I hover, feeling a little spark of disbelief that he's barely looked at Anna.

"Is my dad back?" he asks, returning his attention to me.

"I'm not sure."

Cade replaces the orange juice in the fridge. "I'm heading out for training."

"Oh, what kind of training?" Anna pipes up.

He glances in her direction as if he's already forgotten she's there. "Football."

"Oh my God, I love watching football. What team do you support?"

Cade stares at her with a bewilderment I can almost feel. "Liverpool," he replies before quickly turning back to me. "Is your mum making that chicken thing for dinner again?"

"I don't know. I can suggest it if you'd like."

"It was so nice. I'm not saying anything against my dad, but years of his cooking has taken its toll on my taste buds."

"I'll tell him you said that," I threaten.

"There's no need. He knows how bad he is, and he doesn't need reminding." Cade puts down his glass and raises his eyebrows. "And I hadn't bagged you for a snitch."

"You underestimate me."

"Alex and I would love to come watch you play sometime," Anna interrupts, a slightly desperate edge to her voice.

There's a small silence before Cade replies, "It's been a long time since I played a match. I just train to keep fit and catch up with the lads."

"And speak for yourself," I chip in. "I can't think of anything worse than watching a group of guys kicking a ball around a bit of grass."

Anna glares at me. I'm not sticking to the plan.

"I'm sure you'd find it fun once we were there," she argues.

I smile in an attempt to redeem myself.

"Well, I need to go get changed. I'll see you later." Cade turns to leave.

"Bye. Nice to meet you," Anna calls.

"Yeah, sure," he tosses over his shoulder as he disappears without a backward glance.

Anna heaves a huge sigh as soon as he's out of earshot. "Well, that didn't go according to plan." Visibly deflating, she slumps back onto the bar stool.

"No." I'm still in shock at Cade's lack of reaction to her. This is unheard of. Maybe he hadn't got a proper look at her. He could've just been in a rush to get ready for training.

"Maybe it was the school uniform," Anna suggests. "I knew I should've brought a change of clothes. Next time we meet, I'm ditching the uniform. It makes me look too young and doesn't accentuate my best bits." There's a stout, resolute tension burrowed into her jaw. "I'm not giving up on this one."

I find it hard to hold in the relief that's brewing, as I know it'll be short-lived. Phase one may not have gone to plan, but knowing Anna, she'll have several other phases up her sleeve, all of them needing my help to deploy.

But for now, I'm impressed that Cade appears to have a little more about him than most guys.

SIX

ALEX

"E{\small ARTH} {\small TO} A{\small LEX}." D{\small ONNA} {\small HOVERS} {\small BY} {\small MY} {\small DESK}, bag on her shoulder, her car keys in her hand.

"Sorry, I was miles away." Shaking my head, I turn off my computer and shuffle the papers I've done nothing with into a neat pile.

"And planning to stay the night here, by the looks of things."

"No, thank you. Today has been long enough."

"You can say that again." Donna glances up at the office door that remains closed and has done all afternoon. "Do you think Ian's okay in there? Do you think he needs a food parcel or a sleeping bag?" she asks.

"Who knows."

"Maybe the new guy doesn't eat."

The words are almost out of my mouth, but I stop myself just in time.

I know what Cade eats. I know what he likes and

what he doesn't. I know everything there is to know about him.

Or at least, I did.

As I pull my denim jacket from the back of my chair, Donna continues to talk. "Are you sure you're okay?"

Thrusting my arm into the tight sleeve, I glance at her quickly. "Why wouldn't I be okay?"

With a shrug, she replies, "You just seem a little distracted. Not your usual witty self." She eyes the office door again before returning her gaze to me. "It's ever since the new guy arrived."

"I'm fine, honest. I didn't get much sleep last night."

"Neighbours arguing again?" Donna repeatedly flicks open her car key, her acrylic nails adding to the grating sound that's starting to annoy me.

"Yeah," I lie. For the past few weeks, my neighbours, a young man and woman who've just moved in, have been arguing late into the night. The first time I mentioned it to Donna, I'd come to work with huge bags under my eyes and gripping a large black takeout coffee. When I told her about them arguing, she asked if they'd ever lived together before. I wasn't sure, but they looked young enough for this to be their first house.

"It'll calm down," Donna said. "God, I remember when Ed and I moved in together. We were at each other's throats. I threw a ketchup bottle at him one night when he stacked a load of dirty plates in the sink even though we had a dishwasher and I'd shown him how to load it. It's strange, living with someone for the first time. You get to find out all their annoying habits."

Since moving out of my mum's house, I've never felt comfortable sharing my living space, and I've never felt strongly enough about anyone to want to get to know their habits, bad or good.

The only man I've lived with is Cade.

"So, do you think we're in good hands?" Donna asks.

"What?"

"You know, with the new boss. Do you think the business is in good hands?"

"Sure. Why wouldn't it be?"

I don't hear her reply because I'm back there now, lost in the thought of being in Cade's hands.

Then

Cade hasn't been home long when we're called to dinner. I bag my usual chair as Mark joins us. Cade sits next to me. His hair is still damp from the shower, and the scent of musky shampoo wafts over the table. I'm glad when my mum brings the food in and the smell is replaced with Cajun spices.

"Now, I know I made this the other night, but I understand it was requested." She smiles at Cade as she places the

large dish of spicy chicken in the centre of the table before returning to the kitchen.

"It smells so good." Mark inhales. "Can she cook anything else besides this?" he whispers.

"Even if she can't, it's one more thing than you can cook," Cade points out.

"Hey, I did a good job feeding you," Mark says. "There's nothing wrong with cold beans and a slice of bread."

"I knew you were getting the hang of things when you started warming the beans up."

"God, I wasn't that bad, was I?"

"I'm still alive, I suppose."

Mark is about to throw his napkin at Cade when my mum walks back in.

"And here are the rice and wraps," she sings as she returns to the table, her arms heavy with dishes and plates.

Mark quickly stands up. "Here, let me help." He sweeps around the table to take some things off her, and she smiles into her chest.

"I'm so used to doing it on my own," she mutters.

"Hey, I help out," I say.

"I bet you help out as much as Cade does," Mark jeers.

I wonder if all father-and-son relationships are like this or whether it's just Mark and Cade, but I like it—it lightens the mood around the table.

"Okay, dig in, guys," my mum says.

For the next five minutes, all that can be heard is the scraping of cutlery and the satisfied hum of people enjoying a *good meal on the table. It isn't until we're halfway through our food that anyone speaks.*

"This is good," Cade says, his mouth still full.

"Thank you." My mum beams. "I found the recipe in a magazine about five years ago, and I've been making it ever since. I reduced the spices the first time I made it, as I thought it would be too hot for Alex, but over the years, I've built them up, and she seems to be okay with it."

She glances at Mark, who lowers his fork and looks over at me. I feel about five years old.

"I love spicy food," I say, trying to regain some of my years.

"Well, this is very spicy," Mark adds, aiming a little smile my way.

"Because of Alex's allergy, I've had to monitor her food for so long, it's become second nature," Mum continues.

Cade keeps his eyes on his plate. I want to sink into my seat and slide to the floor.

"It must be hard, Alex, to keep track of what you eat all the time," Mark comments.

I sit up. "I haven't known any different, so it's just the norm."

"I like to think I've trained her to deal with it in the best way possible," Mum says. "That's why we have to be strict about what food comes into the house." She turns to Cade. "I'm sure your dad told you there are to be no Snickers bars or peanut M&M's on the premises."

"Yes, he told me before we moved in." Cade aims a look at his dad, who in turn smiles at his son, and I know that when

I'd told Cade about my allergy, it'd been the first he'd heard about it.

Mark will have been briefed, possibly on their first date. It was probably on her Tinder profile. In turn, she'll have expected him to brief Cade before setting foot over the threshold, but this won't be enough for her. I sense her gearing up for the full allergy low-down.

"Has your dad told you about what to look for and what to do in case Alex has a reaction?" she pushes.

"Mum, he doesn't need to know."

"Of course he does. He's living in this house, and if you have a reaction and you're confused or not able to get to your meds, then what will happen?"

"It's okay," Cade interjects. "She showed me her EpiPen and where it's kept. I think I'd know what to do if she had a reaction."

My mum stops short, her face a picture of surprise. "Well, Alex, I'm very impressed. That was very sensible of you. And thank you for taking it on board, Cade."

He now looks as embarrassed as I do.

"Cade's a sensible kid when he wants to be." Mark chews on some chicken.

I glance at Cade, glad Mark has stopped my mum in her tracks before she gets going.

"I would trust him to act in an emergency." Mark looks at me. "You'd be in safe hands with Cade."

He smiles as I start to think about what it'd be like to be in Cade's hands.

SEVEN

ALEX

Donna and I make it to the car park with still no sign of Cade or Ian leaving the back office. I'm hoping that now I'm out of the shop, the memories will stop attacking me.

Distance.

I need distance.

We've been apart so long, and I've never afforded myself the luxury of wondering what Cade is doing right now, where he is, what life he might be living. My memories are torture enough; I don't need to stick another blade in the wound.

But he's here.

He's back.

How the hell am I supposed to function now?

"Oh shoot." Donna stops midstep as if she's walked into an invisible wall. "I totally forgot. I have to go pick up a cake for my niece's birthday."

"At this time?"

"It's not from a shop. It's a woman my sister knows who makes them. Charges a goddamn fortune for a bit of sponge and icing. I promised I'd collect it for her. She has her hands full with the kids, and the party is at the weekend."

"Can't have a party without a cake."

"Absolutely not. Abigail will have a fit if she doesn't get her unicorn cake."

"Unicorn?"

"Yeah. I just hope the horn doesn't look phallic, or I'm going to have a hard time keeping a straight face."

"You sure know how to taint a kid's birthday party." I swing my car door open and throw my bag into the passenger seat.

"Don't I just. It's the only way to get through these events. You sure you're okay?"

"Just tired." I slide into my car, eager to get away from Donna, from this day, from the memories that are swamping me.

"Get an early night, and sleep with earmuffs on if the neighbours start arguing again." Donna leans on the roof of my car. "Ian's going to be tied up with the new boss for the next few days, so I need you by my side and preferably awake."

Tipping two fingers to my brow, I salute her. "Yes, ma'am."

Donna's hand drops from the roof as she tugs her bag onto her shoulder. "See you tomorrow."

She waves as I fire up the engine and begin to reverse slowly out of my parking space.

"Don't forget your cake," I call just as I swing the front of my car around.

This time, it's Donna's turn to salute.

My house is a fifteen-minute drive from the shop through the small town of Harton I call home. It's an eclectic mix of new and old houses, with modern housing estates cropping up on the depleting green space. It's not so great for the traffic on our winding roads and the school places and local jobs, but for an estate agent, it's a dream.

Passing the Food Emporium and Dante's Shoes, the shops begin to fade and are replaced with some of the older residential properties in the town. They're large and domineering, stonework blackened by years of pollution, towering hedges and trees shrouding them in a mystery that comes with having survived this world for so many years.

To keep my brain in the present, I mentally go through my freezer and the options that await me for my evening meal, but no matter how hard I try, I keep coming back to the unicorn birthday cake and the last time I saw one.

At the tiny roundabout with the beautiful display of colourful flowers, none of which I know the names of, I give in to the memories.

Then

"*Your mum is pretty OTT about your nut allergy," Cade says one morning as we partake in our now school-morning ritual of meeting in the kitchen.*

I roll my eyes. "Oh my God, you have no idea."

"When did you last have a reaction?"

"I was seven, at a friend's birthday party. My mum was there and had brought me my own special plate of food, as I wasn't allowed any of the party food in case it was contaminated." I push my empty cereal bowl away. "So, I'd missed out on the buns and the biscuits and the little party sausages and the slices of pizza. All of which was probably crap, but when you're a kid, it's what matters."

Cade nods as I continue. "The party was for a girl in my class—Katy, I think her name was—but she was obsessed with unicorns, and her mum had had this amazing rainbow cake made in the shape of a unicorn, and it was the most wonderful thing I'd ever seen. It was covered in layers of different-coloured butter cream with multicoloured sprinkles and sparkly glitter. So, when it came to handing out the party bags, I knew I wouldn't be getting any, as my mum always asked them to take the cake out. But at the end of the party, she got chatting to one of the other mums, and I spotted Katy handing out the party bags, so I made a dash for mine before my mum had the chance to intervene. I'd eaten half the slice by the time she noticed. She was frantic and had me in the car within minutes. It was in the back seat on the way home that my lips started to swell, and I began to struggle to breathe." I exhale, remembering the tightness in my chest, the panic on my mum's face, the noises she made as she jabbed the adrenaline into my tiny thigh.

"Wow, no wonder she's a bit crazy with it," Cade says. "But you haven't had a reaction since then?"

"No, after that my mum was on full alert, and she has been ever since."

"But how do you avoid it? What about school?"

"I've never had a school lunch. In fact, in primary school, my mum requested I eat my packed lunch in a separate room from all the other children after one kid brought in a Nutella sandwich. I've never eaten at the school canteen, and when we do eat out, my mum goes as far as inspecting the kitchen. I've never been allowed to go to someone's house for tea, and my mum came with me to all parties until I was about twelve, and after that, she would tell them I wasn't allowed to eat at the party, so pizza parties were great fun."

"Sounds tough."

I shrug. "I'm used to it."

"You hear of people growing out of these allergies, though, so maybe it's not as bad anymore." Cade shrugs.

"I wouldn't know, and it's not worth taking the risk. I just wish my mum would let me take the reins for once."

The familiar tread of my mum making her way down the stairs works its way into the kitchen, and I immediately feel guilty for talking about her.

"Morning, you two," she says as she heads straight for the coffee maker.

"Morning," Cade and I answer simultaneously.

She's flustered, her hair a little out of place and her blouse buttoned up wrong as she scoops coffee into the machine. "Alex, I have to go pick a parcel up before work," she begins. "I'm not sure whether to drop you off before or after. It might make me late if I drop you after." She appears to be thinking aloud.

"Whichever, Mum," I say, knowing she'll make the decision regardless.

"Or she could walk to school with me," Cade suggests.

My mum glares at him as if he's said a rude word.

"I pass her school on the way to mine."

"I don't think that's a good idea," Mum begins, but I see my chance.

"I'd be okay with that." I try not to sound like I'm begging.

I've entered this debate hundreds of times, but this is different. My mum wants Cade and me to get along. She won't want to offend him or Mark by saying no, as this might suggest she doesn't trust Cade. Her argument has always been that I can't walk to school alone, and even the addition of one of my girlfriends has never managed to sway her. I'd even pushed for walking to school with a large group of friends, but she'd dismissed the idea because it would look like I was in a gang, and gangs attracted trouble. So, I'd given up.

Until now.

"It's such a nice morning, and it'd be great exercise."

My mum is visibly grappling with this dilemma as the coffee maker gurgles away. I issue out silent prayers as Cade stares at my mum.

"I don't know." She hesitates. "It would help me out, but…."

"Mum, I'm sixteen in two weeks," I argue but stop as my mum folds her arms. Antagonising her will only backfire. I need this to be her decision; otherwise, I don't stand a chance.

"I walk to school every day, and it's quiet at this time. I'll make sure she gets there," Cade says.

I want to feel angry about my mum and Cade treating me with kid gloves, but I know he's appealing to her train of thought, which is that her fragile daughter needs protecting. I'm too thankful that he's suggested it in the first place to be cross with him.

The ticking of the kitchen clock has slowed as if giving my mum the extra time she needs.

Finally, she speaks. "Okay." She lets it out slowly as if she might retract it at any minute.

I try to withhold the giant sigh. I want to clap my hands and jump around the kitchen, but I contain myself. "Thanks, Mum." I beam.

"But you two need to look out for each other," she adds quickly. "There are weird people about, and I don't want you getting into trouble."

"We'll be vigilant," Cade says.

"And straight to school, no detours." She points at me.

I nod, trying hard to suppress my smile.

"Call me as soon as you get to the school gates."

"I promise." I place my hand on my heart as I slide off the bar stool. "I'm just going to grab my things."

"I'll wait here for you," he says as I leave the kitchen.

Bounding up the stairs, I feel light and buoyant, as if I've been filled with helium, and I'm floating up the stairs. Shoving books into my schoolbag, I can't decide what I'm happier about, the fact that I'm being allowed to walk to school or that I'm walking with Cade.

"Thank you so much," I whisper as we step out the front door and navigate our way down the small front path and onto the street, where we fall into a comfortable stroll. We walk slowly, which I'm glad about—I don't want this to be over too quickly.

"You're welcome, although you owe me now." Cade throws me a cunning scowl.

"I'm forever in your debt." My cheeks start to smart from the smile that won't subside. "I still can't believe she said yes. Although, it wouldn't surprise me if she's following us in her car." I peer over my shoulder, half expecting her red Fiat to be crawling behind us, my mum at the wheel in dark glasses and a wig.

The sun is warm on my face, and I bathe in this time of day which I've never experienced and probably never would have if it hadn't been for Cade.

"Do you walk alone?" I ask, suddenly panicking that he'll meet up with a bunch of friends, and I'll be left feeling like a baby whom he has to escort to school under duress.

"I do now. Before we moved here, I used to walk with my mates, but they're on the opposite side of town now."

There's a sadness in his eyes that stabs at my chest.

"It must be hard having moved away from them all." Why

do I feel like this is my fault? Like I'm the reason he's here and not some shitty landlord who decided to make him homeless?

"Yeah, but we didn't have much choice." He sounds bitter but quickly follows it up with "We are grateful your mum offered us a place to live." Cade stares straight ahead as though some alternative future lies on the corner of the road. His eyes narrow, as if he's uncertain whether it would've been better than where he is now.

"It must be tough."

"It's not so bad." His chest inflates, his voice rising an octave. "I get to walk to school with you now."

There's heat in my cheeks as I cast my eyes to the pavement. "I can't promise to be as fun as your friends. I bet you had a laugh with them."

"Sometimes, but they could also be very annoying. Joss would drink a full can of Coke every morning before school, which always made him hyper, and he would talk non-stop. It wouldn't have been so bad if it was about something decent, but he insisted on talking about his future career as a professional gamer and how he was going to make his millions becoming a YouTuber."

"Does he have his own channel?"

"Yes, but it's not worth watching. It's just him on his PlayStation, yacking on about the latest game."

"I take it you're not a gaming fan."

"No. I prefer real-life games."

Pressing my lips together, I see Cade now—the Man of Action.

"But what about you?" he asks, angling his shoulders in my direction.

"What about me?"

"What do you like to do?"

"Well, actually, I'm a big gamer, and I have my own YouTube channel called Text the Lex. I have thousands of followers, and—" Cade elbows me, and I sway whilst sniggering.

"Okay, very funny."

"I'm not into many things, to be honest. Just the usual. Music and whatnot. I used to dance."

"Really?"

"Yeah."

"What kind of dance?" he asks.

"Modern, pop, a bit of street dancing. My mum enrolled me in ballet when I was about four, and it went from there, but I quit last year."

"How come?"

"I grew up. I was never going to be good enough to compete or take it up as a career, so there seemed no point in carrying on. The shows were a nightmare as well and always interfered with school."

"But did you enjoy it?"

"I did when I was younger, but I think my mum enjoyed it more. She loved being a dance mum. I'd have given it up a long time ago, but I kept at it because it was all she seemed to have, and I didn't want to take that away from her. Do you know what I mean?"

Cade nods. "My dad is a huge rugby fan, so I got dragged

to rugby training at the age of seven. I hated it, but I kept going because I didn't want to upset him. But my real passion was football. I finally persuaded him to let me concentrate on football and drop the rugby, which he was okay with, but I knew I'd upset him."

"It's hard trying to be what our parents want us to be," I say.

"It sure is. Especially when you're not sure what you want to be." A black cat darts from under a bush and disappears under a silver Vauxhall. Cade shivers before saying, "Hey, we haven't done our thing of telling each other a fact about ourselves."

I'm about to argue that I've learned more about Cade in the last fifteen minutes than I have in all the time he's been at my house, but I guess he's trying to take his mind off the cat lurking under the car. "Go on, then."

"I'm a very sore loser."

"That doesn't surprise me if you're a footballer. They're used to winning."

"You'd think I'd be used to losing, the number of times our Sunday league team got beat, but I've never really come to grips with being a gracious loser. I've always been in it to win it." His eyebrows lower, a dangerous look crossing his face.

"I get that."

"Any sportsperson who tells you they're not is lying."

I add Cade the Winner to Cade the Man of Action.

"What about you?"

"My fact or whether I'm a good loser?"

"Both."

"When it comes to being up against other people, I'm a great loser. But when up against myself, I can get a little fierce. And my fact of the day is that I hate people who wear shoes with no socks."

For the first time, Cade laughs. "Really?"

"Absolutely. It's a pet hate."

"What about trainers and no socks?"

"Even worse. All I can think about is how much their feet must be sweating in their shoes, and it's gross." I cringe.

"I'm beginning to wish I'd put socks on now." Cade shakes his head.

I stop walking. "Please tell me you're kidding. I can't walk any further until I know you have socks on." I throw him a stern look, emphasising the seriousness of this situation.

He stands before me, one hand in the pocket of his trousers and a sly smile on his face. "What would happen if I didn't?"

"You'd go down in my estimation."

"And where am I currently in your estimation?"

I pause. Where is Cade? The question rocks me a little, but he's waiting for an answer. "Pretty cool."

"Hm, I wouldn't want to go down any further than that."

"You'll be rock bottom if you don't have any socks on."

"Good job I have, then." He pulls up one leg of his trousers to reveal a black sock hugging his ankle.

I exhale. "Okay, so you're still pretty cool."

"I'm glad I meet your expectations," Cade says as we resume our walk.

As we round the corner, the dark green gates of my school

come into view, and my heart sinks that our time together has ended so soon.

"Well, this is me," I announce, an empty feeling travelling through my stomach at the thought of letting him walk the rest of the way on his own.

Cade stares at the new building that looks more like a smart inner-city office than a high school. "It looks nice, as far as schools go."

"It's okay, I suppose. I've never been this early before. It's so quiet."

"Do you have somewhere to go?" He sounds worried.

"Yeah, the library's always open early for study. I'll go wait in there. I have some work I can catch up on."

"Great. I still have a bit of a way to go, so I'll see you tonight."

Cade walks away.

"Thanks again," I call.

He turns and walks backward, his hands tight around the straps of his rucksack as if he's holding on to the straps of a parachute. "No problem. Same time tomorrow?"

"I hope so." I'll have to pray my mum will let this be a regular deal.

"Bye." Cade gives me a little nod as he spins around.

"Bye." I wave, then slowly begin to make my way down the path leading to the main entrance.

"Lexie!" he suddenly shouts from the road. I turn, and he's stopped, his phone in his hand. "Don't forget to make your call."

"I won't!" I holler back.

I saunter down the main path, almost dancing each step.

I pull my phone from my bag before I hit the no-mobile-phone zone, and I call my mum.

She answers before the phone even rings. "Alex, are you at school?"

"Yes, and I'm fine," *I pre-empt.*

"Good. I've been worried." *I can hear the release of breath down the handset that she's probably been holding ever since I left the house.*

"There's no need to worry, Mum. I'm fine. The walk was great, and I'm here early enough to go use the library to catch up on some revision."

"Well, that is something, I guess," *she murmurs.* "And what about Cade?"

"What about him?"

"Did he drop you right by the gate? He didn't leave you to go meet up with his friends, did he?"

"No, his friends he used to walk with are on the other side of town, so he walks on his own now. I kind of felt sorry for him. I think it cheered him up to have some company." *I let this hang before I continue.* "I was wondering if I'd be able to walk with him every morning."

I can almost hear the crackle down the phone of my mum's inner voice arguing with itself. I glance toward the sky. There's a large, bulbous white cloud rolling across the brilliant blue, the kind of cloud an angel would be right at home on.

"Okay, but only if Cade walks with you, and any sign of this not working, you're back in the car with me."

"Thank you, Mum. You're the best."

"*And I'm still picking you up. Statistics show there're more incidents on the way home from school than there are on the way to school.*"

"*I don't even want to know how you know that.*" I laugh.

"*I'm your mum. It's my job to know these things. I'll see you in the usual spot.*"

"*Okay,*" I agree. "*Have a nice day.*"

"*You, too, sweetie.*"

I press the End Call button and switch my phone to silent. Glancing back up at the sky, I see that the large cloud has moved on, probably on its way to someone else. I smile at it, issuing a silent thanks to the angel who must've been looking down on me.

EIGHT
ALEX

INHALING THE FRESH-PAINT SMELL OF THE GREY Hessian I'd used to spruce up the hallway at the weekend, I drop my bag and kick off my shoes as soon as my front door closes. I bought my two-bed semidetached house several years ago and have been content here. It was a relatively new build when I bought it, one careful owner who purchased it from new, then couldn't afford the mortgage, so they put it on the market when prices were at an all-time low.

I didn't hesitate, not even writing the brochure for it. I put in an offer there and then and have not regretted it since. It's a far cry from the towering ceilings, spacious rooms, and ornate plastering of the Victorian terraced I grew up in. And that was exactly what I needed—something different. Somewhere that wouldn't stir any memories.

But entering the kitchen, I falter. The new gloss

cabinets gleam, the ceramic tiles sparkle, all of it looking as beautiful as it had in the brochure I picked it from a few months ago, but all I can hear is the kitchen designer asking me if I wanted an island.

"The layout of your kitchen is crying out for an island," he'd said as he tapped away on his little tablet, building my imaginary kitchen with his fingers.

"No," I'd snapped. I couldn't do it. Couldn't place an island in my kitchen. It would be a constant reminder of all the times Cade and I met around the one in my mum's kitchen, all the conversations we had, and all the other things we did on that island. It was the pinnacle of so many things, so many moments in my past that I would rather forget for one reason or another.

Glancing at the open-floor space, I take a deep breath.

It doesn't matter about the island. It doesn't matter that I've chosen a house which is the complete opposite of the one I grew up in. It doesn't matter that I've spent the last sixteen years avoiding Cajun chicken and cats.

Because he's back.

He's at my workplace, my domain, my nine-to-five.

But he's not here.

He's never been here. This is the one place I should be able to forget him.

I head upstairs to the bathroom and shower, hoping to wash the day from my skin and the memories from my mind. It was surreal seeing Cade again today and having him standing in front of me, to the point where I'm starting to doubt if it was real. Was he just an illusion I'd created? Will I go to work tomorrow and the whole thing will have been a dream, Cade replaced with some old, balding executive type?

Do I want that?

My head is a mess, the present and the past tangling themselves into a ball.

After slipping into my favourite hoodie, I wander downstairs in the hope of finding something on TV that will rid my brain of all thoughts.

I'm on the sofa, under a soft blanket, the remote in my hand. I watch pictures flickering on the screen of a drama I'm not paying any attention to, as the lead female is irritatingly wooden, and her plight of having a cheating husband seems banal compared to my own dramatic day.

It's when I start channel-hopping that I hear them.

The noise is low at first, the familiar rumbling of the argument brewing before the shouting really begins. The lie I told Donna this afternoon has come back to haunt me.

Pulling the blanket up to my chin, I increase the volume on the TV. This is the third argument they've had this week, and as their voices climb the walls, so do my memories.

Then

Staring at the TV screen, I hug my knees to my chest and pull the soft grey throw around myself even though I'm far too warm. Why had I turned the lights out? It'd seemed like a good idea—the house to myself, a scary film, the dark room. But now, halfway through, I'm regretting this.

It's an old movie I found on Netflix that had great reviews. Normally, I'm not bothered by horror films, but for some reason, this one is getting to me. I should just turn it off, but I don't want to give in to my fear.

The front door slams, making me jump. The remote control I've been clinging to clatters to the floor, startling me further. There's a shuffle of feet in the hallway, and my ears strain to make out whether it's my mum and Mark or Cade. I don't care either way, just as long as they're human and amongst the living.

"Hey, what are you doing?" Cade asks as he enters the living room. "Has there been a power cut?"

"No, I'm watching this film." I scramble for the remote.

He bends down, picks it up, and hands it to me. I pause the movie.

He stares at the screen. "I've seen this. They all die in the end."

I glare at him as a grin creeps across his face. "Very funny."

"I take it my dad and your mum aren't back yet?" he asks as he perches himself on the edge of the adjacent seat.

"No, my mum texted, saying they didn't get a table until

late, and then I think she put something about going to a gin bar after the meal."

Cade makes a gruff sound. "I can't see my dad in a gin bar."

"The things people do for love," I sing.

"God, I know. It's weird, isn't it?"

"What people do for love or the fact that it's your dad and my mum?"

He considers this before answering. "Both."

"Are you telling me you've never done something out of the ordinary for someone you liked?"

"No, I can't say I have."

My heart prematurely deflates before he adds, "But I've never met anyone I liked enough to do something crazy for. What about you?"

"Me? God, no. I've done enough stupid things for Anna, let alone myself."

"Anna?"

"My friend I introduced you to last week." This would be a perfect opportunity to bump Anna up in Cade's estimation, to sell her to him, and if I was any kind of friend, I'd be doing just that.

"Why do you end up doing stupid things for her?"

"When she decides she likes someone, I'm usually involved in the orchestrating of their meeting or of them getting together. I'm like a director. For example, when she had a crush on Dean Foster, I had to accidentally on purpose bump into him in the corridor, dropping all my books, one of which was a magazine on skateboarding, so when he stopped to help me pick them up, he would see the magazine and say, 'Hey, I didn't know you were into skateboarding,' to which I would've replied, 'Yeah, but not as much as my friend Anna'—cue introduction to Anna, the beaming blonde who is kitted out head to toe in skater gear."

Cade looks perplexed. "And did it work?"

"No. He didn't stop to help me pick my books up—he just yelled, 'Watch where you're fucking going,'" I say in my best Neanderthal voice.

"Nice guy."

"He was one of the better ones."

"Can she not ask someone out on her own?"

"Girls don't usually do things alone. We're always in pairs."

"I can see that now you've mentioned it."

A little silence filters into the room before I glance back at the screen.

"I suppose I better watch the rest of this, although I won't be able to sleep tonight."

"Then why are you watching it?"

"I can't give in to a fictional storyline that holds no bearing on reality."

"It's not a challenge."

"It is. I've started, so I'll finish. I won't let it get the better of me."

"I hate horror films." He shivers.

I lean back into the sofa, my eyebrows raised. "Wow, really? I thought you'd be a diehard horror fan."

"When I was about eight, I was over at a friend's house,

and he had this great idea of watching The Exorcist. *I had no idea what it was, so I went along with it. I could barely watch, and I think I started crying at one point, saying I didn't feel well and wanted to go home. It traumatised me. I couldn't sleep. Even my dad noticed something was up, and when I finally told him what it was, he went nuts and told me I couldn't go to my friend's house anymore."*

"Jeez."

Cade smiles and then sits back in the chair.

I stare at him. "Are you staying for this?" I point the remote at the screen.

"I can't very well let you watch it alone. It'd be a massive dent in my manhood, and where would I go in your estimation?"

"My estimation of you is faring well, as I see you're wearing socks, so there's no need to worry in that department."

"Fair point, but I'm still not leaving you to watch this alone. Besides, it's been years since I watched a horror film, so it's about time I gave one a go, but we may have to sleep with our doors open and our lights on."

He sinks into the chair, and I un-pause the movie, not feeling afraid anymore.

My head has barely hit the pillow when I hear noises coming from downstairs. It must be Mum and Mark coming back from their night out.

According to my phone, it's one in the morning. My mum

has never stayed out this late, and I hope it's a sign of a good night, but as the voices downstairs rise, I start to think otherwise.

The clattering makes me sit up. It's as if there's a heavy-handed chef down there who's decided to prep a three-course meal. Normally, I can't hear what's going on in the kitchen, being two storeys up, so the fact that I can hear it at all is worrying.

I pull my phone out of the charger and recheck it, like there might be a notification from Sky News about what's going on in my own kitchen.

My bedroom door is wide open. Cade had endured the remaining hour of the film, and we'd headed up to our separate rooms around midnight. We'd agreed we would leave our bedroom doors open and the lights on just in case. I've not wanted to admit the comfort I've felt in knowing he's just opposite me with his door open.

Fishing for my headphones, I'm about to drown out the din with some music when I freeze. Am I mistaken? No, I can definitely hear swearing. Are they watching a movie, and the sound is coming from there? No, I know what I can hear—the acoustics are enough to tip me off that this isn't some TV drama. I know the shrill, accelerated sound, the antagonising volume, and the nit-picking tone.

I know what my mum sounds like when she's drunk.

My stomach vaults.

I tell myself that this doesn't happen very often—Christmas parties, birthdays, and the odd summer evening in the garden with a bottle. I have little experience with drunken people, but I know that people are either happy drunks or depressed drunks, either of which I think would be far easier to deal with than the aggressive monster my mum turns into after one gin too many.

The first time I saw her turn into this raging beast, she'd come home tipsy from the leaving do of one of her work colleagues.

Grandma had left after having babysat me, telling my mum she needed to drink a glass of water and go straight to bed, but as soon as the door had closed, Mum had pulled a bottle of something out of the cupboard. I'd crept downstairs after getting out of bed, unaware of what transformation she was going through.

At first, she'd been welcoming. "Alex, my beautiful girl, come sit with Mummy. Come keep me company." But as the bottle had got lighter and the glasses emptied, her presence became something more sinister. Her hug was too tight, her breath sour, and her face a contorted gargoyle, every word delivered with a venomous sting.

At six, I couldn't understand where my mum had gone.

"Never rely on a man, Alex. You want something doing, do it yourself. They're all a set of bastards, every single one of them. Don't ever get involved with a man. He'll just break you. They're all fucking shits," she'd spat, her head lolling as if her neck had lost its rigidity.

I recall the beep of Mum's phone, the text message that had been the detonator. She peered at the screen before erupting into what could only be described as a war cry and hurtling the phone across the living room. Instinctively, I'd shielded my head with my arms, my tiny nightdress rising above my knees and sending a chill over my skin. Mum had stood from the sofa, her legs unsteady, her body swaying as if there were a hurricane in the room. She'd grabbed the large candle that'd been a Christmas gift and launched it against the living room wall. The glass shattered, the candle bounced, and the scent of jasmine and honeysuckle filled the room.

I fled back upstairs to my room, but not before I'd seen the look on her face—the raging eyes, the bared teeth. Jumping into bed, I pulled the duvet over my head, grabbed my favourite bear, and held it so tightly that my arms hurt. And I'd shivered under the covers, wondering what'd happened to my mum, where she'd gone, and whether that monster would still be there in the morning.

As I've got older, I've become more accustomed to these outbursts and have been able to read the signs and know when it's time to lock myself away in my room and leave her with her internal anger.

I'd hoped Mark would never have to see this side of my mum, but judging by what I can hear going on downstairs, it seems the moment has landed.

"Hey." Cade appears in my doorway, the brightness of the landing light behind him making him appear like a shadow.

"Hey." I grimace a half smile, embarrassed by the shouting coming from downstairs.

"Do you know what's going on?" he asks as he pads into my room. He's wearing an old football kit, shorts, and a T-shirt, the lettering faded and the numbers partially disappeared.

"No, but it doesn't sound good, whatever it is." I pull my knees up to my chest, the duvet coming with them.

"Do you think we should go down?"

"God, no. Whatever it is, they need to sort it out themselves." I don't want Cade to see my mum like this. It's bad enough Mark witnessing it. "I'm sure they'll stop soon."

Soundlessly, he perches on the end of my bed like it's his natural place.

"It feels weird," he says. "Like they're the kids and we're the grown-ups."

"Maybe we should go down and threaten to bang their heads together," I joke. "Do you remember your parents arguing at all?"

"No, never. I mean, they used to bicker, but it was just the usual mum-and-dad stuff—nothing like that." Cade nods toward the open door to where the shouting is still raging.

"I was six when my mum passed away," he continues. The room takes on an enormous silence despite the racket from downstairs. "She died suddenly one morning of a brain tumour. My dad said she woke up with a headache. She'd been complaining about them for a few weeks but had put them down to the stress of working and raising a family. He'd gone downstairs to get her a cup of tea, and by the time he came back up to the bedroom, she had died. There was nothing anyone could've done. It was just one of those tragic things. So, we've been on our own for a long time. What about yours?"

The enormity of what he's just told me weighs so heavily in the room, it takes me a second to answer. My mum told me Cade's mum had died when he was younger, but she hadn't told me how, and for some reason, I get the feeling that he's never really spoken to anyone about his mum.

"I've never known my dad. My mum was quite young when she had me, and she said my dad didn't want a baby."

"That's too bad."

"You can't miss what you haven't had."

"I guess."

Even though the shouting downstairs is so loud, my room feels too quiet.

"I was about to listen to some music to drown them out." I hold an earphone out to him.

"Sounds like a plan, unless you're listening to something terrible." Cade scoots up the bed to sit beside me. I shift over to make room for him. His skin is so warm as he leans in and takes the earphone from me.

"Just a bit of Girls Aloud." I grin.

Cade's face drops as he holds the earphone.

"I'm kidding. It's just a playlist of chart songs on Spotify."

"I was worried for a second that you were going to go down in my estimation."

I raise my eyebrow. "And where am I now in your estimation?" I ask.

Cade places the earphone in his left ear and looks at me. "Pretty cool."

We settle down to listen to Daniel Powter singing about a bad day whilst the war rages on in the kitchen.

NINE
ALEX

AFTER RESORTING TO TWO SLEEPING PILLS, I'D finally slept a dreamless, heavy sleep with no Cade, no memories, and no arguing neighbours gracing my dark slumber. But as I fumble with the alarm on my phone, the morning sunlight forcing its way through the gap in my blackout curtains, my head feels like it's filled with dirty dishwater. It could be the after-effects of the sleeping pills, or it could be the stress of yesterday or the anticipation of what today will bring.

Whatever it is, I have no choice but to get up and face the day. I've worked hard to get where I am, and my job is the only thing that keeps me grounded. The rest of my life is a jumble sale of not knowing where I belong or what I should be doing. I've tried to take up hobbies, but I'm not into crafting or baking or joining a group of people who want nothing more than to poke into your past. The only thing I like doing is walking, and I will often don my walking boots and waterproofs on my days off and explore our local woods or canals, but even that only highlights how incredibly lonely I feel. I'd love a dog, but it wouldn't be fair with the hours I work; I crave a companion, someone who would love me unconditionally, who wouldn't ask any questions and wouldn't want to know how I've ended up in the dark place I'm in.

I find my way to the kitchen, then switch the kettle on and stare at the wall separating my house from next door.

My neighbours' argument had lasted over an hour, and I can't help wondering what their kitchen looks like this morning, what the air feels like, and whether any evidence of their dispute remains. I know only too well what afterward can look like.

Then

In the morning, I wake to find Cade has gone. I don't remember falling asleep or the noise stopping downstairs. All I remember is Cade's chest rising and falling beneath his T-shirt as he sat next to me, the music travelling between us as the chaos ensued downstairs.

My phone and headphones have been placed neatly on my bedside table, and the silence downstairs floats up to my room like smoke from a dying fire.

I check the time, then leap out of bed, remembering it's Saturday and Anna is due here any minute.

It's time for phase two of her plan.

Anna arrives looking fresh-faced and excited. Her skinny jeans are tighter than ever, her belly top barely reaches under her large bust, and her hair is painstakingly curled to perfection. I'm even more annoyed at her glowing presence, given how my sleep-deprived grooming has left me looking dishevelled.

The morning has been difficult. We've spent it treading on the invisible eggshells that litter the kitchen floor after the argument last night.

Mark got up first and went straight out, and my mum is still in bed.

God knows how long the argument lasted. But sitting with Cade, him leaning into me to hear the music from the tiny earphones, had calmed me. I'd been a mixture of emotions last night. I felt sick at the thought of Mum and Mark arguing but also contentment that Cade had been with me and I wasn't suffering alone.

Anna's expectant face irritates me as she reels off her latest plan to snare Cade. I feel nothing but distaste for my friend. I try to shake it off; it's just a lack of sleep and the fear of what will happen when my mum finally gets out of bed. But lately, I've been annoyed by her demands over Cade. Text messages asking what he's doing and who he's doing it with. What's his favourite colour? Will he like her wearing the tight jeans, or is he more of a skirt man?

"So, he's still in bed?" Anna asks, fluffing her hair up whilst sliding into position on the bar stool.

"I didn't say he was still in bed," I snap. "He's just still in

his room." I try to change my voice from ice-cold milk to hot chocolate.

"God, I hope he's not one of those lazy guys who stay in bed all day."

I glance at the digital clock on the oven door. "It's only quarter to eleven," I state. "Besides, we had a late night."

I can almost hear the snap of Anna's neck.

"When you say 'we,' do you mean, like, all four of you?"

The panic is written across her face in eyebrow pencil, and I know the power I hold, but even though she's getting on my nerves, I would never be that cruel to my best friend.

"Yes, all four of us." This isn't a lie, even if my mum and Mark had been on a different floor of the house.

"It must be weird going out with Mark and your mum and then fit Cade tagging along. I don't think I'd be able to cope." Anna fans herself with her hand like some Victorian maiden.

"It's getting less weird."

"Really?"

"Yeah. Cade's nice, and I'm kind of used to having him around now."

"Oh, well, that's good, I suppose." Anna returns to her reflection in the mirrored oven door. "Oh my God, is that him?" Her hands freeze above her hair as the creaking of floorboards trickles down from above.

We strain our eyes on the ceiling, Anna praying it's Cade, and for once, I join her, as the thought of facing my mum with a hangover sends an army of ants running over my skin.

If the last encounters are anything to go by, it will be a

surreal experience. Mum will trudge into the room, denial written all over her face, complaining about the inaccurate measures of the drinks in the last bar, the strength of the alcohol that had been served, or even claim that she's suffering from a migraine that arrived out of the blue and knocked her for six. It's never her fault. It's never the last drink she shouldn't have had or even the one after that. She'll smile at me, but it'll be the kind a guilty child throws to convince a parent they haven't misbehaved, a messy smile that looks like bad stitching. There'll be no mention of the things she said, the items she threw, or the ornaments she broke. They'll be cleaned away, swept under the carpet along with the incident, never to be spoken of again.

And none of it ever matters. I'm the sole witness. Who's going to argue with her? Who's going to question her about her behaviour? A six-year-old me? An eight-year-old me? A twelve-year-old me?

But this is different. Mark and Cade now know. Other people will ask the difficult questions and hold her accountable. What will the repercussions be of last night?

Whatever happens, I don't have the patience for my mum this morning. Not on top of Anna drooling over Cade.

I hear her intake of breath as he walks into the kitchen wearing grey sweatpants and a white T-shirt. He hasn't gelled his hair, and the smell of his body spray could easily knock us out.

"Hey." He nods at me without looking at Anna.

"Morning," she chirps like a cheerleader on the bench.

He glances over and nods before looking back at me. It's a

strange moment, an unspoken conversation between Cade and me that I'm certain Anna is oblivious to.

"I'm making a coffee. Anyone want one?" He pads over to the coffee machine.

"No, thanks," I reply.

"Coffee would be great," Anna says, straightening her back and pushing out her chest. She never drinks coffee—she thinks it's bitter and reminds her of Mr Jenkins's breath, our English teacher from last year, who arrived at every lesson with a full Thermos flask that he would slurp slowly throughout the entire double period.

Cade rattles around the kitchen, finding cups and spooning granules whilst waiting for the kettle to boil. I'm lost in watching him perform this simple task, but my moment of solace doesn't last long, as I feel Anna's stare boring into the side of my head.

Dropping my shoulders, I give in and look over at her. Anna's eyes widen, her head tipping to the side as she nods in Cade's direction.

I sigh. This is my cue to initiate plan B.

I push the stool back, cringing at the scrape of the legs, and stand before shuffling over to the glass of water that's been sitting patiently on the counter for the last twenty minutes. I pick it up, premature embarrassment washing over me as I move toward Anna. She's like a dog waiting for its dinner, her eyes round, her chest at attention—the only thing missing is her panting. Her eyes flitter over to Cade to check what he's doing before she nods at me.

I'd endured the rehearsal not twenty minutes ago, and that

had been bad enough. I'd walk past Anna with a glass of water, I'd trip or stumble, and the water would tumble down her front, putting her first in line for a wet T-shirt competition. Anna would shriek, Cade would look and be faced with her heaving bosom beneath her now see-through top, and the job would be done. Cade snared.

But even with such planning, I find myself unable to commit to the role, and the actual event comes across as amateur and clumsy as I pour the water down her front.

Anna, on the other hand, performs with gusto as she shrieks at the genuinely cold water running down her cleavage.

"Alex!" she hollers.

As predicted, Cade turns and sees Anna with her top soaked to her skin and me standing like an idiot with a glass in my hand.

"Sorry, I must've slipped." My words sound deadpan.

Cade's eyes dart between me and Anna. She slips from the stool and starts to bat the water down her front, which only results in pressing her top further onto her skin. The black bra she's wearing underneath is like a beacon, and in that second, I can forgive Cade for being drawn to it. As plans go, it'd seemed lame, but standing here now with Anna's wet front and heaving cleavage, I have to hand it to her—what guy would be able to resist?

I've prepared myself for him to be glued to her large chest, gawking with his eyes wide and his tongue hanging out, hypnotised and rendered helpless under the power of Anna's double-C cups. But he isn't looking at her.

He's looking at me.

Cade is normally hard to read, but I can almost hear his thoughts whirling as he stares at me. He isn't stupid, and after what I'd told him on the way to school, he's quickly worked out what's going on.

"Oh my God, look at me, I'm such a mess!" Anna declares, but his eyes remain on me.

"Are you all right?" Cade finally speaks.

"I'm fine, thanks, but…," Anna begins, but as she looks up, she realises he isn't talking to her at all. He's talking to me.

"Yes, I think I just tripped on the leg of the stool," I answer awkwardly, aware of Anna's stare now penetrating me.

"You're probably tired after last night," Cade suggests.

"Probably," I agree, uncertain where he's going with this.

Anna's transfixed, wondering what is going on and why her chest is not the centre of attention.

It's then that the devilish flash in his eyes sparks, lighting his face and making my toes curl.

"I should've gone back to my own bed sooner. You might have slept better." He picks up Anna's cup of coffee. "Your coffee," he says as he puts it down on the counter in front of her.

My cheeks are on fire and my breathing shallow. I keep my eyes on him, not able to tear them away, not daring to look at Anna. The awkwardness of this new situation is now clinging to the walls.

Anna glares as Cade walks out of the kitchen.

There's a moment of unreadable silence. She's clearly in shock, whilst I'm a hot mess. Does Cade realise what he just said? He must—otherwise, why would he have said it? He must've known what Anna was up to and how I'd been used, so he'd thrown the comment out there to... what? Put Anna in her place? Embarrass me? To put a stop to her flirting? Or is he just being downright cruel?

"Oh. My. God." Anna lets the three words roll out slowly, her mouth exaggerating each one as her disbelief follows. "What the hell did he mean? Why was he talking about sharing your bed? What is going on?" Her face is drawn and her eyes stark. She looks like a victim of a natural disaster, standing in my kitchen with her top soaked to her skin. I have no idea how to proceed.

"Nothing's going on," I begin, but Anna's already shaking her head.

"Don't give me that."

"Okay, it's not what you think."

"What I think is that something is going on between you and Cade, and what pisses me off is that you let me go through with this ridiculous plan, knowing that." She flaps her arms by her sides and pulls at her wet top just in case I'm unsure which ridiculous plan she's referring to.

"Nothing is going on between me and Cade," I protest. "We were up late listening to music on my bed, and I fell asleep."

"You expect me to believe that?"

"It's the truth."

"Why was he in your bed, listening to music late at night? It's not the normal kind of thing you do with your brother."

Anna's dented pride is now baring its teeth, and I'm starting to get annoyed.

"He's not my brother," I snap. "And if you must know, my mum and Mark came home late and were having a massive row in the kitchen, which woke both me and Cade up. He came into my room, and we put on some music to try and drown the noise out. I fell asleep. He was on top of my covers. Nothing happened."

Anna blinks, looking for cracks in my account. Then she sits down on the bar stool, her shoulders slumping and her chest deflating. "Why didn't you tell me?"

"I didn't want you to know about my mum and Mark. Besides, there's nothing to tell with regards to me and Cade. We were just drowning out the shouting."

She toys with this new scenario before saying, "I didn't mean to overreact, and I'm sorry about your mum and Mark arguing."

"It's okay. And nothing is going on between me and Cade."

Anna assesses me. "Are you sure?" she asks.

I sigh.

"I'm not accusing you of lying. I believe you when you say nothing is going on with you. What I'm asking is if you're sure he doesn't have feelings for you."

"What do you mean?" It's my turn to be shocked.

"I think he likes you. Maybe a little bit more than the regular like."

"No, no, not at all," I argue. The idea just seems so ridiculous. "He's just being nice and trying to fit in here."

"You really believe that?" Anna pushes.

I think of all the things Cade has done and said over the past week. The offer to walk me to school, the getting-to-know-each-other chats, and the fact that he'd endured a horror movie with me. Was he just being polite? Was he trying to get his feet under the table?

I flop onto the bar stool.

"Trust me, Alex, I know what I'm talking about when it comes to guys." Anna folds her arms, goose bumps having risen over her damp skin. "And I think he likes you."

The whole idea that Cade likes me is like a Lilo I'm trying to straddle in the pool but keep slipping off. I'm embarrassed by it but can't understand why.

"I'm not sure." My head swims. I'm unable to look at my best friend.

"Trust me, I'm right on this one," Anna says more sternly. "But I suppose what really matters is whether you like him."

My eyes find hers.

"I like him. Of course I like him—he's nice, he's friendly, he's made an effort to get to know me. But…." I trail off as I slide off the Lilo, my body a dead weight in the water.

"But?" Anna pushes. "How much do you like him?"

"I don't know. I haven't thought about him in that way."

My voice is quiet inside the chasm of my head. Have I thought about him in that way? No, but maybe that's because I haven't let myself. But it's out there now. Anna has branded it and put it on a billboard. No matter where I look, I can see the slogan flashing in neon letters: Cade likes you.

"Well, I think it's something you need to think about," she says, "because there could be the recipe for love here."

"What are you talking about? What about Operation Snare Cade?" I try to pull myself back from the land of make-believe.

"Hey, I know when I'm defeated." She holds her hands up, palms facing me. "Besides, I'm not so sure about him. He drinks coffee and plays football. I hate coffee, and I hate football." She makes a face, and I smile, relieved that she doesn't seem too cross about the whole thing.

"We need to start a new plan," Anna declares. "Operation Alex and Cade."

"No, really, I'm not sure that's a good idea."

"Really?" She raises an eyebrow. "Actually, you're probably right. I don't think you need my help at all. He's already yours. All you need to do is take him."

IT TAKES SEVERAL MINUTES FOR ME TO REALISE THAT staring at my maths book isn't going to make the correct answer appear. Once Anna left, I'd stayed up in my room, figuring that when Mark returned and my mum got up, they might need a bit of space to talk about what happened last night.

What did happen last night? What was their fight about? Will they manage to sort it out? What if they don't?

The door to my room is ajar, so when Cade knocks, it swings open, revealing him. I pull my earphones out, not failing to notice how strong his upper arms look, how his body takes up the full height of the doorway, and how dark and intense his eyes are.

What has Anna germinated in my brain?

"I hope I didn't cause too much trouble for you with your friend," he says.

I try to play it cool. "What makes you say that?"

"I got the impression that she was up to her usual tricks. I know you're not that clumsy."

He knows I'm not that clumsy.

I'm beginning to wish Anna hadn't said anything.

"There's not much that gets past you, is there?"

"I don't know." Cade shrugs. "I can be pretty clueless sometimes."

"Well, not this time."

"That's a relief." There's a beat of silence before he continues. "Was your friend okay about it?"

"Which part? The rejection or the fact that she now thinks something is going on between us?"

"Both."

"She took the knockback on her chin. You're a drop in the ocean where Anna is concerned."

"I'm hurt." Cade grabs at his heart. "And what about us?"

"What about us?" I twirl my pencil, trying my hardest to look unfazed by this conversation.

"What did you tell her?"

"What's there to tell?"

"You could've told her we were madly in love with each other."

His eyes find mine, and I hold my ground, staring right back at him as my heart beats furiously against my ribcage, reminding me it's in there.

"I could've, but I didn't."

A cheeky grin spreads across his face. "Shame." He shrugs, then walks out of my room.

I exhale deeply, the air rushing from my lungs, heat balling in my stomach as I fling myself back against my pillows, my heart fluttering like it's trying to keep up with the tempo of a fast dance song.

Shit. Anna is right. I can't ignore this.

Do I want to ignore this?

What does this mean?

I'm so out of my depth.

TEN

ALEX

After pulling into the car park, I kill the engine and remain in the quiet confines for several minutes. Yesterday was hard enough with Cade arriving in the shop and unleashing a cavern of memories I thought I'd managed to forget. He stirs up so many things inside me, things I can't control, things I don't want to control. Can I survive another day of him?

Will Cade already be in the shop?

Did he even leave last night?

Will he and Ian still be there in yesterday's crumpled clothing?

I'm not sure I'm ready to see him again. I'd had no choice when he'd arrived yesterday as if from another universe, his presence as alien as a life form from another planet. But today, I know he's going to be there and I'm going to have to look at him, be next to him, breathe the same air as him, and pretend I know nothing about him. Pretend I don't know what his touch feels like, what his words do to me, and that they aren't rooted in my heart.

Pretend.

I'm going to have to do a lot of pretending.

I grab my bag and am readying myself to get out of the car when I spot movement on the other side of the road.

There's a small Italian restaurant across from the car park. A tall, thin man in a crisp white shirt and dark trousers is setting up tables and chairs outside in the hope of the good weather continuing. I've never been to the restaurant, but it doesn't stop the memory taking hold.

Then

The atmosphere in the restaurant is as strained as the dim lighting that fails to illuminate my birthday meal. It's early evening, and Mark, Cade, and I are the only people in the sea of tables besides a family who've just arrived with a helium balloon in the shape of a number one. There are six adults, two of whom look to be the parents of the toddler who is babbling away to the remaining four, who I guess are grandparents.

"Not the only one celebrating tonight," Mark says, eyeing the balloon as they approach the table next to us.

I smile as the parents try to stuff the chubby toddler, who I presume is the birthday boy, into a child seat, the pair manhandling a tubby leg each. The toddler is adamant that he won't be confined to this little wooden jail, his legs resembling the jaws of an alligator.

"I've spoken to the chef, and he assures me there are no peanuts on the premises," my mum broadcasts as she returns to the table, her electric-pink satin shirt glaring at us all.

I grimace.

"I bet they had a right laugh in the kitchen when you asked if there were any nuts on the premises." Mark sniggers, eyeing Cade.

Mum slides into the booth next to Mark, pulling on the front of her shirt. "It's no laughing matter," she snips. "My daughter's life is no joke."

Mark sighs and glances at me. "I didn't mean any offence," he apologises.

"None taken. I thought it was funny."

My mum glares at me as I hide behind the menu.

The first few days after my mum and Mark's argument had been precarious, the atmosphere in the house a little off, but as the days have gone by, they seem to have softened, and things have slipped back into how they were before that night. No one has mentioned it—it's an unspoken thing that we now carry with us, and for once, I'm not shouldering it alone.

"Well, when everyone's done laughing at my expense, then we can order." My mum bristles, picking up her menu and giving it a disdainful look.

Mark throws me a guilty look, but I shake my head, silently telling him not to worry about it.

"Have you had a nice birthday?" Cade asks, putting his menu down on the table.

"As nice as you can have when you have double biology," I reply.

"I think they should bring a rule out where you don't have to go to school or work on your birthday for the whole of your life," Mark joins in.

"That would be great," I agree.

"I don't think that would be very practical," my mum intercepts. "What would all the single mothers do when their kids had a day off school because it was their birthday, but they needed to go to work?"

She's in no mood for fantastical discussions, which is a shame, as I'd hoped we would enjoy our first night out together, seeing as it's my birthday.

Since Anna had suggested there might be something between me and Cade, our interactions have become something entirely different, and I'm not sure if it's just me who is picking up on it or whether he feels the shift also.

Our walks to school have become insular, as if we're the only two people in the entire world. I've managed to convince Cade to eat a slice of toast before setting off and also rescued him from a confrontation with a ginger tom who'd leaped into our path.

"What do you think they were arguing about?" he'd asked one morning.

"I don't know. Could've been anything." I shrugged.

"I don't think I've ever heard my dad shout like that before."

I looked at the pavement and tried to avoid the cracks. "My mum can get a bit hot-headed when she's had something to drink," I said at last.

"So, you think it was your mum's fault?"

"I'm not saying she would be solely to blame," I explained. "Just that it wouldn't be the first time too many drinks have set her off."

"So, she's got a drink problem?"

"I wouldn't go as far as that. She doesn't drink often enough for it to be a problem. It's just that when she does, it brings out the worst in her."

Things have calmed between Mark and my mum since the argument, but I know there are only so many things that can be swept under the carpet before it becomes impossible to walk on.

By the time we finish our main course, the restaurant has begun to fill. I was underwhelmed by my hunter's chicken and envious of Cade's burger, which is what I really wanted to order but felt my sixteenth birthday was too big of an occasion for just a burger.

"So, are you doing anything else to celebrate, Alex? What are you up to with your friends?" Mark asks when the dessert menus arrive.

I glance at my mum, but she's too busy studying the dessert menu. She'd suggested a party, but I couldn't think of anything worse than my small group of friends standing aimlessly in the local golf club with a few lame banners and a cake with a ballet dancer on, my mum fussing all the while from one dilemma to the next.

"I'm having a few friends over on Saturday night," I reply. I'd wanted to go out somewhere with my friends, like to a restaurant or a pizza place, but there was no way my mum would let me in a restaurant without her, so I'd suggested having Anna and Kadijah over for the evening. My mum had been keen on the idea, even offering to spruce the garden up, hire a hot tub, and make mocktails for us. I'm happy with this. Mum can fuss behind the scenes.

"Remind me to go out on Saturday night." Mark winks at Cade. "Maybe you'll come with me, Cade."

"I'm sure I can find somewhere to be." He smirks.

"Will it be all nail varnish and facemasks? Is that what you girls get up to?" Mark asks.

I giggle as Cade mouths, "I'm sorry," shaking his head at his dad.

"Mum hired a hot tub," I tell him.

"A hot tub?" Mark raises his eyebrows. "I've never been in a hot tub before. I might stay in after all. What do you say, Cade? Might even dig out my budgie smugglers."

I nearly spit out my drink with laughter.

"You won't be laughing when you see him in the budgie smugglers, trying to bomb the hot tub," Cade adds.

I'm really laughing now when I notice something is missing.

My mum hasn't confirmed the plans for the hot tub or gone over the mocktail menu she's designed, nor has she reprimanded Mark for being vulgar at the table.

Instead, she's staring at the table next to us, where the chubby toddler, still stuffed in his highchair, is now clapping his hands in delight as a waiter brings over a colourful birthday cake, one little candle dancing to the tune of his family singing "Happy Birthday" to him.

My mum is transfixed.

"Mum? You okay?"

"I don't believe this," she mutters, lowering her menu but still looking at the family.

"Do they not have your favourite?" Mark asks, referring to the dessert menu now redundant in her hand. "If it's spotted dick you're after, then you'll be disappointed. I've already looked, and it's not there."

I want to laugh, but the look on my mum's face stops me.

I know that look.

"I'm just going to speak to the manager." She wiggles from the booth.

The three of us stare as she strides over to the small bar. I look away, the embarrassment already beginning to leak into my face.

"What's the problem?" Mark asks. "If she's going to complain about my jokes, then she's not going to get much joy from the manager." He chuckles.

Cade stares at me. "What's the matter with her?"

I sigh. "The family at the table next to us has brought a birthday cake in for their child."

"Is that bad?" Mark asks, still confused. "Is she upset because she didn't bring you a cake?"

"Is this to do with your allergy?" Cade asks.

"Shop-bought cakes can't guarantee they're nut free," I explain, my chest tightening.

"But we aren't eating it. So, it doesn't matter, right?" Mark says.

"It's been in the kitchen. They've opened it to put the candles on. The waiter has touched it," I say.

The singing from the table next to us finally stops as the toddler attempts to blow the candle out but ends up blowing a sloppy raspberry instead.

"Oh." Mark nods, still not understanding why my mum is so cross. "It's okay, though, isn't it?" he asks me. "Just as long as you don't eat the cake."

"I can react to anything that has touched a peanut, even a person. I don't necessarily have to have eaten it."

"I see." Mark narrows his eyes as if he doesn't really see at all.

"It isn't a problem, really, but my mum is just a bit OTT with it all."

She's on the other side of the restaurant, flapping her arms at the young manager, who looks perplexed as to what exactly she wants him to do. Luckily, I can't hear her, but I imagine she's saying how irresponsible it is to let people bring in possibly contaminated food whilst knowing they have a diner with an allergy on the premises. I know she called ahead first to warn them, but I doubt they thought a birthday cake would be an issue.

I glance around the room, grateful that none of the other diners seem to have noticed what's going on, especially the family next to us, who appear to be basking in the joy of their child's first birthday.

We sit in silence, waiting for her return. Cade keeps glancing at me as if trying to tell me something.

"Right, we're leaving," my mum announces when she finally returns. She pulls her coat from the back of her chair and beckons me to do the same. Her cheeks are flushed, and the veins on her neck are pulsing from beneath her skin.

"But what about dessert?" Mark asks, still confused at the turn of events.

"I have a cake at home. We can eat that."

"You should've brought it with you," he says innocently, nodding toward the table next to us, still oblivious to the drama their shop-bought cake has caused. "They would've brought it over and sung 'Happy Birthday' to Alex and properly embarrassed her. Isn't that what birthdays are all about?"

Mark is desperately trying to rescue the evening, and I want to thank him for trying.

"I didn't bring it because I didn't want it contaminated in their kitchen, and it's a good job I didn't, as they have no idea what cross-contamination is."

She's struggling into her jacket as I slide from the booth.

"What about the bill?" Mark asks as we begin to follow my mum toward the exit. At the bar, the manager stands, arms folded, glaring at us.

"I'm not paying them," she snaps. "I've refused on the grounds that they could've killed my daughter with their incompetence."

Words fight to get to the surface. I want to tell her it's fine, since I have my EpiPens, and I don't think a shop-bought cake on the table next to us is a big deal, but this is not the time to point that out. I'm going to have to learn to live in the big bad world, and unfortunately, peanuts are part of that world; I can't expect them to disappear for me.

I hang my head, adding "criminal" to my list of shame.

We bustle out the door, my mum like a racehorse taking up the lead with Mark jogging behind her, still trying to understand what's just happened.

"Are you all right?" Cade asks as he trots up next to me, his hands thrust deep in his pockets.

"Great. Never better. Just how I wanted my birthday to end."

"Is it always like this when you go out for something to eat?"

"We don't ever eat out." A despondency washes over me as we make our way over to the car.

We head home and assemble in the kitchen whilst my mum fiddles about with candles and a lighter, her anger still radiating through her fingers. The cake has been made by a local baker, one who assured her there were no nuts on the premises. They sing "Happy Birthday," Mark breaking out his baritone singing voice as they near the end, and I smile as I blow out all sixteen candles.

"Have you made a wish?" Cade asks as the smoke rises, twisting in between us like dancers in the air.

I answer, "Yes," before my mum starts cutting into the cake.

Complaining of a headache, she goes to bed early, and Mark finds something to watch on Netflix. Cade announces he's going out, so I skulk off to my room to end my birthday by myself.

I'm halfway through my book when I hear a knock at my door. Not waiting for me to answer, Cade pushes the door open. Letting my book flop onto my lap, I sit up.

"Hey," he says as he closes the door softly behind him. He looks odd, his jacket zipped up, his posture all wrong.

"Hey."

"I could see how upset you were in the restaurant," he begins, "and I didn't want you to end your birthday like that." He starts to unzip his coat. My eyes widen as I clock the brown bag. "So, I broke all the rules of the house and have sneaked you a McDonald's."

"Oh my God!" My hand goes to cover my mouth.

"I did ask at the counter, and they said they don't have nuts on the premises, but they can't guarantee it hasn't been near a nut in its past life. And I knew you wanted a burger."

"How?"

"I just knew. The way you were watching me eat mine. The way you pushed that dry chicken around your plate."

He starts to unwrap the food. My mouth waters as the smell of melted cheese and fries wafts into the room.

"My mum would hit the roof if she knew."

"But she doesn't, and what she doesn't know won't hurt her."

Cade passes me the burger. I take it and grin.

"Would now be a good time to tell you I've never had McDonald's?"

"If you'd have told me that a few weeks ago, I wouldn't

have believed you, but knowing your mum like I do now, I'm not surprised."

"It's only because she cares." My head drops as I grip the burger, guilt working its way in.

"I know. But you're sixteen. And you can't stop living because of something like that."

A palpable sadness washes over him, and I wonder if he's thinking about his mum and how short her life had been and what she's missing out on.

"I also went on a nut allergy social media group, and there were people on there who have eaten McDonald's all their lives and have never had a reaction, but it's up to you. I understand if you don't want to take the risk."

"It's fine. I have an EpiPen just in case. And thank you for giving me a McDonald's for my birthday."

"You're welcome. I just hope you like it."

I take a bite. I don't care what I'm eating or how it tastes. I just know this is the best burger I've ever had.

ELEVEN
ALEX

THE TAPPING ON MY CAR WINDOW STARTLES ME, AND I look up to see a smiling Donna waving at me.

"Were you asleep with your eyes open?" she asks.

I shake my head and grab my bag. Hauling myself out of my car, I feel like my body weighs a thousand tonnes. The effort it takes me to exit my vehicle feels unreal.

"No. I'm just tired."

"Still? What were you doing all night if you weren't sleeping?" She nudges me as we walk.

"Get your brain out of the gutter. I slept fine. A little too fine, actually, as I took a couple of sleeping pills."

"Just the two?"

I shoot her a look.

"It's just, you look shattered."

"Did you get your niece's cake?" I ask, changing the subject.

"I did, and there's no phallic horn, so all is well. Although, I called my sister last night, and she's having a mini meltdown, as my niece has now announced she wants a hot-tub party."

Missing my bag, my car key drops to the floor.

"Hey, butterfingers. You sure you're okay?"

"Of course."

"Is it nerves?"

Donna hands me my key, and I stuff it forcefully into my bag.

"Why would I be nervous?"

"Because *I'm* nervous. This is the first full day with the new boss. Are you sure you don't know him?"

"No," I snap, then add a little softer, "No, I don't know him."

I *knew* him.

"So, anyway, my sister has to find a hot tub by the weekend. Know anywhere that rents them?"

The pavement vanishes, Donna's voice drifting into oblivion. And I'm gone.

Then

"When's the hot tub arriving?" Cade asks as he closes the front door behind him.

I push through the small front gate, feeling a sense of relief as my feet hit the pavement. I've spent all morning spraying cheap body spray around my room, trying to get rid of the smell of fried food. If my mum finds out Cade smuggled food in for me, then he and Mark will be homeless. He got rid of the bag and wrappers and assured me that she won't find out. But I know what my mum is like.

"It's being delivered this afternoon. My mum's booked the afternoon off work to wait for it to come. I hope it isn't too complicated to set up."

"I'm sure my dad will help out."

"Is he any good with things like that?"

"He's quite handy when he wants to be."

We round the corner and fall into step with each other like we have done every morning for the past few weeks. This has quickly become my favourite part of the day, just Cade and me and not a nut in sight.

"If you could change something, anything at all about your life, what would it be?" he asks as we amble past the large semidetached house with the circular window on the top floor.

I pull my bag further onto my shoulder. One of my textbooks digs into my back.

"I don't know." I shrug. "I often think it would've been nice to have a brother or a sister. But then my friends who have siblings do nothing but complain about them."

Cade stares at the ground.

"What about you?"

"I wish my mum hadn't died." He holds on to the strap of his bag with two hands as if it's keeping him upright.

"It must've been awful."

"It was strange. I was so young. At the time, I just went

along with what was happening, never really considering the long-term effects or how things would change for me and my dad. It's only as I've got older that I've started to ask questions, questions I know there aren't any answers to, but even so, I feel like somebody should be able to answer me, to justify what happened."

"What about your dad?"

"I always thought he was some sort of superhero, that he was invincible, given how he kept us both together and never seemed to falter. But now I see the pain he's carried, the brave face he's put on, and that he's just a man who lost someone he loved."

"He makes me laugh," I say, unsure of an appropriate response.

"That's the one thing you can rely on him for." Cade slows his pace as if the conversation is holding him back.

"Have you never wanted to know about your dad?"

"I've asked about him, but I get the impression that my mum doesn't want to talk about him. He was just a teenager. He didn't stick around long. I don't think he wanted to play happy families."

"He could be out there, anywhere, and you wouldn't know. Doesn't that bother you?"

I think about this. "Not really. He didn't want anything to do with me, so why should I think about him?" I glance at Cade. "Does that seem odd to you?"

He shrugs. "I don't know. I find it harder to understand how your dad can walk around knowing you exist but isn't part of your life. I know I couldn't do that."

I push my hair behind my ear, feeling the anger reverberating off Cade. I've never seen him angry, but he must have a temper, as I've seen the evidence for myself. Is this why he plays so much football, physical activity being a good outlet for his emotions?

"It just doesn't seem fair," he says after several minutes.

"What doesn't?"

"That your dad got a choice when my mum didn't."

THE GARDEN LOOKS AMAZING. THE LONG, THIN OUTDOOR space is littered with balloons and bunting. Laminated photos hang along the fence. The first picture ever taken of me, a tiny, red-faced bundle nestled within a white blanket and held preciously in the arms of my mum, who doesn't look much older than I am now. Then a photo of me as a toddler squashed in a pushchair with ice cream smeared all over my face along with a huge grin, and a photo of an eight-year-old me in a tutu and ballet shoes, standing gracefully at a ballet bar.

Mum has draped fairy lights amongst the shrubs and dangled them from the lower branches of some of the larger trees at the bottom of the garden, which will add a touch of magic once the sun goes down.

The arrival of the hot tub had been stressful. It wouldn't fit through the house, so the delivery men had to go around and try to squeeze it over the back gate, knocking one of the fence panels over in the process. Mark managed to prop the panel back up, whilst Mum haggled with the delivery guy over compensation for the damage.

In my eyes, it's been worth it, as it now stands in pride of place on the patio area. Mark was the first to get in, announcing that someone needed to be the guinea pig. Even though the water hadn't quite heated up, he stayed in, saying he could get used to this kind of life, but before my friends arrived, my mum shooed him out and told him to clear off for the night.

Anna and Kadijah got here at seven, both seeming excited for the evening ahead. They've been frisked at the door by my mum, a box of chocolates removed from Kadijah, who looked positively frightened at the thought of having brought contraband.

"You'd have been better off bringing a bottle of vodka," Anna jokes as we pile into my room. "Alex's mum would've been fine with that."

"I'm sorry," Kadijah apologises for the fourth time. "I'd forgotten about the peanut thing."

"Don't worry about it," I tell her, pulling my bikini from the bottom drawer.

"Nice two-piece," Anna notes as she grabs a bikini with far less material than mine from her beach bag, the strings looking thin and flimsy.

Kadijah clasps her hand over her bag, wary of getting her costume out.

"Anna, you can get changed in the bathroom and Kadijah in here. I'll go in Cade's room."

"Is he in?" Anna flashes me a look, one that I feel.

"No, he's gone out, and so has Mark."

"Good," Kadijah pipes up. "The only reason my mum let me come was because I told her there were no men in the house. She'd have a fit if she thought I was parading around in a swimming costume in front of living, breathing men."

I smile, knowing Kadijah comes from a devout Muslim family.

"Will Cade mind you snooping around in his room?" Anna asks, her eyebrow raised as if trying to suggest something.

"No," I say quickly. "And he won't even know."

Anna looks at me like she's analysing the page of a book before she tugs her bag onto her shoulder and makes her way out of the room.

"Will you be okay in here?" I ask Kadijah as I follow Anna.

"I'll be fine."

I close the door to my room, and Anna disappears into the tiny shower room as I'm faced with Cade's bedroom door. He's taken to leaving it open, but today, it's closed. I haven't been in his room since he moved in. He's always come into mine.

I flip open the cover on my phone and type out a quick text.

> Am I OK to get changed in your room pls?

I wait, wondering what Cade will make of this. There are plenty of other rooms in the house I could use, but none are as convenient as his.

His reply appears on the screen.

> Yes, just don't be offended by all the posters of naked women.

I smile, replying with a laughing emoji. I've walked past his open door enough times to know there are no such things.

Pushing open his door, I bundle inside before closing it behind me and surveying the room that used to be my dumping ground. There are trophies on top of a chest of drawers and a signed football shirt framed and hung on the wall. His bed has been roughly made with grey bedding.

There's something strange about being here in here without him.

Slipping out of my clothes, I struggle into my bikini.

I feel different now, my bare arms and naked legs exposed to Cade's room. I wriggle my toes into the soft carpet and have a sudden urge to lie on his bed and feel his sheets on my skin. I sit on the edge of his bed, his musky smell worming its way into my nose. Glancing over his bedside cabinet, I notice a small picture in a silver frame. I pick it up, the frame heavier than it looks.

The photo, I presume, is of Cade as a toddler, nestled in the arms of a smiling woman. I can see the resemblance, the dark features, the intense eyes.

It's Cade and his mum.

I put the photo down, a profound sense of sadness washing over me as I make my way out of the room.

ONCE MY MUM SORTS THE MOCKTAILS OUT, SHE LEAVES US to enjoy ourselves, which gives Anna ample time to add a little gin to our drinks.

"It's some sort of flavoured stuff my mum got for Christmas and will never drink," she says as she pulls the brightly hued bottle from her bag.

"None for me, thanks," Kadijah says, putting her hand over the top of her glass as Anna unscrews the cap.

"I don't think we need any gin. These are pretty good," I add.

"Oh, come on, live a little. You're only sixteen once." Anna sloshes the violet gin into her already full glass.

We drink and laugh and discover that karaoke in a hot tub is no easy feat when trying to keep our phones dry and not drop them in the water. And with no microphones to amplify our off-key attempts at Rihanna's "Umbrella," we just sound like a bunch of caterwauling cats. And it's nice to forget our up-and-coming exams, my mum and Mark, and my feelings for Cade, even if only for an hour or two.

I've drunk a fair bit and am feeling quite light-headed by the time the party winds down. Kadijah had been collected at eleven, just before Cade arrived home, and Anna left shortly after.

Just before midnight, my mum heads off to bed. I've contemplated going to bed as well but can't quite bring myself to end the night. So, against my mum's instruction of not getting in the hot tub unsupervised, I climb back in, contemplating how many dead skin cells are now floating on the water.

"Are you out here on your own?" Cade calls as he appears in the back doorway.

"Yes, don't worry, they've all left," I reply as the bubbles froth between my fingers.

"Not much of a party if it ends before midnight."

"Kadijah isn't allowed to stay out late, and Anna has some family get-together tomorrow that's miles away, so they're setting off early."

"Are you going to sit in there all night?" Cade pads over, his right hand jammed in his pocket.

"Need to get our money's worth. It's being collected on Sunday afternoon, and it might rain tomorrow." I stare at him. "Why don't you get in? You know you want to."

Cade grimaces. "I can't remember the last time I wore a pair of trunks. In fact, I'm not sure I even own any."

"You'll be okay in a pair of shorts," I suggest, meaning football shorts or something, but I watch as Cade stares at the water and then, using one hand, pulls his T-shirt up and over his head. My stomach flips.

"Have you guys been drinking?" he asks as he begins to undo his trousers.

I'm gawking, but I can't help it.

"My mum made mocktails, which we spiced up a little."

"What with?" he asks, kicking his jeans off.

I'm transfixed. I've seen guys in shorts, but this is different. This is Cade in tight boxer shorts.

"Some flavoured gin Anna brought. I think it was Parma Violet."

Cade mimes being sick.

"Are you not a gin drinker?"

"Can't stand the stuff." He peels off his socks and makes his way over to the hot tub.

"Are you getting in in your boxers?"

He surveys his designer underwear, the black shorts hugging his muscular legs. "You said shorts."

"I meant football shorts." I shake my head. "Never mind. They'll do."

As if granted entrance, Cade climbs into the hot tub and lowers his body, the water shifting to accommodate him. He settles on the little seat opposite me, and I'm suddenly conscious of where my feet are and whether they're touching his. He places his arms around the outer edge, seeming happy.

"Actually, this is nice," he says after several minutes.

"You sound surprised."

"It's not really what guys do, sit in hot tubs."

"I forgot you were only happy with a spear in your hand," I joke.

"You know what I mean," Cade says. "I don't mean it like in a sexist way. It's just…."

"It's just not very manly," I finish for him.

"Exactly."

"Well, wait until I get you a face pack out."

"Not a chance."

I take a sip of my drink.

"Are you sure I can't get you a drink?" I offer.

"No, thanks. I've already had a few with the lads, and gin isn't my thing."

I picture Cade sitting with his mates, drinking.

"Where do you go?" I ask.

"There's this pub not too far from here. It's an absolute shit-hole, but it's the only place that doesn't ask us for ID."

"I think you look eighteen."

"It's easier for girls. Bit of make-up and high heels and they're in."

"Do you meet up with any girls?"

"A few."

I bite the side of my glass.

"You should come out with me one night," he suggests.

"As if my mum would let me," I scoff.

"She wouldn't have to know. We could say we were going somewhere else."

"She's only just let me walk to school with you."

"It's worth a try. Unless you don't want to come out with me." His eyes twinkle, the reflection of the water making them look like they're shimmering.

"I think I'd cramp your style."

"I'm not sure I have a style, and anyway, I think it would be the other way round."

"The other way round?"

"I think I'd be cramping your style." Cade's eyebrow rises as he gives me a sly grin.

"As if," I tut. "I'm not allowed anywhere without my mum and an EpiPen. I don't even think I'd know what to do in a pub."

"You just sit around a table and drink and talk shite until they tell you to go home."

"Sounds great." It comes out sarcastic, but I'd love nothing more than to spend time talking to Cade.

"We should give it a go," he says.

"And tell my mum what? Where would I say we were going?"

"You could tell her it was a date."

I laugh, but Cade doesn't.

"What's so funny?" he asks.

"I don't think she'd believe that." I place my drink on the small table my mum put next to the tub. The bubbles have stopped, the timer having run out, and the water is still and silent, the distorted image of our bodies swaying under the surface.

I thrust my hands under the water.

"Why not? Am I not good enough for you?" Cade looks serious, his light-hearted banter having evaporated along with the steam from the tub.

"No, no," I stammer, shaking my head. "Nothing like that. I just don't think she'd believe that you would want to take me out on a date. You're older than me, and—"

"Not much older," Cade intercepts.

"No, but even so. You have friends and you go to the pub and you're a popular guy, and I'm…."

"You're funny and witty, and I like spending time with you."

The sheen on his forehead from the heat of the tub is glistening in the fairy lights. He's deadly serious, whereas I feel as if I've stepped into a fairy tale.

When I don't say anything, he adds, "And you're exceptionally beautiful."

We stare at each other. There's a funny sensation in the pit of my stomach, and I wonder if it's the gin.

"Ah, this is where the party is!" Mark's voice erupts from the back door, breaking our stare.

We turn in unison, the water rippling at the sudden movement.

"You're home," Cade says, eyeing his dad.

"The wanderer returns," Mark replies. "Where are all your friends, Alex?"

"They've gone home," I reply, trying to push my back up against the side of the hot tub.

"And now you're stuck with my Cade." Mark makes a tutting noise as I smile. "It could be worse, I suppose," he continues. "You could be in the kitchen, stuck in between two annoying aunts with a plate of congealed trifle in your hand."

I look at Mark, feeling bemusement spread across my face like butter.

"Here we go," Cade moans, rolling his eyes before looking at me. "You're about to hear about my dad's sixteenth birthday and how it traumatised him for the rest of his life."

"There was none of this hot-tub business in the garden in my day. I don't even think we had a paddling pool."

"Next you'll be telling us you didn't have running water and electricity," Cade says. "He acts like he was born in the Victorian age."

"Very funny," Mark bites back. "I'm just trying to say we

weren't as privileged as you kids today, with your mocktails and your parties. We had very little."

"What did you do for your sixteenth?" I ask Cade, whipping my head around to face him.

"Nothing much," he answers. "I'm not much of a party person."

"Don't let him fool you that I didn't try to have a big party for him because I did, but the stubborn mule wasn't interested."

I find it hard to imagine Mark organising anything.

"Me and some mates went to watch a football match, and then we went for pizza," Cade tells me before looking at his dad. "It was great," he assures Mark. "Exactly what I wanted to do."

"You see, lads are a lot less complicated than you girls." Mark whistles. "We're happy with the simple things in life—a bit of sport, a bite to eat, you get the idea."

"So, what do us girls need?" I challenge him.

Mark scratches his chin. "You need lights." He sweeps his arm around the garden, signalling at the fairy lights. "You need glitter and glamour, an entrance, an exit, and a standing ovation. It's more about the performance with you ladies than the actual show."

"That's very philosophical of you at this hour," Cade says, throwing me an apologetic look. "How many beers have you had?"

"Not enough, son, not enough," Mark answers.

"Well, I would've been more than happy to go for pizza with my mates rather than all this," I tell Mark.

"Well, it's late," Cade says, "and I'm way too hot in here now."

He pulls his body out of the water, and I stop breathing as it runs down the front of his chest, his shorts having shrunk, leaving nothing to the imagination. I wasn't hot before, but now I am. He levers himself out of the tub.

"Did you get in in your boxers?" Mark asks.

"I don't own a pair of trunks," Cade replies as he grabs a large towel from the pile my mum deposited on a small fold-out table.

"What about the pair you had when we went to Benidorm?"

"That was about seven years ago, and they had Power Rangers on them," Cade scoffs.

Mark pulls a face.

"I should get out as well. I think I'm going to shrink if I stay in any longer." I wade through the tub to the other side.

Cade secures his towel around his waist before leaning over and handing me one.

"And what do we need to do with this thing overnight?" Mark enquires, looking at it like it's an alien spacecraft that's landed in the garden.

"Mum said we just need to put the cover on."

"I'll sort it," Mark says. "You kids go get dry." He nods for us to go inside.

Cade stamps over to the back door, trying to dry his feet in the process. I follow, shoving my feet into my sliders and wrapping my towel around my chest.

"I'm sorry about my dad," he says as we enter the kitchen. "Sometimes I think he was born in the wrong century."

"It's okay, really. He's funny."

"He's just very old-fashioned."

"That's what makes him so funny."

"Yeah, well, he has his moments."

We stand in the kitchen, water pooling beneath us as it runs from our bodies.

"I'm going to head up," I say as I hear Mark swearing from the back garden.

"I'd better go help him," Cade tuts. "He's probably fallen in."

I smile as he heads back into the garden.

The gin has made my legs feel heavy as I climb the stairs. I feel giddy yet tired, Cade's words dancing around my gin-laden brain.

"You're beautiful."

I've never been told that by anyone. Was he being serious?

As I close the door to the small bathroom I now share with Cade, my eyes land on his toothbrush. Regarding my reflection in the mirror above the sink, I clutch the towel that's covering me. The hot tub has brought out the colour in my cheeks, making me look a sweaty mess, as if I've just climbed a thousand steps on a red-hot day. And my hair has seen better days. I've piled it on top of my head and secured it with a clip to keep it away from the water, but the humidity has enticed the tiny new growth and the straggly bits to pop up randomly over my head.

I try to pat it down.

What constitutes beautiful? What does Cade see that I don't?

After stripping off my wet bikini, I go to hang it on the small radiator in the shower room, then decide against it. Cade won't appreciate looking at my wet clothes. I pull the towel around myself and then head into my room, dropping the bikini on my own radiator instead as I leave the door open. My pyjamas are soft and comforting, and I climb into bed, my head sinking into the pillow like it's made out of dough.

It's been a long night, and as I drift off into slumber, the image of Cade taking his clothes off replays in my head on a continual loop.

TWELVE
ALEX

I'M UNSURE WHETHER IT'S A RELIEF OR disappointment that Cade is nowhere to be seen when we arrive at the office, and I envy the way Donna launches herself into work as if the whole office has not just been turned upside down by his arrival.

Ian arrives shortly after us in a dark suit I've never seen him wear and a tie I'm pretty sure he bought from the charity shop on the way here.

As the kettle boils, he starts to fill us in on his long meeting with Cade yesterday and how he hadn't left the shop until well after seven. He looks drained, his skin pale against the new suit, his eyes weary.

"It sounds like it was full-on," Donna says, sinking into her chair and firing up her computer.

"He wanted to see every file, every property we have on our books, every policy. He looked over the website and all the brochures, new and existing. He was relentless." Ian scratches his head like he's just witnessed a tornado and is now assessing the aftermath.

Ian's words tug at my insides as I hover by my desk. It's the same as I left it yesterday, with the addition of a Post-it Note stuck to the side of my monitor detailing a property viewing booked for today at twelve thirty under the name of Mr Gainsborough. It's not Ian's slanted writing or Donna's either, as she always ends every note with a kiss, so that only leaves one person who would've taken this booking. The handwriting looks different from what I remember from his schoolbooks that contained the hurried scrawl of someone who didn't really care about the words he was writing. These letters are neat and purposeful, as if the hand that formed them has grown up. I peel the note from the screen and examine it, imagining his hand as he'd written it, how his fingers must've gripped the pen, and what he must've been thinking about when he wrote it.

"Alex." My name reaches me. "Anyone at home?" Donna mocks from her desk.

"Sorry, yes. What were you saying?"

"I asked you if you wanted a sandwich ordering." She flaps a piece of paper in my direction. "You know we won't get our lunch if we don't put our order in early," she reminds me.

We order our lunch every day from Foyles Deli, which is just around the corner. It's a small shop run by a husband-and-wife team, and their food is to die for. Every small business within a one-mile radius orders their lunch from them every day. I recite my regular order of a turkey salad sandwich on brown bread as Donna scribbles it down.

"You sure you only took a couple of those sleeping pills?" she asks.

"I'm sure."

She shakes her head.

How the hell am I going to get through this? How am I supposed to function when he's not even in the shop and I'm already lost, the sight of his handwriting enough to send me into a dazed stupor?

***

As I approach the detached bungalow, my heels clack on the block-paved drive. I check the time. I'm fifteen minutes early for the twelve thirty viewing.

The property has been vacant for some time, and I need to get rid of the stagnant smell that will have begun to permeate the walls and carpets. I hate showing people around empty houses. Some people can't see past the bare shell. They see a house and not a home. I wish I had a bit more time and a few items of furniture to spruce the place up.

I'm in the bathroom, making sure the taps work, when I hear the front door open. Quickly, I make my way to the front of the house, curious as to who would've just let themselves in without knocking.

Entering the hallway, Cade closes the door behind him.

My breath catches on the cobwebs.

Had I known when I saw the note? Had I hoped?

He turns and faces me. He's beautiful.

"Mr Gainsborough, I presume?" I fold my arms across my chest as if I'm expecting a full-frontal attack.

"For the moment."

"I should be annoyed at you wasting my time, but you're paying me."

"You've not lost that witty mouth of yours." Cade pushes his hands into his pockets.

I want to laugh, to smile. I want to pick up where we left off sixteen years ago when we were one, just the two of us and no one else, but I can't erase the day it all came crashing down, the screaming, the shouting. So much anger.

It hadn't always been that way.

"Why are you here?" I ask, the angry beast stalking inside me.

"Because someone up there is having a fucking laugh at our expense," Cade says, casting his eyes skyward. "I need you to know, I had no idea you worked here. You don't get a list of employee names when you buy a business. I'm as shocked as you are."

"I'm more shocked that you ended up being an estate agent."

"No more shocked than I was."

"I thought you'd be a PE coach or something."

"Things change."

"No shit." I'm trying not to be too defensive, but if I let my barriers down, I'll be putty in his hands, and he knows this. I can't let that happen.

"You look—" Cade begins, but I cut him off.

"Don't."

"Tired," he finishes.

My eyes are drawn to his mouth. I can't be here. I cut to the chase. "How the fuck is this going to work?" Pushing my hands through my hair, I try not to recall his hands doing the same thing.

"I think we need to start by clearing the air."

"Clearing the air?" I laugh. "Is that some sort of managerial bullshit talk?"

"Lexie—"

I hold my hand up. "That's not my name. Don't call me that." I can't handle that name.

His head dips. "I can't call you Alex." He glances back at me, his eyes full of the past. "I think we need to talk about that afternoon."

"No, absolutely not. That afternoon is the last fucking thing I want to talk about."

"Hey, I don't want to go there as much as you don't, but if we're going to work together without this atmosphere, then we need to address it."

"To address it? There you go again with your business mouth."

"We were young. It was a long time ago."

"And in here"—I stab at my chest with my hand—"it still feels like yesterday."

It's so clear. All of it. Every last memory chiselled into my brain as if the last sixteen years had never existed.

"You think I don't feel it too?" His eyes narrow. "You think I don't lie in bed at night and replay the whole fucking thing, wondering what happened, where everything went wrong?"

He takes a step closer, his hand coming out of his pocket, and I freeze. He sees my body balk.

He steps back, his shoulders dropping, his hands out flat in front of him, a sadness replacing the anger. "The last thing I want to do is drag this all up, but if we're going to move forward, we need to talk about it. And I need you to know that I spend every single day wondering what would've happened to us if that afternoon had never existed."

I'm silenced, his thoughts mirroring my own.

"I'd give anything for it to have never happened."

"Me too," I whisper, pain spearing my heart.

He straightens, his shirt pulling against his chest. "We're going to have to work together, and I don't know about you, but I can't work like this. The other staff have picked up on it."

"So, what's the plan? You get me here to tell me I

have to be all smiles and happiness when you're in the shop?"

"Look, I know this isn't ideal, but we have to try and make it work."

It was sixteen years ago, and in all that time, Cade has never gone anywhere. He was with me when I left high school. He was with me when I went to university. He was with me when I kissed Ronnie Walsh in the cinema and all I could taste was popcorn on his breath. He was with me when I slept with Harry Denver in the back seat of his Nissan Micra and all I could do was stare at the tree-shaped air freshener hanging from the rear-view mirror, wishing Harry was Cade. He was with me when I let Kirsten Roberts kiss me, wondering if I was gay because I never felt the way I did when I was with Cade.

He's always been with me.

"I'd better get back to the office. They'll be wondering where I am." I glance at my watch without registering the time.

Cade nods, then turns, readying to leave. He stops. Turns back and stares at me. "For what it's worth, I'm sorry. I'm so fucking sorry, it hurts."

I gulp. "So am I."

He turns then and walks out the door. Moving to the window, I watch him climb into his car. The way he moves, the way his suit hangs perfectly on his frame is torture, seeing him now after all this time.

Love overwhelms me. It comes in waves when I least expect it and leaves me drained.

Our time together had been bliss. I'd never known happiness like it. I'd wake up every morning, and my first thought would be him. I'd go to bed every night with thoughts of him wrapped around me as I drifted off to sleep.

And in a blink of an eye, it was all destroyed—the delirious delight, the fairy-tale dream my life had become—all gone.

It had been so painful, like I'd had my heart ripped out of my chest cavity and shown to me, the beating mass of blood and veins slowing with every second I'd stood in that room. My eyes burned, and my breath came in rasps. I'd wanted to scream, but somehow the silence had taken over, penetrating my eardrums with its deafening irrevocability.

And I vowed I'd never see him again.

My breath gathers on the window as I watch him leave the house, still not believing he's back.

The pain in my chest gets worse with every step he takes.

But it can't be any other way.

THIRTEEN
CADE

As I grip the steering wheel, the familiar feeling of a hurricane stirs inside me. The shame that's consumed me all this time has reared its ugly head. All these years, I've tried to push it down until there's almost nothing left of it. But now she's here, and every time I look at her, something uncoils. A memory springs to life, and I can't help but remember.

It had taken all my resolve yesterday not to grab her when she stood up from behind her desk. At first, I'd thought she was just someone who looked like her, Lexie's double greeting me, but the look on her face told me it was her—the disbelief, the shock, the recognition.

And I recovered quicker than she did, the mask slipping into place as I introduced myself as her new boss.

The urge to touch her was overwhelming, every

instinct telling me to do it, to claim what was mine and forget this whole work thing. But I had a job to do, one I couldn't fuck up, so I'd put my managerial head on and locked myself in the tiny office with Ian, trying to fill my head with everything I needed to know about the business.

But it wasn't easy knowing she was mere feet away and was going to be for the foreseeable future.

Most of the memories are amazing, the best of my life. The long walks to school when we would hold hands without a care in the world, talking about how we'd move in together once we were old enough. Running my hand up her leg under the dinner table, my dad none the wiser. Lying on top of her covers after having sex, the room full of heat and hormones. My mouth on hers. Her hands on me.

If I concentrate hard enough, I can still taste her.

Our talk hadn't gone as planned. I'm not even sure what I thought would happen. I know what I would've liked to have done, and that involved Lexie spread-eagled on the countertop with my head between her legs as she screamed my name, but that was never going to happen.

But it's worse than I thought. She's shut down, banished that day from her memory, and I don't blame her, but I know she's never going to deal with it that way. She must face it. *We* must face it. If not now, then soon, because if we don't, us being in the same town, let alone the same office, is never going to work.

FOURTEEN

ALEX

"So, what's this new owner like?" Shawn Bowling asks as he rolls over on the bed, instinctively grabbing for his cigarette packet. He hasn't wasted any time. I knew he'd want to know about the takeover, but I thought he'd wait a little longer post-sex before he threw it out there.

"You can't smoke in here," I tell him, leaning over the side of the bed trying to find my bra.

Shawn takes a smoke out anyway.

"We wouldn't have this problem if you let us do this in your house," he mumbles. "I don't know why you insist on a Travelodge every time we meet."

"You know why we can't meet at my place."

"Yeah, and it's dumb."

"We agreed from the start that this is sex, nothing more. No hearts, no flowers, no soppy text messages.

You don't need to come to my house, and I don't need to come to yours."

Shawn doesn't reply. Instead, he chews on the end of the cigarette, clearly wishing it were lit. He doesn't want me at his place as much as I don't want him at mine.

There's no hiding why he's here. I've known from the minute he walked over to me in the bar last month what his agenda was.

I'd started drinking early, a girls' afternoon that'd turned into evening, and I'd been pretty drunk by the time Shawn had made his way over to my table. We knew each other, of course. Who didn't know Shawn Bowling, son of Mathew Bowling and our biggest competitor in the estate agent world? He'd used that to get his foot in. I'd looked at his blond hair, his blue eyes, his winning smile and, with the help of more vodka, convinced myself he was actually quite attractive. I can't remember what we talked about or even if we talked at all. I do remember the hurried sex down the side of the nightclub, my heels skidding on the pavement as he pushed me up against the wall. It'd been quick, erratic, and something I could've quite easily forgotten.

I'd filed it away, never to be referred to again, but he'd called two days later and wanted to meet up. I'd been a little stumped. We'd already had sex. That little milestone had been achieved, and from my recall, it hadn't been earth-shattering, so what other purpose did Shawn have for his pursuit of me? My witty banter? My astounding general knowledge? Maybe I could've convinced myself of one of the above, but his question now confirms it.

He's here for information.

He wants to know about the new owner of Malcolm and Co.

He wants to know about Cade Westwood.

He's hoping I'll spill the beans on the company's big takeover and what new initiatives the big-city boss man has put in place.

Was it chance that Shawn Bowling arrived in the bar two weeks after the company's purchase was announced? I think not.

He thinks I might leak some important information concerning the world of estate agents.

What he doesn't know is my past with Cade Westwood.

Shawn has hit the jackpot. I could give him what he wants and more. I could give him a scandal that would ruin Cade Westwood before his feet are even under the desk.

It wouldn't surprise me if Shawn's father sent him personally.

Bowling Sales is Malcolm and Co.'s biggest rival, and Cade Westwood is a new threat to their business.

But that's not what concerns me. What worries me is what I'm doing here.

After slipping my bra on, I grab my top and trousers and dress hurriedly.

"You got somewhere to be?" Shawn yawns, swinging his legs off the bed.

"Anywhere but here." I slink over to the window and pull the curtain back. The sunlight dazzles the room as I continue holding the curtain. I stare at the bronzed workmen on the far side of the car park with their high-viz jackets on and bare chests underneath. They're nothing to look at, not considering that I know Cade Westwood, but it's what they're doing that has me snared.

They're tearing down some old rotting fence panels that have seen better days whilst the new ones rest patiently against their pick-up truck.

And I'm gone.

Then

"Did you have a nice birthday weekend?" Cade asks on Monday morning as I attempt to scrape mud off the side of my shoe.

"Yeah, it was okay. Just a bit embarrassing when the men came to pick the tub up."

"How come?"

"My mum started going on at them about the fence panel, and the guys were like, 'Hey we're just here to collect it, lady. If you got a problem, you need to call management.' It was very

embarrassing." I roll my eyes, but Cade is smirking at my terrible impression of a delivery driver.

"I'm sorry I missed it."

"You obviously had a better offer."

"Just a bit of Sunday morning football," he replies.

We've barely seen each other this weekend. Cade always seems to be out with his mates, doing whatever lads do, or I'm out with my mum or revising for my exams. She'd taken the weekend off so we could go shopping, which I hadn't enjoyed, as my mum appeared to go out of her way to not like any of the clothes I'd picked up.

"Did you mean what you said about going out together?" I ask as we round the corner of the street. There's an awkwardness to the question that's been plaguing me all weekend, but Cade doesn't seem to notice.

"Of course," he says. "I wouldn't have said it otherwise."

"It's just…." I glance at my feet, my cheeks stinging against the fresh morning air.

"Just what?"

"I have an idea, that's all, about how to get around my mum."

"Go on."

"Well, on Friday there's this dance organised by my school as a little incentive to get us all through this last month before our exams start." I steal a look at him, trying to remember the lines I've rehearsed. "It's a fundraiser or something like that. The ticket sales go to a charity." I pause, aware I'm waffling. This had seemed so much easier in my head.

Cade appears worried.

"Oh, don't panic," I jump in. "I'm not asking you to come to some cheesy dance."

"I don't think I'd fit in," he says.

"It's at the civic centre, and with it being organised by the school, my mum is actually letting me go, but everyone is talking about going out somewhere after it finishes."

"I see." Cade stares at the ground.

"So, I was thinking we could meet up and go somewhere if you'd like."

"And what about your mum?"

"I haven't invited her," I joke.

Cade grins. "You know what I mean," he says. "What will she say?"

"It starts at seven and finishes at eleven, so I was thinking I could go for the first half hour and then meet you somewhere. Just as long as I'm home by eleven."

"What about your friends?"

"What about them?"

"Will they be coming with us?"

"That's up to you. If you bring your mates, then I'll bring mine, although I can't promise they won't freak out at being out in a pub. They aren't the most experienced at adult socialising."

Cade thinks about this before replying. "Better keep it just me and you, then."

Neither of us has said the D-word, but this is the closest I've ever been to going on a date.

I exhale slowly, trying to contain the smile brewing from deep inside me.

As soon as I get in my mum's car on Friday after school, I know something isn't right. There's no "How was your day?" or "Do you have any revision?" She's perched in the front seat, her grip on the steering wheel like that of a rally driver.

It's my turn to ask the questions.

"Have you had a nice day?"

She snorts like she has something stuck up her nose. "Depends what you mean by nice."

"Is it work?" I probe, already mentally planning my make-up and hair for tonight.

I'm wearing a dress to the dance, a black one I bought last year which is nothing fancy, but then I'll change into jeans and a top that I'm going to stuff in my bag. I need to look older without trying to. It's going to be difficult, but I've watched a few make-up tutorials, and my heels will give me some added height. I've been panicking about what will happen if we get turned away from somewhere because I don't look old enough or they ask me for ID.

"It's just life, Alex" my mum moans, grinding the gears and spinning the vehicle around like she's riding a bumper car.

Staring out the window for the rest of the journey, I contemplate the night ahead and try to ignore the almost visible seething coming from the driver's side of the car.

It's when we get home and the bottle of gin comes out that I start to worry. The kitchen feels suddenly too small, and I'm making an obscene amount of noise simply finding a snack before I get ready. I want to say, "Bit early for that, isn't it?" But that wouldn't go down well, so instead, I ask where Mark is, thinking it safer territory.

"Who knows where he is!" My mum flounces as she mixes a very disproportionate amount of gin to tonic.

"Has he not come home from work?"

"He texted to say he was going straight out with some mates after work." She sighs.

"Is everything okay with him?" Now is not the time to be asking this question, but I have to say something.

"It's fine." Mum shakes her head. "You don't want to listen to me moaning." She grips the glass, her arm resolute. "Isn't the dance tonight?" She flashes me a plastic smile before raising the glass to her lips.

"Yeah, I'm going about half six, so I'd better start getting ready." I eye the glass nervously.

"Off you go, then." She thrusts the glass in the direction of the stairs, her grin already melting.

As I leave the kitchen, I work out how many hours it is until I have to leave and how much gin is in that bottle.

FIFTEEN

ALEX

"You're still sticking to the story that there's nothing between the pair of you?" Donna asks as I bring her a cup of coffee. Gone is her special mug; instead, I place down a grey, nondescript travel mug that lacks character and feeling. This is just one of the many changes Cade has brought into the office. No one is allowed a hot beverage in an uncovered cup for health and safety reasons.

It's been two weeks since he arrived, and I'm surprised he's still here. I thought he would've poked his nose around for a few days before returning to one of his other branches. No such luck. He's been in this office every day, making changes here, overseeing things there. It's like torture. Look but don't touch. Every goddamn morning, he's arrived looking hotter than the previous day, the sexual tension sizzling with every stolen glance, every muted word, and each instance of forced conversation. This afternoon I've been granted a small reprieve, as he's gone out to value a property, but Donna has wasted no time with her interrogation.

"Nothing is going on between us." Returning to my desk, I make sure Donna can't see my face. She's been like a bloodhound with the scent of rabbit in her nose for the past two weeks, and it's draining.

"Okay, but there was at one time."

One time.

"Nope, sorry, wrong again."

"I don't believe you," Donna huffs. "The atmosphere when you two are in the same room is weird. It's like there's an electrical current going through you both, and the whole room feeds on it."

"That's very insightful of you."

"I mean it. I think there's more to it than you're letting on. Either that, or you knew each other in a past life, and the present you is trying to tell you this, but you're choosing to ignore it."

I flash Donna a look of disbelief. "Do you want me to fetch you a dishcloth to tie around your head whilst you rub your crystal ball?"

"Come on. You could've been Cleopatra, and he could've been Mark Antony."

"Didn't he stab himself because he'd heard she was dead?"

"Yeah. That's true love for you."

Opening a new client file, I roll my eyes at the

screen. "You're imagining it. Whatever it is that you think is going on between us is all in your mind."

"Ian thinks so too."

"And what does he know? He wouldn't be able to pick up on an atmosphere if it wrapped itself around his face and starved him of oxygen."

"I'm going to find out. You know that, don't you?" Donna scowls at the travel mug as coffee spits out from the lid and burns her lip.

"You'll be disappointed." My computer screen stares at me. I know what Donna is like once she has an idea in her head, and she's ruthless at getting to the bottom of things if she thinks there's something to be unearthed.

But how would she find out? Maybe she'll tackle Cade, glean some information from him, and go from there. But he won't say any more than I will. It would be a dead end. Donna will find nothing out and will eventually get bored and drop her theory—or so I hope.

SIXTEEN
ALEX

WE SHUT UP THE OFFICE FOR THE DAY, IAN LOCKING the door and Donna checking the lights are out as we bundle together out onto the street.

"I can't believe we have to go for drinks," I tut, pulling my hair out of the back of my jacket.

"Just one of the many things our lovely new boss has introduced," Donna says. "I can't imagine George having taken us all out for drinks after work, can you?"

"God, no," Ian joins in as he catches us up. "And if he did, it would've been in the Dog and Gun for a Guinness and a line of dominoes."

We all laugh.

"How did Rachel manage to get out of it?" I ask. Rachel is a trainee who we took on a few months ago and works part-time during the week.

"No one to pick the kids up from the childminder," Donna says.

"Why didn't I think of that?" I huff.

"You don't have any kids," she points out.

"I could've borrowed some."

Ian and Donna shake their heads.

Sticking my hands in my pockets, I drag my feet down the road. I've been dreading this little soiree ever since Cade suggested it at the beginning of the week. "It'll be great for a bit of team bonding and office morale. Statistics show teams who socialise together perform better in the workplace," he'd told us all via an email.

It was optional, though. Cade had made that clear.

My gut reaction was to think of some excuse, but Donna was one step ahead of me.

"I take it you aren't coming for drinks on Friday," she'd said whilst making coffee in the tiny staff room.

"And what makes you think that?" I'd replied, fishing my boxed salad from the tabletop fridge.

"Just with you and Cade and the weird thing between you two. You won't want to come because you can't stand to be in the same room as him, let alone share a drink in a bar. And him, well, I'm not sure he'll be able to keep his eyes from you for long enough to down a pint."

My spinach salad was like dried paper in my mouth, clinging to the back of my throat.

"Well, that's where you're wrong. Of course I'm coming," I'd declared, knowing I would then have to attend the dreaded drinks.

"Are Sonya and Michael coming?" Ian enquires as we round the corner.

"They're meeting us there," Donna answers.

Michael and Sonya are the weekend staff who also cover holidays and busier periods.

We're about to cross the road when the door to Bowling Sales opens.

Shawn steps out, his grey suit looking overly shiny like it's been ironed within an inch of its life, all the material burned away. I often think he was born in the wrong decade. His hair looks like something from the eighties, and his dress sense needs modernising.

"What's this, then?" he asks as he begins to lock the door. "A little work outing?" He smiles like he's trying to be friendly but fails miserably.

Ian grimaces. "Good evening, Shawn."

"Just a few drinks after work, that's all," Donna informs him.

"Hey, sorry about the Coleridge property today." Shawn turns to Donna. "My client just wasn't happy with the offer. You know how it is." He flashes her one of his sickly grins.

"No problem. All part of the job." She manages a more authentic smile even though her eyes say otherwise.

One of her clients had sold their house today, then went to view a property up with Bowling Sales. The house had been a little out of their price range, but Donna had encouraged them to go view it, explaining that they had sold their house and held all the cards. They'd loved the house and made an offer, ten thousand under the asking price, and had been knocked back straight away, which was to be expected. They'd increased their next offer, already pushing themselves, only for it to be refused again. After a call to their mortgage adviser, they'd put in a final offer, only to be told by Shawn himself that it was the asking price or nothing and not to call back with anything under.

Donna had been furious.

"The arrogance of that man!" she'd huffed as she'd put the phone down on him.

"Might be the vendor who's being difficult," I'd suggested, unsure as to why I was defending Shawn when I knew how pathetic he could be.

"Bollocks," Donna had spat back. "I bet he hasn't even put the last offer to them. It's just one of his silly games. He's so greedy, it makes me sick."

"We've had a lot of interest in the house," Shawn continues, even though it's been on the market for over two months. "I advised them not to settle for anything under the asking price. I'm sure your couple will come back with the asking price tomorrow if they want the house."

Donna holds her smile, knowing full well they won't—they can't afford it. More fool him.

"It's a popular street," she agrees, her teeth almost biting into her lip.

"Well, have a nice night." Shawn bids us on our way before grinning at me. It's not a look of love, lust, or even hunger. It's a look of triumph.

SEVENTEEN

ALEX

WE GATHER AROUND A LARGE TABLE IN THE CORNER of the All Bar One, the only bar in our small town. Sonya and Michael arrived first and look as eager to be here as we are. The atmosphere is bustling rather than busy, the off-white shirts and sensible shoes giving away the workers who've met for a pre-weekend drink and to celebrate the fact that they've all survived another Monday-to-Friday shift. Ariana Grande is playing over the speakers just loudly enough that we can still appreciate a conversation.

Everyone is talking shop, which annoys me. I don't want this to feel like an extension of work. I want to kick back and forget about three-bed semis and bungalows with scope for improvement. But it does feel like work. We've been summoned here by Cade, who has yet to arrive.

He's been out of the shop all afternoon, some business to attend to in another branch, which I've been grateful for. It's getting harder to be around him in so many ways. I have to avoid the staff room when he's in there, which, luckily, is rarely. He's commandeered the office at the back of the shop, which is where he spends most of his time. But to get to the office, he has to walk right by my desk. It sounds like a minor inconvenience, but to me, it's torment. I've trained my eyes to remain on my computer screen and not be drawn by his toned figure and expensive suit. I've learned how to hold my breath so I don't inhale any of his sharp, spicy aroma. I've mastered the art of shutting myself down so I'm immune to him.

It isn't easy, but I have no choice. There are parts of him embedded in me, the times we spent together etched in my brain. I need to forget them, to be cleansed of those moments. Like the time I lay on his naked chest, my ear to his heart, listening to it beating beneath me. And the times he would sneak into my room in the middle of the night and climb into bed next to me, his skin so warm, his body like a shield, and I'd drift off into the most blissful sleep. Even the time I was throwing up in the bathroom after eating some dodgy chicken, and Cade had knelt behind me, holding my hair and rubbing my back, telling me it would be okay, that he was here. That he would look after me and would never leave me.

Then that afternoon in my kitchen comes back to me like a dark curtain falling over the bright happiness, my Disney film replaced with the opening credits of a Tim Burton one, Cade's face unrecognisable. Silence, then the screaming as I shoved my hands over my face, trying to hide from what was right in front of me.

And I had to let him go.

He was supposed to be my happily ever after. But I was wrong. That day in the kitchen, my dreams shattered along with everything else like an optical illusion.

I had to let him go.

Donna eyes me from across the table as I take a large swig of my wine. I wish I could tell her. I imagine it would feel good knowing someone else in the office is aware of what I'm going through. But if I did, I'd have to reveal a whole lot more of myself than I'm willing to share.

EIGHTEEN
CADE

THE LAST THING I WANT TO DO ON A FRIDAY evening is sit in a cheesy bar and talk about houses with a bunch of people I barely know, but needs must. Too much rides on this job for me to fuck it up.

And then there's Lexie.

Every day is agony.

Sharing the same air as her is like working in an opium den, her enticing fumes swirling in my brain, making me want to succumb. It's been harder than I thought. So fucking hard to sit there day after day with her on the other side of the flimsy plasterboard wall, wishing I could walk out of the cupboard they call an office and fuck her right there in her chair.

But I can't.

Those days are gone.

She doesn't want me anymore.

She's made that perfectly clear.

And now I'm expected to sit with her in a bar and keep my hungry eyes and lurid thoughts to myself.

It's going to be hell.

She said she's coming tonight—I'd overheard her talking to Donna—but I don't expect to see her. I've been here before, expecting her, waiting for her, only for her not to show up. And look how that turned out.

Then

The civic centre is a concrete monstrosity, probably built in the eighties when grey breeze block was all the rage. Giddy teenagers arrive in their parents' four-by-fours as I loiter outside in black jeans and a white T-shirt. The lads all look the same, each wearing a crumpled shirt of dubious colour, mismatched with the only pair of smart trousers they own. The girls look very different. Some have gone all out, arriving in flouncy dresses and complicated hairstyles. Others have kept it low-key yet still manage to look like they've spent a week getting ready. I'm glad I don't have to contend with these unfathomable things just for a Friday night out.

Lexie had said eight o'clock. It's now quarter past, and there's no sign of her. She could be dancing, having a good time, and I don't want to interrupt her if she is.

But she'd said eight.

I need to move before people start to wonder what I'm doing here. Will she hear her phone if I call her? What if her battery has died? Has she just lost track of time?

Something doesn't feel right.
Pacing the road, I open my phone and dial her number.
She answers straight away, barely letting the phone ring.

NINETEEN
ALEX

IT'S TWENTY MINUTES LATER, AND THE CHAT AROUND the table has moved on from the current housing market, which would've been a welcome relief if the new topic hadn't been Cade.

"Some of his ideas make sense," Ian says, his tie having loosened somewhat since his arrival.

"Yeah, I can appreciate some of the things he's done," Michael agrees. "Take the website, for instance. The adjustments he's made to the search criteria have meant we're getting a lot more hits on a lot more houses."

"And the changes he's made to the brochures have made a difference. The photographer he uses is brilliant. The brochures look a lot classier," Ian adds.

"Kind of upset old Simms when he brought the new guy in, though," Sonya pipes up.

"Simms is way over the retirement threshold, let's

be honest." Michael lowers his pint. "He should've packed his camera away years ago."

"What, and stayed at home all day with Mrs Simms? You've got to be kidding." Sonya laughs.

"Hey, I can forgive his motivation on that count." Michael chuckles.

The conversation ripples around the table, everyone dissecting Cade the Businessman, the Managing Director, and the Guy with all the Good Ideas.

None of them really know him.

Cade the Man of Action.

Cade the Knight in Shining Armour.

Then

He calls at quarter past eight.

"Hey, it's me," he says, then waits for me to speak, but the words are lodged in the back of my throat, a huge lump of disappointment and anger keeping them at bay. When I don't say anything, he continues. "It's after eight, and I'm outside the civic centre. I thought we were meeting here."

There's silence followed by a ruffling noise as I press the phone to my ear.

"I'm not there," I say at last. "I'm not going to be able to meet you. I'm sorry. I have to go."

"Wait, what do you mean, you're not here? Where are you? Has something happened?"

"I'm at home. It's nothing. Don't worry about it. You go on and meet your mates. I'll see you later."

"I'm coming back," Cade says.

"No. Please don't. Honestly, it's fine. Go enjoy your night. And sorry for messing you about."

I cut the call quickly, imagining Cade standing on the street, staring at his phone.

"HEY, SPEAK OF THE DEVIL," MICHAEL SHOUTS AS Cade arrives by the side of the table.

The whole party looks his way, me included. He's wearing a dark blue suit, but his tie is gone, his top button undone, and his sleeves rolled up.

I shiver.

"All good things, I hope." Cade smiles, his grin illuminating his already perfect face.

"Of course," Ian assures him. "We were just all agreeing on what a good job the new photographer is doing." He looks around the table for confirmation.

"Well, I'm glad you all approve, but let's not talk about work." Cade sweeps his gaze over the table at them like they're children and he's the teacher explaining what he wants them to do, until his eyes land on me. Then his shoulders drop and his face sharpens.

Cade

They're sitting at a round table in the corner of the bar like knights awaiting King Arthur. I don't feel like a king, let alone *their* king. The air is humid, too many bodies packed into too small a space. "Closing Time" by Semisonic plays over the speakers, and I wonder just how late I am.

They spot me as I approach their table.

Smile. Be polite. Go through the motions. Be the boss they want you to be.

I do all the above until my eyes find Lexie.

She's here. And I can't explain what it feels like to see her. Relief. Joy. Fear. She evokes something in me that has never gone away. I feel it all over again like it was only yesterday.

Then

It doesn't take me long to get back to the house. When I arrive outside, I'm surprised to find none of the lights on downstairs. Silence oozes from the house, which sends a rivulet of cold down my back. Has Lexie decided to watch another horror movie on her own rather than our planned night out? Somehow, I doubt this.

I open the front door and step into the darkness of the hall-way. I'd been right about the silence—the house is draped in the stuff. But it isn't just the lack of noise surrounding me— there's something else. Like an echo trapped in the walls, some-

thing is reverberating from inside, warning me of what has happened. Not wanting to disturb the quiet or rouse the echo, I close the door carefully, resisting the urge to call out.

There's a sliver of light around the edge of the kitchen door, illuminating its rectangular shape, and I immediately think of the film Poltergeist. *I edge toward the door, trying not to step too loudly, wondering what I'm about to disturb. I push open the door, the creak unnaturally loud, and she's there.*

Alex

He hadn't expected me to be here.

I hadn't expected to be here.

"What can I get you to drink?" Ian asks, half standing as he pulls his wallet from his back pocket.

Cade puts his hand up, signalling for Ian to sit back down. "No need. Drinks are on me. What can I get everyone?"

Everyone sits up, shifting in their seats at the offer of a free drink as they start to reel off their orders.

Cade's gaze reaches mine, and I feel its pull, the lure of those beautiful green eyes.

"A white wine, thanks." I quickly look away.

"I'll give you a hand," Ian offers now he's out of his seat.

"Thanks." Cade nods, and the pair of them make their way over to the bar.

Donna catches me taking a deep breath, and even though she's on the other side of the table, I can feel her energy, her ears pricking up, her nose twitching at the scent of something in the air.

"What?" I mouth.

She smirks and shakes her head. "Nothing."

"Whatever." I drain my glass, relieved another is on the way.

Ian returns and hands out several drinks before Cade follows with his drink and mine. I stand up and lean over the table to take it from him. He holds my gaze as our fingers brush against the cold glass. I snatch the glass like I've just been electrocuted whilst Donna watches us as she takes a sip of her red wine.

Everyone shuffles to accommodate Cade, who draws up a stool. Awkward silence trickles across the table, our previous topic abandoned now he's joined us.

Ian tries to flood the emptiness. "So, where's everyone headed this year for their holidays?"

Holiday chitchat is not my territory. I sit back and try to keep my eyes off Cade, but he's directly opposite me, and my gaze is relentlessly being tugged in his direction. He barely touches his drink as he follows the conversation of his new workforce. He looks like he's listening, and I wonder whether he is or if his thoughts are, like mine, wandering into the past.

Then

He finds me in the kitchen, sweeping brush in my hand, some large rollers in my hair, and my beautiful black dress on. When the door is fully open, I stop sweeping.

"I told you not to come back," I say, shaking my head as I go back to sweeping.

Cade walks around the edge of the island, his shoes crunching with every step.

He looks at the floor. "Is that glass?"

"Be careful," I tell him.

He scans the floor. It's everywhere.

"Why is there glass on the floor?"

"It's not important." My voice is as flat as the dustpan I'm sweeping the glass into.

"What happened? Why didn't you go to the dance?"

"I don't want to talk about it."

He studies me as if the events of the past few hours are written on my face. Beneath the make-up, my skin is blotchy, my mascara having smudged under my eyes as I'd tried to wipe it away.

"Where's my dad?"

"He's gone out with his mates from work. That's all I know."

"And your mum?"

Silence creeps out from underneath the cabinets, the kind that wraps itself around your ankles and doesn't let go.

"She's upstairs." I can't hide the anger in my voice.

"Is she all right?" Cade asks, his eyes still roaming the room.

"She's asleep."

His gaze lands on the empty gin bottle standing on the counter like a loaded gun.

After tipping the contents of the dustpan into the bin, I place the brush back in the corner of the room before I stop and finally look at Cade.

"What happened? Was it your mum?"

My eyes close momentarily, flinching at the memory of the glass hurtling through the air and smashing against the back wall.

"I think they've had some sort of falling-out," I say, making it sound like kids in the playground.

"Who? My dad and your mum?"

I nod.

"Were they here?" Cade surveys the room again like he missed something the first time around.

"No." I shake my head. "Your dad went out straight from work. I haven't seen him."

"So, it was just you and your mum?"

I nod again.

"How do you know they've fallen out?"

I glance at the empty bottle.

Cade's eyes follow mine. "Right." He sighs. "Why didn't you just leave her to it and go to the dance?"

It's my turn to sigh. "I didn't have much choice." I shiver as if the angry monster is still lurking in the halls.

"Of course you did," he protests. "You should've just walked out the door."

"Does your dad drink?" I shoot the words across the room.

"Yes, every weekend."

"And what's he like when he's had a few? I bet he's jolly, the life and soul of the party," I say with a sneer.

"Not all the time." Cade's shoulders drop. "He can get pretty down on occasions."

"Does he get angry?"

"No, not that I've seen."

"Well, then, you wouldn't understand." I pick up a cloth and begin sweeping it across the top of the counter, the tiny shards of barely visible glass forming a small mountain by my hand.

"Are you hurt?" he asks.

"Not this time," I say as I scoop the glass up and place it in the bin along with all the rest.

"And what about your mum?"

"A few cuts, that's all. She's out cold. I managed to get her upstairs and onto her front."

Cade watches as I slump onto a bar stool and pull the large rollers from my hair.

"How'd you get her upstairs by yourself?" His eyes narrow, his weight shifting from one foot to the other.

"I managed."

His fingers flex, his face darkening. "It's not the first time, is it?"

Raking my fingers through my hair, I answer, "No."

"Fuck." Cade lets out a breath, running his hand through his hair, anger brewing beneath his cool exterior.

"I'd better go get changed." I slip off the stool. "No point in having this on now."

"Wait," he says, stepping forward and blocking my path. "I'm not having her ruin your night."

"Bit late for that," I scoff.

"It's never too late." Cade takes my hand, the sudden contact making me shiver. "I want you to go get ready. Finish doing whatever you were doing. Just give me a few minutes, and then come back down." He studies me, and I can see the concern, the anger, the hurt behind his eyes.

"Okay."

He drops my hand and watches me leave with my shoulders down, my head low.

Holding back the tears, I finish my hair, pinning half the loose curls up and leaving half trailing down my back, and then I patch up my make-up, working the smudged mascara into a smoky eye which I'd not intended. When I'm ready, I wobble down the stairs in my high, strappy sandals. A thin veil of the most expensive perfume I own trails behind me.

Missing the dance had not upset me. It was just a stupid school dance. It was the other part of the night, the plan to meet up with Cade and go out for the first time. And as soon as the bottle of gin had come out of the cupboard, I'd known my night was not in my hands anymore. And I hated my mum for it.

"You're going to the dance, then? Leaving me here on my own when I'm upset?"

The look on her face had been sour, my heart plummeting as I tried to get ready.

"You go out, have a good time. I'll just stay here on my own. I'm used to it, as everyone ends up leaving me."

I ignored the comments and remained silent, not bothering to answer because there was no point.

But I couldn't ignore the breaking glass. And my mum knew this.

I enter the kitchen where my mum is gone, the glass in the bin like nothing ever happened. The swell of anger I've been trying to suppress now has a life of its own as it threatens to rage in full force at my spectacularly ruined evening—then I spot the bowl of crisps and a half-eaten bag of Haribo sitting on the island. My empty stomach protests. I should be starving, but I'm too full of emotions to tell the hunger from the hurt.

"You're ready," Cade says as he emerges through the patio doors and into the kitchen, rubbing his hands down the front of his jeans, his skin a little flushed.

"We can't go anywhere. I can't leave her." I gesture upstairs, my face contorting as the resentment threatens to bloom again.

Taking my hand, he smiles. "We don't need to go anywhere. Everything we need is right here." He picks up the bag of Haribo and presents me with it.

I dig my hand in and pop a couple into my mouth, the sugar hitting my taste buds. Bringing the bag with us, he leads me out the doors and into the garden.

The first thing I notice is the lights—the ones my mum

put up for the hot-tub party last week and hasn't yet taken down. She'd draped them lavishly over the plants and branches, whereas Cade has placed them, almost individually, amongst the foliage to the point where they look like part of the plant.

Candles burn on the patio. Some of the larger lanterns my mum had bought a few years ago and never used now house flickering flames, giving the garden an almost medieval feel.

"I'd like to lay claim to the petals on the patio," Cade says as he moves behind me. "But they were already there."

They belong to some large plant that flowers for a few days every year; deep, vivid pink petals erupting amongst the elongated leaves, the weight of them far too heavy for the stem of the plant—an evolutionary error, I always think—before they droop and hang like defeated boxers, their petals abandoning them.

"It looks beautiful," I whisper, my eyes still wandering the garden.

"I was tempted to hang toilet roll from the trees, but I only had fifteen minutes, and I thought I might be cutting it fine."

A smile emerges at the corners of his mouth, which I catch.

"Well, I'm glad you ran out of time." I face him, the candles shimmering in my peripheral vision.

"Why have you done this?" I ask, my eyes feeling heavy, guilt coating me, but for what, I'm not sure.

"Because I wanted to." He moves closer. "Because you deserve it."

Shame replaces the guilt, and I look away.

He picks up my hands. "You're sixteen, Lexie. You should be living your life, not stuck inside looking after your drunken mother. You should be out with your friends without your mum in tow with her EpiPen and overbearing fears. You should be taking control of your life, not letting her live it for you."

I glare at him, ready to fight my mum's corner. She's been a single parent for so long. She's cared for me, kept me safe, and loved me like a parent should. But there's a part of me that knows he's right.

My chest deflates, my shoulders giving up on me. Whose corner am I fighting exactly? Tiredness sweeps over me. I've done enough fighting tonight.

"I don't want to talk about her." I sniff. "She's done enough damage tonight."

Cade pulls me closer, his arms wrapping around my shoulders, and he holds me as I steady my breathing, fighting the tears. He brushes my hair away from the side of my head, scanning my face like he's discovered a treasure map.

"You look beautiful, by the way," he says, his fingers trailing down my cheek making goose bumps erupt over my arms. "Are you cold?"

"No." I shake my head as his hand runs up my arm, the warmth from his palm coating my skin. "Thank you," I whisper, blinking away my embarrassment at his attention.

"Shall we put some music on?" He strides over to the Bluetooth speaker he's brought outside and begins to scroll through his phone. "The acoustics might not be as good as at the civic centre, I'm afraid, but it's the best I can do."

"I'm sure it'll be fine." I don't care about the music. I don't care about the civic centre.

"Shall we dance?" Cade extends his hand.

I take it, my face relaxing as I step into his hold. The music is some folk song I've never heard before and would not have associated with him, but I like it. Somehow, it matches the garden and the mood.

"Now, I can't promise to be as good a mover as you," he jokes. "I have footballer's feet, I'm afraid."

"I'm sure there's not much difference." I rest my hands on Cade's shoulders. His arms are wrapped around my waist. "I'm sure football requires some sort of fancy footwork that's probably not dissimilar to dancing."

"I never thought of it like that, but I suppose you're right."

We sway gently as if the breeze is orchestrating our movements. I'm surprised at how natural this all feels, almost like I've been here before, but this time, Cade is real.

"I didn't have any lessons in ballroom. Just a bit of ballet and modern dance."

"Well, that's a relief. I was worried you might break out into a Viennese waltz, and I'd be expected to keep up."

We dance for several minutes, the music wrapping itself around us and blanketing us from the world and everything in it.

It's several minutes before I speak. "What's happening here?"

"Here, or in there?" Cade nods toward the kitchen.

"I don't want to think about what's going on in there," I reply. My mum and Mark's relationship is a worry. "I don't want to think about what might happen if things don't work out between them."

"Me neither." Cade's eyes leave me for a second before

returning even more intense than before. "I know what I think is happening here, though." His face is serious, the tone of his voice low as if sharing some conspiracy theory.

"Go on," I push.

His eyes twinkle in the candlelight. "I can only speak for myself, you understand."

I nod.

"Ever since I met you, you've been in my head. It's like you've crept inside and taken over the controls."

"Is that a good thing?"

"It's good and bad," Cade answers. "It's good because I want you there. I'm happy you've entered this desolate place which had nothing to occupy it other than football." He pauses, taking a deep breath.

"But it's bad because…?" I prompt, unsure of just how bad this bit is going to be.

"Because I'm getting to the point where I can't imagine my life without you."

The swaying stops as if Cade's words have anchored us to this moment in time. We stare, silently trying to read each other's faces.

"But like I said, I can only speak for myself," he says at last, the silence too heavy to hold. "You might think there's something completely different going on."

I'm floundering. Words seem complicated and cumbersome. How am I supposed to sum up what I think is happening when my brain doesn't understand it? The complexity of it all is overwhelming, like my emotions are running on some sort of energy drink.

But as I gaze at Cade, the fairy lights, and the candles whilst contemplating the fact that he's here in the first place and not out with his mates, something dawns on me, the simplicity of it sharp and definitive.

"I think you're falling in love with me," I say, my voice soft and delicate.

"I think you might be right," he agrees.

I gulp. "So, what happens now?"

"That depends," Cade says.

"On what?"

"On you."

"Me?"

"It depends how you feel about me."

Me. How do I feel? I've spent so much time orchestrating Anna's love life that I've never contemplated my own. I've never really fancied anyone at school. Yes, I've had boyfriends when I was younger, but nothing since hitting my teenage years.

"I've never been in love with someone before," I begin, "so I'm not sure what it feels like, but I know you make me feel happy. You make me smile the minute you walk into a room, and I feel sick when you leave. When I see you, I have this urge to touch you, like you're too far away even if you're right next to me, and no matter how long I've been with you, it isn't enough. It's never enough."

His eyes narrow. "Hm, I'm no expert, but it sounds as if you might be in the same boat as me."

My body sways as if our imaginary boat is bobbing on open water, and there's nowhere I'd rather be.

"So, what do we do about it?" I ask, my heart fluttering to its own random rhythm.

"I know what I'd like to do."

"What?"

"I'd like to kiss you," he says, his head dipping toward mine as he closes the gap between us.

"I'd like that," I reply, my heart stopping momentarily.

As he takes my head in his hands, his lips meet mine, and it's nothing like I'd imagined. I haven't been kissed very much. There'd been a fumbling kiss with a boy who Anna tried to set me up with—only because he was the friend of the guy she was trying to get with. It'd felt messy and rushed. He shoved his tongue into my mouth and flicked it around as if he were checking my teeth for fillings. The whole experience had been unpleasant, his mouth tasting of cheese and onion crisps that had put me off my favourite flavour for a long time.

This is nothing like that.

This is gentle, his lips soft, his mouth tasting of sugary sweetness.

We begin to sway again, my hands tightening around the back of Cade's neck. When he finally pulls away, I'm breathless, feeling as if a warm breeze has been blowing in my face.

"This complicates things somewhat," I say, dropping my arms down along his and resting them on his forearms.

"See, that's where I disagree. I think it makes things a whole lot easier."

"How do you work that out?"

"We just need to be together."

"But what about my mum and Mark?"

"Do you think it'll be a problem?"

"For my mum, yes. I've never had a boyfriend, and I don't know how she'll react. She might move your bedroom down to the tiny box room. She might stop us walking to school together. She might never leave us alone in the house again." My breath comes back in chunks, a tiny panic beginning to well inside as I imagine my mum on high alert, me never left unsupervised ever again.

"We don't tell them, then," Cade suggests.

"Like, keep it a secret?"

"Exactly. They don't need to know we are madly in love with each other."

His eyes flood me with such warmth, I can't help but smile. "It won't be easy." My smile drops as the reality of it registers.

"No, but I didn't think being in love with someone would be easy."

"I guess not."

As we hold each other, the enormity of what we've just agreed takes hold.

"How long have we got before your dad gets back?"

Cade checks the time on his phone. "Couple of hours," he guesses. "He won't come back before closing time."

"Good," I breathe. "I want to show you something."

Grabbing him by the hand, I lead him from the patio and down to the bottom of the garden where the conifers are large and overbearing.

I thrust my hand between the dense branches in exactly the right spot and part the leaves like an explorer in the jungle.

Dry leaves crunch under our feet as Cade follows dutifully, my toes curling up at the feel of soil in my sandals.

We emerge into a small square plot. The conifers continue around the outside, framing the large and very old trampoline sitting in the centre.

"No way," Cade exclaims, letting go of my hand and walking around the outside of it. "How did I not know this was here? This must add another ten feet onto your garden."

"The gardens are really long, and you won't have seen it from the house, even from the upstairs windows, as the bathroom backs onto it and you can't see out of that window, and then there's the box room that I don't think you've ever been in."

"No." He shakes his head, running his hand up the rusty pole. "Why is it here?"

"My mum got me it years ago, but she didn't want it spoiling the lawn or her garden, so she cleared this bottom part and let the trees grow around it. It used to be lovely, but it's been neglected since I stopped using it."

"Are you wanting to have a go now?" Cade smirks.

"I'm not dressed for it." I pull at the hem of my dress. "I want to show you something else."

My ankles wobble as I unstrap my sandals. He puts his hand out to steady me, and I slide them off and climb onto the trampoline.

"Come on," I urge.

Cade follows, struggling to fit through the small zip in the side of the netting.

"You need to lie down here, next to me." I guide him as I

lie down on the trampoline, my dress fanning out around me. He settles next to me. We must look like two snow angels.

"Now look up at the sky." My eyes are already set on the black void above us.

We stare up, silence hugging us as the tiny stars wink, the clear sky showcasing the entire spectrum of constellations.

"I used to lie here for hours just looking at them and wondering how far away they were," I reminisce. "Sometimes, my brain would start to hurt when I tried to think about what was up there."

"It's mind-boggling," Cade agrees.

"But beautiful," I add.

He turns toward me, propping his head on his hand as he gazes at me.

"Very beautiful," he whispers as I turn to face him. His hand finds its way onto my cheek, his fingers smoothing my skin as my eyes become heavy. "Don't close them," he warns.

I quickly open my eyes.

"Keep them open," he insists, his head dipping toward mine. He kisses me softly, our eyes still looking at each other.

I roll into him, and Cade pulls me on top of him, our arms locking around each other. We stay like this for what feels like hours, the stars twinkling above us, the trees shrouding our bodies as if keeping us from the world and everything in it.

TWENTY

ALEX

IT'S FIFTEEN MINUTES LATER WHEN A SMALL WOMAN walks up behind Cade. She's petite and birdlike with thin blonde hair framing her face. She stands behind him, and Ian and I are distracted by how close she's approached. Cade's attention is on Sonya as she tells the group about the caravan she shares with her mum on the East Coast, so he doesn't notice the woman until she places her hands over his eyes. Winking at us like we're in on her surprise, she smiles, shushing us with her lips. His hand quickly shoots up to hers as he swivels on his stool.

"Surprise." She grins, leaning back as Cade clocks her.

His face drops, and he lets go of her hand. "Jess?" He shakes his head, confusion swamping him. "What're you doing here?"

"I thought I'd surprise you."

"No kidding."

For a second, we've been forgotten.

"Aren't you going to introduce me?" Jess beams, casting her eyes at our table.

Cade turns slowly, his body stiff and on alert.

"Everyone, this is Jess." He nods, his face cold and hard.

"Hi." She gives us all a dainty wave.

Michael extends his hand and introduces himself. The rest of the table follows suit, the women giving a little wave, the men clasping Jess's hand and shaking it profusely. Donna manages to shoot a look at me, but I'm too busy contemplating who this woman is to pick up on what she's trying to say.

I'm last to introduce myself, nodding, my name feeling foolish. Jess looks at me fleetingly, her small, beaklike nose making me imagine her sitting in a tree, triumphantly tweeting out a little song. She's pretty. Her blonde hair is neatly parted on the side and sits on her shoulders, her make-up minimal and her frame slight. She looks intricate, like she's been carefully assembled in a tiny workshop by a master craftsman.

"So, Jess." Sonya inflates herself like the barrage of questions about to come out is mounting inside her. "Do you work with Cade? Are you from another branch?"

"God, no," Jess replies, her comment like a little slap to our faces. "No, I'm Cade's girlfriend."

I grip the side of my glass as Cade sighs heavily,

and I hope to God a pin doesn't drop, as it'll be deafening.

Jess flashes us a look, her face soft, her smile spreading like the wings of a butterfly.

"Look, Jess." Cade stands up and takes her by the arm. "Why are you here?"

"Why?" Her small frame spins around as he begins to move her away from the table.

"If you'll excuse us." He bows his head as he ushers her away.

We wait until they're at a safe distance before anyone speaks.

"Well, I didn't expect that to happen," Donna says, her wide eyes sweeping over us.

"No." Sonya shakes her head. "Who is she?"

"According to her, his girlfriend," Michael points out.

"Yeah, but he doesn't look happy to see her." Donna stares at me.

"Looks like they're having some stern words." Ian flicks his eyes over to where they're standing by the other side of the bar.

I've been trying not to look, but I can't help it. My head feels light, as if it's filling with helium, the panic button inside me blaring at me to get up and leave, whatever has invaded me making me feel sick and panicky.

His girlfriend.

This shouldn't rock me. He's a good-looking guy.

Did I expect him to remain celibate for the last sixteen years?

Girlfriend.

And she touched him. Her hands were on his face, roaming his skin, her body pressed against his back. She will have kissed him, tasted him, seen him in the flesh, all of him.

I think I'm going to be sick.

Then

We hear the door close, the sort of noise when someone is trying to be quiet but fails badly. We'd tidied the garden up and moved into the sitting room, turning the TV on for effect, but our greedy hands and mouths have been busy for the past twenty minutes.

At the noise of the door closing, Cade jumps up and scoots over to the sofa opposite me whilst I pull at my dress, tucking my feet underneath it.

"You didn't need to wait up for me," Mark says, appearing in the doorway. His words are lazy, but there's a sharpness to him that surprises me. I've only ever seen my mum drunk, so his alertness is something new.

"We didn't. We were just watching telly." Cade's lie slips out too easily.

"I'm going to bed," I say, smoothing down my dress, my eyes darting to Cade, panic rising that I'm being too obvious. How can Mark not tell we spent the last hour kissing?

"Was it something I said?" Mark jokes.

I throw him a quick smile, no hard feelings, just before I reach the doorway.

Mark moves out of my way. "Goodnight, then," he says.

"Night."

I try not to run up the stairs.

TWENTY-ONE
CADE

I'M CURSING THE SMALL BAR THAT HAS NOWHERE for me to take Jess where we can have some privacy.

"You're hurting me," she snaps as I manoeuvre her away from their prying eyes.

"What the fuck, Jess?" I hiss, my voice a guttural growl. "What the fuck are you doing here?"

"Like I said," she spits, "I came to surprise you. I thought it'd be nice, seeing as it's been so long since we've seen each other."

"I'm working."

"That doesn't mean I can't come see you."

"You can't just turn up. You could jeopardise everything."

"How? Having a girlfriend isn't going to mess with your work. If anything, it might help. Besides, what am I supposed to do when I haven't heard from you in days?"

"You know how we left things. We agreed on a break."

"*You* agreed on a break. I did no such thing."

"Don't give me that bullshit." I press my hand to my forehead, my patience wearing thin. "You can't be here. You shouldn't be here."

She takes a step toward me, her smile dropping, her eyes sharpening. "But I am here, and I don't see the problem."

My face is inches from hers. "You need to leave. Now."

"Or what?"

"What do you mean, or what?"

"I could march over there and tell your new little friends exactly how we met."

My body freezes, and my hands clench. Fuck. This is all I need.

"You wouldn't dare."

"Just try me." She bares her teeth, and I know she isn't bluffing. "Now, we're going to go over there, and you're going to introduce me to them as your girl-friend, and you're not going to say another word, or I'll tell them everything they need to know about their shiny new boss."

She stands on her tiptoes and plants a kiss on the end of my nose. I pull away. "Be a good boy, Cade, and play nice." She smiles, then turns and heads back to the table.

Fuck.

I've never been afraid of confrontation. When I was younger, I would actively seek it out, raring to have a pop at anyone who thought they were hard enough or man enough to take me on.

But that was a different time, a different me. I can't risk everything by having a bust-up with Jess in front of everyone. I've always preferred to keep my arguments behind closed doors.

My mind races back to the night Lexie and I got together, the night it all seemed to fall into place for us, whereas my dad and Jacquelin were falling apart.

Then

"Are you going to tell me what's going on?" I ask as soon as Lexie has left the room.

My dad untucks his shirt and pulls at the collar as if it's been strangling him. "What do you mean?"

"With you and Jacquelin. Lexie said her mum was upset when she got home. Have you fallen out?"

"You make it sound like we're kids." He chuckles, avoiding my gaze.

"That depends on whether you're acting like a child," I say.

He stops pulling at his shirt. "And what's that supposed to mean?" His lip curls slightly.

"You know exactly what it means," I shoot back. "We have a good thing going on here. We don't want to fuck that up, now do we?"

My dad draws his breath in long and slow. There's no smart comeback, no hilarious joke to chase this with, so instead, he shakes his head and pats me on the back like some old football chum.

"You've nothing to worry about," he declares, a drunken smile spreading across his face. "Just a little lovers' tiff. Nothing that won't be forgotten in the morning." He sways, blinking at me before turning and walking toward the kitchen, probably for a pint of water and a pre-emptive paracetamol.

I spin around and walk over to the sofa where, moments before, Lexie and I had been making out. It isn't the first time I've made out with someone, but doing so with Lexie is something else. I'd struggled to behave myself and keep my hands under my command.

Arriving at the top of what I now consider to be Lexie's and my stairs, I note her door is open, the small glow of the lamp telling me she's not asleep. I enter my room, strip off my clothes, and put on some old shorts before making my way into the bathroom.

When I'm finished, I step out into the hallway and peer at Lexie's open door. Not thinking it through, I gently tap on the door, pushing it open before I've even heard her voice.

TWENTY-TWO
ALEX

Jess arrives back at the table, her smile wide and triumphant.

"Hey, you're back," Ian says, trying to hide the fact that we've all been talking about her.

"Yeah, sorry about that. Cade likes to play the fool sometimes, although I'm sure you guys have already picked up on his annoying little habit." She laughs to herself.

The rest of us are dumbfounded. No one has witnessed Cade playing the fool, and I know he's never adopted that persona. Quite the opposite, which sparks my interest as to what exactly is going on here. Who is this woman? What's she doing here, and what hold does she have over Cade?

"Have a seat, Jess," Sonya says as she adjusts her chair to make room whilst Ian grabs Jess a chair from the empty table next to us.

Jess perches herself in between Ian and Sonya, pulling at her jacket as if she doesn't want it contaminated by her surroundings.

"What line of business are you in?" Sonya asks when the silence becomes too dense.

"I'm a psychologist."

The silence tries to return, but Sonya is on the case.

"Wow, that must be interesting. What kind of therapy?"

"All sorts of therapy, really, but I specialise in dealing with trauma. I have a lot of patients with PTSD…." Her voice trails off before she adds, "Post-traumatic stress disorder," like we're all a bunch of morons.

"So, how long have you known each other?" Sonya continues.

"Cade and I have been together for a few years now." Her smile is tight, her eyes wide, as if she's daring us to challenge her.

Cade arrives back at the table, his jaw firmly set, his eyes like daggers.

The atmosphere is thick, like treacle coating the back of everything, leaving sticky hands in its wake.

Cade hovers, staring at me across the table.

The atmosphere seeps under my skin, making it feel like I've been sitting in the sun too long and my skin is now red and blotchy. I'm hot. I need to move, need to get out of here.

What's wrong with me? Why do I feel like I've been humiliated? Why is this woman irritating me so much? I'm being naive if I think Cade hasn't been with anyone since me, but I don't want to be presented with the idea in the form of the oh-so-annoying Jess.

Why can't it be like it was before when it was just me and him, no one else?

Then

Getting ready for bed slowly, I don't want this night to end. I can't believe how badly the evening had begun and how elated I now feel. But amongst the fever of Cade's kisses, his declarations, and grand gestures, there's the fear of the future, fear of my mum and Mark, fear of what will happen beyond tonight.

Pushing these thoughts away, I tell myself that Cade is right. I deserve a bit of happiness, and I'm not going to let my fears for the future spoil this magical evening.

I climb onto my bed, straining my ears to hear his feet on the stairs, my stomach fluttering at the sound.

Patiently, I wait, hoping my open door will speak to him.

"Hey," he says, walking into my room after I heard him finish up in the bathroom.

I'm on top of the covers, my hair cascading down my shoulders in large unruly waves, my make-up gone, my dress replaced with a long T-shirt that barely covers me.

"Hey," I greet him, putting down my phone. "Did you ask him what had gone on?"

Cade plants himself on the end of my bed. "He said they'd

just fallen out, but it was nothing serious. Said it would all be okay in the morning."

"Do you think it will be?" I shift my legs, my T-shirt riding up. His eyes wander over my skin. Goose bumps erupt everywhere his gaze touches. Running my hand down my leg, I suddenly want my hands to be his.

"I'm sure it'll be fine. Couples fall out all the time." He watches as I push my hair behind my ear, the little move distracting him.

"I've had a really nice night," I tell him.

"Me too."

"But I'm not sure I'm ready for it to end." I'm starstruck, and not just from the stargazing.

He slides over the bed, reaching for my face as he pulls me into him. His kiss is slow and purposeful. A pulsing builds inside me. I don't know what it is. I've never felt it before, but it's here, now, growing with every second. Then he touches me, running his hand up my leg, and it's bliss. I grab onto his arms as he runs his hand back up my leg and it finds its way under my T-shirt.

He quickly pulls away, looking shocked.

"Sorry," he apologises. "I don't trust myself." He exhales heavily.

"Have you done this before?" I ask, afraid of the answer.

"Yes," he confirms, "but it wasn't an experience I want to replicate in a hurry."

My body deflates, although I'm not surprised. There's no way a guy like Cade would be a virgin.

"I'm not sure I want to, then, if it's as bad as that," I joke, turning my head away.

"It was more a case of the wrong person. I'm sure with someone who I actually have feelings for, it'll be different."

"It's funny, because I've always imagined my first time being disastrous, a brief fumble with some random boy somewhere, him trying to shove it in and me just gritting my teeth until it's all over, then crying as soon as I get home." I've pictured it many times. I'm under no illusion about the momentous occasion. Anna had brought that dream crashing down with her real-time re-enactments.

"That sounds scarily familiar." Cade sniggers before adding, "But it doesn't have to be that way."

I shuffle over to him, my lips dangerously close, my eyelids heavy. Lazily, I kiss him, caressing the side of his face, my body beginning to sing.

"Lexie." My name leaves his lips like it's meant to be.

I move closer, climbing on his lap, my legs on either side of him.

"I can't be trusted here. I want you too much."

Pulling back slightly, I examine him. His face looks desperate, like a recovering drug addict holding a syringe.

"You can have me," I say as I pull my T-shirt up and over my head.

He stares at me, his eyes captivated. "What if someone comes in?"

"There's no way my mum is making it up another flight of stairs any time soon, and I don't think there's any danger of your dad coming into my room." I stand up and head toward the door, my tiny pants barely covering me. I feel Cade watching me. I drag the chair from beneath my desk and shove it under the door handle before returning to him.

"I haven't got anything," he stammers, panic lacing his words that this could spoil the entire moment.

I pull open a drawer in a small cabinet and riffle through the mass of hair accessories, roll-on deodorants, and old headphones until I find the silver packet.

"I've had this since I was fifteen." I smirk. "Anna gave it to me. I don't know why, but she said I might need it someday." If she'd been in the room, I would've kissed her myself.

"Are you sure?" Cade says as I clamber back onto his lap.

"Well, it goes out of date next month, so we better use it; otherwise, it would be an awful waste."

His smile tickles at my insides. Then he's kissing me, his hands wandering over my skin like it's Braille.

He rolls me onto the bed. I lie flat beneath him, my hair fanning out on either side of me. It's like I'm floating on the surface of a pool.

"I've never met anyone like you." He exhales this into the air as he towers over me.

"Likewise."

He lowers himself, his lips returning to mine, our bodies becoming entangled to the point where it's impossible to tell who is who.

And it is bliss. All of it. Our time together is the most perfect of my life. And I know, deep down, it will end. All good things come to an end.

I just didn't realise it would end so fucking horribly.

TWENTY-THREE
ALEX

Nausea rolls through my stomach, and I stand up quickly.

"Where are you going?" Donna shoots over at me.

"Refill," I reply, keeping my head down. Shimmying out from behind the table, I don't bother to ask if anyone else needs another drink.

As expected, Cade follows me.

I lean on the bar, fishing in my back pocket for my debit card.

"Everything all right?" Cade asks as he appears on my left.

"Sure. Why wouldn't it be?"

"You tell me."

"There's nothing to tell." Jess is in my head. Her little beak, her thin lips. I think about Shawn, but he has no right to be in my head, so I push him out. All I can see is Cade and Jess, and my blood boils.

Leaning back, I brace myself. "Jess seems—"

"Don't," he snaps.

"Don't what?" I reply. "I was only going to say she seems nice." My voice betrays me, the raised pitch laced with sarcasm. It's my only line of defence here for the hurt that's developed since Jess arrived and put her hands on Cade's face.

"Then you'd be lying to me."

He's gripping a ten-pound note, his voice scraping the back of his throat and almost bringing me to my knees. I study the bottles on the shelves behind the bar, wondering if I should order something stronger.

The bartender saves me. "What can I get you?"

"White wine, please." I glance at Cade, who adds a bottle of beer to the order.

The bartender busies himself.

"A psychologist?"

It's Cade's turn to study the bottles on the shelf.

"Is she *your* psychologist?"

"No."

"Oh my God, she is, isn't she?"

"No."

"Holy shit. You're fucking your psychologist?" I hate the words as soon as they leave my mouth, but it's all the ammunition I have. I hate this. I hate the fact that he's been fucking anyone other than me. I know I'm being unreasonable—I can't expect him to have stayed celibate all these years—but that doesn't stop it from uprooting my heart like a gardener pulling up Japanese knotweed.

"What did you need a shrink for?" I laugh, but it's cold, brutal. I don't want to do this to him, but I can't stop myself.

"We're not doing this now."

"What's she doing here?"

"It's a long story."

"I'm all ears."

The bartender places a beer in front of Cade, who nods his thanks. He picks it up and turns to me.

"Not here." He stares at me, and I swear my heart stops. "It's a conversation for another time."

My wine arrives, and we have no reason to continue standing here.

Cade walks away.

Let him go. Just let him go.

"Does she know about us?" My question comes from nowhere, like a lasso. I'm hoping it'll pull him back.

Cade holds my stare, the bottle hanging loosely in his hand. "She knows what happened."

"You talked to her about it?"

"I didn't have much choice."

We stare at each other, a moment that comes and goes in a second, but even a bystander wouldn't fail to notice it.

"What's that supposed to mean?"

Cade glances over at the table where I know we're

being watched—if not by Donna, then by Jess or even Ian or Sonya, who will be wondering what the hell is taking so long to get two drinks. His eyes fall back to me, something in them now that I've not seen before—a wildness, a darkness ready to consume me.

"I said your name."

"You said my name? Why would you say my name?"

He edges back toward me, closing the gap between us. "You really want to know?" he challenges.

"Yes." My voice lacks conviction now. What the hell is he going to say? Did he say my name whilst they were arguing? Did he write the wrong name on her birthday card?

Do I really want to know?

He leans in. He's so close, I can feel his breath on the side of my face.

"Because whilst I was fucking her, I was thinking about you, and as I came, I said your name, not just once but over and over again."

The glass nearly slips from my hand as Cade walks back to the table.

Gripping the glass, I close my eyes for a second to ensure I don't slide to the floor. *What the fuck?*

It takes all my courage to return to the table.

The conversation is flowing. Jess is under the tight scrutiny of Sonya and Donna. I don't look at Cade. I don't trust myself. How am I supposed to process the image of him fucking someone else whilst thinking about me? Jess's silky blonde hair doesn't move. Her sweet smile stays rigid on her face, and I want to slap her. She's done nothing to me. I should feel sorry for her. Cade obviously feels nothing for her, but even so, I can't let go of the anger that she exists, that she's tasted him, that she's felt him inside her.

"I'm only up here for the weekend," Jess is telling everyone. "Cade is spending so much time up here, I've barely seen him, so I thought I'd visit."

"The takeover is a bigger project than I anticipated," Cade adds, trying to rein some normality back into this evening.

"He's had to buy a small apartment up here, which I told him was silly." She laughs in a way that suggests there's nothing funny about this. She's airing an argument.

"What's silly is the commute," he counters, a sharpness in his tone that raises an eyebrow or two. "I can't keep driving all this way whenever I need to deal with something. This way is much easier."

"Well, if there's one thing this man knows, it's property," Ian says. "Look at it as an investment."

The rest of the table nods in agreement, but we're all thinking about how much money he must have to be able to buy an apartment up here just to avoid a long commute.

"So, how did you guys meet?" Donna asks, her legs crossed as she clutches her knee.

"Oh, we met through friends," Jess answers.

I'm not the only one who sees the look Cade gives her, the one telling her to tread carefully.

"They introduced us, and we hit it off straight away."

"Some things are just meant to be." Donna swoons.

"I think we should give poor Jess a break now," Sonya says. "She's survived our interrogation."

There's a small ripple of laughter, but it doesn't reach me.

"Where's the best place to eat around here?" Jess asks no one in particular, but Sonya is ready.

"Depends on what you're after. Indian, Italian, Turkish?"

The chat takes off, everyone having their own opinion on the best place to eat out. The thought of food makes my stomach heave. I can't focus with Cade sitting opposite me. The intensity of him is too much — the way he holds the bottle, the tiny hairs on his forearm, the rise and fall of his chest beneath his shirt. I haven't been this close to him in years, and it stirs things in me I've worked hard to suppress.

Cade eyes me, his stare boring into me like a challenge for me to look away. I stand my ground, keeping my eyes locked on him until the heat starts to build and his words fill my body.

"Because whilst I was fucking her, I was thinking about you."

I throw my wine back like there's a hole in the bottom of the glass.

Everyone seems oblivious to this battle of wills continuing over the table until Sonya stands up. She edges her way from behind the table as Jess and Ian pull their chairs in to let her out. When she finally makes it, she turns to ask if anyone needs a refill.

A man is behind her, three glasses clutched between his hands, his debit card clasped between his teeth as he steers his way over to his pack on the far side of the bar. Sonya isn't looking, too busy trying to memorise the drinks order. She turns at the same time as the man walks past, and she collides with him, beer sloshing over the edges of the glasses, all down his shirt and all over Sonya's front.

There's a three-second silence whilst the damage is assessed and mood asserted.

He puts the three glasses down on the end of our table and shakes the liquid from his hands, then retrieves his card from his mouth to unleash his anger.

"Jesus, you need to look where you're going, for fuck's sake." He takes a step back as if trying to get away from his wet shirt.

Sonya tries to appease him. "I'm so sorry. It was an accident."

"Well, you've spilled three drinks and ruined my shirt in the process. What the fuck are you going to do about it?"

The scrape of Cade's stool against the floor reverberates. "If there's a problem here, why don't we take this outside?"

He's here now, the Cade I remember, the Don't-Fuck-with-Me Cade who resides inside Cade the Businessman. Anger stalks behind his good looks—the anger that's always been there.

The guy turns to Cade, and his face drops. "Hey, man." He shakes his head, the colour draining from his cheeks.

Cade is taller by several inches, his chest broader and his stance resolute, but it's none of these things that makes the guy back down. It's the fire in Cade's eyes, the snarl on his lips, and the intent behind his offer. The Businessman is nowhere to be seen.

"S-Sorry, I just…," the guy stutters, then looks at Sonya. "Sorry, I didn't see you. It's a new shirt."

Cade's shoulders drop, and the Businessman is back. He slides his hand into his trouser pocket and pulls out his wallet. "This'll pay for a new shirt." He takes out a wad of cash and stuffs it into the top pocket of the guy's sodden shirt. "And pay for another round of drinks."

The guy shuffles off back to the bar, probably wondering how he managed to get out of that without getting his head kicked in.

"God, what a dick!" Michael exclaims as soon as the guy is out of earshot.

"I'll pay for the drinks, Cade. Please, let me. It was my fault," Sonya says.

"It was no one's fault," Cade says, still looking at the back of the guy. Even without a smile, his words put Sonya at ease, and I want to scream so fucking loud.

"Thank you," Sonya mouths quietly, looking a little shaken.

Cade deflects her attention. "No problem."

"What a complete jerk," Michael repeats as if no one heard him the first time.

"Absolutely," Ian agrees.

"And what was he wearing? I've never seen a man dress like that before," Michael adds, clearly feeling the need to belittle the guy to make up for his lack of action in defending Sonya.

"He was certainly very fashion-conscious," Donna says. "Those jeans looked like they'd been sprayed on, and I'm sure the shirt was designer."

"Who comes to a bar dressed like that?" Michael continues. "He looks like he needs a visit from the fashion police." He sniggers, safe now the guy has long gone and Cade is still on alert. "Did you see what he had on his feet? Were they loafers or boating shoes? And he wasn't wearing any socks."

"You should never trust a man who doesn't wear socks with his shoes," Cade says, then takes a swig from his bottle of beer before his eyes land on me.

"Is that so?" Michael laughs.

"Is that some sort of proverb?" Ian chuckles. "If it is, I've never heard of it."

"No." Cade shakes his head, a small smile growing at the corner of his mouth. "Just something someone once told me." He holds my gaze, and I need to run.

"Well, it's sound advice, if you ask me, and proven right tonight," Michael says, and the rest of the table is in agreement.

But Cade and I have left the conversation. We're locked in each other's sights, the past igniting like a flare. I'm being swallowed by it, my whole body beginning to drown in Cade, and I'm not sure I can breathe.

"I think I'm going to call it a night," I announce, finally tearing my eyes from him as I push myself away from the table, my legs wobbling beneath me.

Cade stands up instinctively. Jess glares at him.

"Are you sure?" Donna asks, looking at her watch.

"Yeah, I have an early start in the morning," I lie as I begin to shuffle out from behind the table, Michael and Donna adjusting their seats to let me out.

"Okay, well, I guess I'll see you Monday," Donna says.

"Yeah, see you Monday," Ian adds as Sonya waves.

"It's your round next time." Michael laughs, tipping his near-empty glass in my direction.

"How are you getting home?" Cade asks as he follows me out of the bar with everyone watching us. There'll be looks exchanged, glances thrown, and questions to be answered on Monday.

"I'll call a taxi," I answer as I reach the door and step out into the car park.

"I can drive you home. I'm still under the limit."

"I don't want you to drive me home," I huff, searching in my phone for a taxi company. "Besides, what would Jess say?"

"Fuck her."

"You've already done that," I snap.

"I can't profess to have lived like a monk for the past sixteen years, but I can tell you that every time I've fucked a woman, I've been thinking about you."

"Stop." I try to turn away, but he pulls on my arm.

"Why?"

"Because I don't want to hear it."

"What don't you want to hear? The fact that I can't get you out of my head? That you've never left?"

"No," I lash out, the frustration of the past hour rising to the surface. "I don't want to hear about all the women you've slept with, how you've touched them, how they've seen you like I have."

"Trust me, Lexie, no one has seen me like you have."

A sadness creeps in.

"You'd better go back inside," I tell him. "They'll be wondering where you are."

Without another word, he turns and heads back into the bar.

Why am I always left staring at his back?

Letting out a deep pent-up sigh that's been crushing my chest the entire evening, I look at my phone, where the taxi number glares at me. I switch to text and tell my thumbs to type.

Are you busy?

I wait for the reply which I know will come.

No.

I respond.

Do you want to meet?

His reply is quick.

Sure. Where?

My thumb hovers over my reply. I can't afford another hotel, but I also can't go home alone tonight, and although Shawn Bowling's company is second-rate, it's the only way I'll push Cade from my thoughts. I need to feel numb. I need to feel nothing. I need to wipe this evening from my thoughts, and what better way than to spend it fucking some shit guy who I don't care one bit about. The sex is mundane and boring, but it's all I've got because what I need, I can't have.

I type out my reply.

My house.

TWENTY-FOUR

CADE

"Well, that was an experience." Jess sighs as she sits in the passenger seat of my Audi.

Ignoring the bait, I fasten my seatbelt and check my mirrors.

"I could have a whole new caseload of clients just from that table," she continues. "I don't think I've ever met anyone as intrusive as Sonya. All the questions suggest to me she's insecure about something."

"Or maybe she was just being polite. It's human nature, is it not, to be inquisitive?" I say, but Jess isn't listening.

"I suspect Donna has an abusive husband, the way she flinched when that guy came over and started shouting at Sonya. Her reaction was that of the classic victim, and Michael, quite clearly, has a drinking problem. The guy must've drunk double what we did."

"Have you quite finished?" My patience is waning.

I'm used to Jess dissecting people. It's what she does for a living, and she seems unable to turn it off even after office hours. But I don't need this tonight.

"I'm just saying, they're a bunch of very dysfunctional people."

"They're just normal people doing normal jobs and enjoying a normal drink in a bar after work. Why can't you just take things for what they are for once and stop analysing everyone."

"You should be thanking me. These are your new recruits. Don't you want to know if Michael might come into work drunk one day? If Donna may call in sick because she has a bruise on her face she can't cover? If Sonya will keep losing sales because of her insecurities?"

"I get what you're saying, but that still doesn't dispute the fact that it's pure guesswork on your part."

"Are you questioning my abilities as a psychologist?" she scoffs. My eyes are on the road, but even so, I know her nostrils will have flared.

"No, I'm just saying that sometimes things are not what they seem." I wait for her next comment. I don't need to be a psychologist to know where this conversation is leading.

"And what was going on between you and that Alex woman?"

"Nothing." She'd been watching me at the bar. She's always watching me.

"Whatever." Jess rolls her eyes. "I watched the

pair of you. It was as if there was a silent argument going across the table. Have you had a run-in with her in the office? Have you had to discipline her? I got the distinct impression that she can't stand to be around you."

"You got all that, did you?"

"It wasn't just her reaction, though. Why did you go after her when she left?"

"I was just making sure she had a way of getting home. I asked them all to come out for drinks after work, and I felt obliged to make sure they all got home safe."

"Would you have followed one of the men?"

"No, I would not, so there it is—I'm a sexist pig."

"All I'm saying is that if it had been one of the other women, I don't think you would've batted an eyelid."

"And your reason for thinking that?"

"I'm not blind, Cade. Alex is clearly a looker."

"Oh, I see. So I only made sure she had a lift home because she's an attractive woman. Great, now I'm a chauvinist and a letch as well as a sexist."

"You didn't pay Donna as much attention."

"Donna rang her husband—sorry, no, her abusive husband—who came to collect her, and Sonya shared a taxi with Michael and Ian. Alex was the only one who left alone." I flash Jess a look as I change gears. "Now who's being insecure?"

"Can you blame me?" she shoots back.

Here it comes.

"You disappear up here for work, not even saying goodbye. You never consulted me, never even asked me what I thought or how I felt about it."

"I wasn't aware I had to consult you with regards to my business arrangements—and we talked about a break. I need a break."

"It has nothing to do with the business, Cade. It's the fact that you've bought an apartment up here. This is not a break. It's like you're not coming back."

Steering into a tight bend, I accelerate, the car pulling beneath me as I ease into the corner.

"Maybe I'm not."

TWENTY-FIVE
ALEX

Waiting for a spark of arousal, I examine the ceiling as Shawn pushes himself inside me. By the noise he's making and the speed he's going, I know he's nearly done. My teeth grind as I grip the sheets and block out his ragged breathing.

As he writhes away, I take my cue and clench my body, simulating an earth-shattering orgasm as Shawn reaches his own pathetic end.

Without looking at me, he climbs off the bed and heads straight into the bathroom.

I pull the sheets over my body, knowing I'll have to change them before I can sleep in this bed tonight. Why the fuck did I let him come over to my place? This was a bad idea, the backlash of the stupid drinks.

"So, how was your little gathering tonight?" Shawn shouts from the bathroom.

"It was just a couple of drinks after work."

"Was the new boss man there?"

"It was his idea."

"Really?" He emerges from the doorway, his jeans in one hand and a cigarette in the other.

"You're not smoking in my house. You'll have to go outside."

Shawn shoves his leg into his jeans, hopping as he sticks the smoke in his mouth. "And what was the reason for this social gathering?"

"Just to get to know each other outside of the office."

"And why would you need to do that?"

"I don't know. I didn't ask him."

"Hm, seems a bit nonsensical to me. The workplace needs to remain the workplace. You can't muddy the waters by getting to know one another. You can't mix business and pleasure. That's the first rule of the business world."

"Is that so?" I perch on the side of the bed, pulling a T-shirt over my head.

"The work environment won't function if staff start airing their dirty laundry. Take us, for instance." Shawn glances at me.

"Us?"

"Why haven't you told any of your work colleagues about us?"

I think about this carefully. I need to compose the right answer.

"Because it's none of their business."

"Exactly. It's none of their business. And what would happen if they knew you were screwing me?"

I flinch. Even though I'm relieved at his interpretation of what's going on between us, I still don't like to be reminded of what a shit fucking idea this is.

"I don't know." I shrug, contemplating Donna's reaction of complete and utter horror.

"Oh, come on." Shawn exhales. "You know as well as I do it would fuel the office for weeks. The fact that we're fucking would be front-page news."

"You think too highly of yourself," I tell him.

He picks up his phone, dressed and ready to make his exit now he's had what he came for. "I bet your new boss wouldn't be happy if he knew you were fucking his biggest rival." Shawn smiles like some sort of gruesome doll.

I look away. What would Cade think? If my reaction to Jess is anything to go by, then I dread to think what Cade's reaction would be if he knew about Shawn.

TWENTY-SIX
CADE

SITTING ON THE BALCONY OF MY NEW APARTMENT with a whisky in hand and the night air for company, I'm grateful for the quiet. The argument had lasted long enough that it was too late for Jess to check into a hotel, which was what I'd suggested, so she's asleep in the spare room.

Bringing her back here had only fuelled her anger. In her mind, I'd bought a small apartment, somewhere just to call base at the end of the day. In reality, I've bought a plush apartment by the canal. The converted mill is not only architecturally stunning but also decorated and finished to the standard I'm used to.

Jess had instantly hated it. "What a waste of money," she'd spat. What's the point of a beautiful view if I'm hardly going to be here to enjoy it? What's the use of a six-seater dining room table when I'm never going to have guests around? Her words, not mine.

After downing the rest of my drink, I head back inside, closing the sliding door and shutting away the scenery. I put the glass in the sink, then make my way to the master bedroom. On passing the spare room, I note the open door, a tactic on her part, I'm sure.

Guilt invades me.

Even though I hadn't been her patient, she'd helped me through the worst of it. She'd made me realise I wasn't at fault. And I'd mistaken it for something else. She'd been a comfort, someone to talk to who understood what I was going through. We'd both been through so much. Two damaged souls pushed together.

I thought it would be enough, that I could move on.

But I was wrong.

And now what?

I head for the bathroom and brush my teeth, all intent on going to bed, but my legs won't move.

I reach for my phone, for something to start me off, but I don't need it tonight. Reaching inside my boxers, I stroke myself, images of Lexie flooding my brain like a euphoric drug.

TWENTY-SEVEN
ALEX

Long after Shawn left, I lie on fresh sheets, fighting the feeling growing between my legs. The more I push it away, the more it burns. Slipping my hand under the sheet, I let my fingers explore.

I'm spoiled for choice with the memories I can conjure, but tonight, I select the time my mum and Mark had left me and Cade alone to go to a casino.

We'd started in the bath, the water spilling over the edge as he'd washed every part of me, his mouth following where the sponge had been. We made it out onto the landing, my wet hair soaking into the carpet as I'd lain on my back and Cade had begun.

Even though it was sixteen years ago, I haven't forgotten the feel of his tongue between my legs, the soft licks he would drive me wild with, his hair tickling the inside of my thigh as I pushed myself toward his mouth. I still feel the ghost of his fingers sliding inside me, rhythmically pulsing as he'd worked me into a frenzy. Every time, I'd try to hide how close I was, but he'd know. And just as I was about to come, he'd pull away, leaving me burning and raw.

"Not without me," he'd say before pushing himself inside me and turning my world into a dazzling myriad of lights and colours where there was no end and no beginning, only *now*.

I can still feel him when I climax. His face, those eyes, those hands—and amongst the pleasure, there's pain making me want to cry.

TWENTY-EIGHT
ALEX

THE WORKLOAD FOR THE DAY STARES AT ME FROM my to-do list. I'm feeling hungover despite the lack of alcohol.

The front door opens, and my stomach lurches as Cade walks through the door looking devastatingly handsome in a dark grey suit, his stubble framing his face, his eyes rich and powerful. The words on my to-do list dance before my eyes.

"Morning, Alex," Cade utters as he passes my desk.

Focus on the words.

"Morning."

"I need a word with you in my office."

My list of jobs is now impossible to ignore.

"I'm kind of busy," I tell him.

He turns.

Bergamot and apple waft under my nose, loosening my muscles and softening my resolve.

Giving in, I glance at him.

"Whatever you're doing can wait."

Shit.

"Can I get you a drink?" he calls as he disappears into the small kitchen.

"No." There's nothing strong enough in there to prepare me for being in close quarters with Cade in his office.

Several minutes later, he emerges with his travel mug and stands by my desk. The coffee smell is trapped inside the mug, so I'm assaulted again by his fruity cologne, which only lulls me into a false sense of relaxation.

"Shall we?" He tilts his head toward his office.

Gulping, I push my chair back and follow him. He opens the door and stands aside to let me pass. I hold my breath as I slide into the room.

He closes the door, then strides across the office and takes up his position behind his desk. "Sit."

I glare at him.

"Please," he insists.

Lowering into the small chair opposite his desk, I remind myself not to scowl.

"I've had a complaint about you."

My hands knot in my lap.

"Staff or client?" I ask.

"Client."

"Let me guess. Mrs Wells."

"Yes," Cade confirms.

"Is it worth mentioning how rude she was to me? Would you like a list of the names she called me just because her house hasn't sold yet?"

"You put the phone down on her."

"I had good cause."

"You know you can't hang up on clients." His eyes soften as he leans forward in his chair, his arms resting on the desk.

"I don't get paid enough to take the shit she was giving me."

"I agree," Cade says. "So you should've passed her on to me."

"You weren't here."

"You have my number. You could've patched her through. I will always answer your call." He studies me.

"I didn't want to bother you," I lie.

"I think we both know why you didn't call me."

"We do?"

"You're avoiding me."

"Am I?"

"You know you are."

Silence.

"Which is fine up until something like this happens. And it's not just this."

The room shrinks around me.

"Your sales have declined since my arrival. Your work performance has slowed."

"And what did you expect? Did you think you could just walk back into my life and we'd smile nicely at each other and carry on as normal?"

"Of course not."

"I've managed to forget as much as I could. And then bam, you arrive, and everything comes flooding back. It's like living in a recurring nightmare."

He sits up, his eyes ablaze. "Was it all that bad?"

What are his memories like compared to my own?

"No, and that's what makes it so hard," I explain. "Most of it was the best time of my life. I loved you—I mean really loved you—and then…." The room blurs.

"This is why we need to talk about it," Cade begins, leaning over the desk.

"I'd rather we didn't."

"We were teenagers. It was the worst time for us to be dealing with everything we had going on. Maybe now we can look at things differently. The longer you put it off, the harder it'll get."

"I'll leave, then." I stand up, straightening my shirt.

"Sit down," Cade says softly.

"Or what? You'll fire me?"

"I'll do no such thing."

"Then what?"

He rises and unbuttons his jacket, and I suddenly wish I hadn't said anything at all.

"Sit down, Lexie, or I'll make you sit down. You

know I can. And I'll do it—right here in this office if I have to."

My face burns. My hands wish they had something to hold on to. His voice so soft, so silky that I can almost feel the words brushing against my skin.

"You wouldn't dare."

He steps closer, his head lowered. "Try me."

Fuck. I can't breathe, can't move.

"You won't."

"I will," Cade declares as he hovers before me.

My eyes close.

"I haven't forgotten, Lexie, and I know you haven't either." His fingers graze the side of my cheek, so gentle, so smooth. "I'll stop when you sit down or you tell me to stop. It's your call."

His fingers undo me as they slide slowly down the side of my neck. I know these fingers, know what they can do, and I've missed them so fucking much, but I can't let him win, can't show him how weak he makes me. The word *stop* forms in my brain, but my lips remain clamped shut, my mouth mute.

"Just tell me to stop, and I will," he repeats as his hand moves to my collarbone.

My body responds. I try to shut it down, but it's like a siren has been set off. I bite my lip.

"I'm hoping no one has touched you like this since me," he growls.

My groan catches in the back of my throat.

I can't let him do this, can't let him take me, because once I do, there's no going back.

It takes every ounce of energy to make myself sit down.

As soon as my bottom hits the chair, he pulls his hand away.

This is not a fair game. He knows me too well.

He stalks back to his chair.

"This is exactly the reason I can't work here anymore," I say.

"I disagree."

"I'll look for a new job."

"No," he asserts.

"One of us has to go, Cade, and as the CEO, I don't think you're a viable option. It'll have to be me."

"I won't accept your resignation."

"You won't have a choice."

"Look, there has to be a way. I'm not going to be the cause of you quitting your job, a job you're very good at."

"Like you just said, I'm not at my best here. This is the only way."

"Let's not do anything hasty. Surely you have bills to pay."

"There are other estate agents. Maybe I'll go work for Bowling."

Cade stares, his face frozen. "Absolutely not."

"You're just saying that because they're your biggest competitor."

"No, I'm saying it because of what I've heard about Bowling and the way they run their business."

"Everyone knows what they're like."

"Do they?" His eyebrow arches, making me wonder what he does know.

"What do you mean?" I straighten in my chair.

"Nothing. Forget I said anything. Just don't go sniffing around there. You belong here, and I won't be the reason you quit your job."

"I think we both knew this was never going to work."

"But we can make it work. I'll make it work."

But my mind is made up. I can't be here with him. I stand up and head for the door before turning and looking at him. "But I think we both know this will be for the best," I say before leaving the room.

Returning to my desk, I pick up my list of jobs, tears obscuring my vision, my hands shaking, my heart in bits. I don't want to quit my job—I've been here for years—but I also know I can't go on like this. The incident with Mrs Wells is evidence of that. My emotions are being hammered daily, my heart constantly requiring a reboot after seeing Cade, hearing his voice, or simply knowing he's in the next room.

I thought it would get easier, that I'd learn to function as a robot, mastering the basic daily commands to get me through the day. But that hasn't been the case. It's getting worse. Every day that I'm exposed to him, the weaker I'll become until the day will arrive when I have nothing left.

And then what?

Cade

I slam my fists onto the desk, my fury balling like a tornado in my stomach. I want to charge after her and beg her to stay, but I can't. She's right. It was never going to work. We can't share the same air, let alone an office. And it's killing me. It's ripping me apart. We can't be this close, yet so far away. The sensible thing would be to let her go, try and move on with my life, and concentrate on what I came here to do, but I don't think I can. Fate has thrown us together again, like it has unfinished business with us, and I'm sure as hell not going to let her push me away again.

I will fight for her if I must.

I will do whatever it takes to keep her.

Whatever it takes.

TWENTY-NINE
ALEX

MY NECK ACHES AS I STARE AT THE POSTER CADE has pinned on the noticeboard in the staff room.

"Who's your plus-one going to be?" Donna slinks up behind me like a shadow. "You are coming, right?"

The words on the poster blur, my brain only picking out the important information.

Celebrating the takeover.
Saturday 6:00 p.m.
Kiki's restaurant.
I hope you'll all be there.

But it's the opening sentence that's now responsible for my sweaty palms and sudden headache.

You and your partners are invited to...

"I don't know." I exhale too loudly. "I don't have anyone to bring."

"Sure you do," Donna says, elongating the words for emphasis. "What about the mystery guy you've been seeing? Or did you make him up just to stop me trying to fix you up with random guys?" She laughs, but it quickly trails off as if she realises there might be an element of truth to what she said.

"He exists. I'm just not sure he'd be welcome." I imagine their faces if I showed up with Shawn.

"He can't be that bad, surely?" She waits for me to respond, but my eyes remain glued to the poster. Realising I'm not going to indulge her, Donna leans over and joins me in inspecting the invitation. "Hm, formal attire," she reads, squinting at the wall. "Kiki's. I've never heard of this place. Have you?"

"No."

"God, I'm going to have to dig Ed's suit out." She groans as she makes her way over to the kettle. "That relies on it still fitting him, of course."

"He only has the one?"

"He's not really a suit-and-tie guy. And he's going to need a full MOT. Haircut, nails trimmed, nostril hair removed. There'll be nothing left of him by the time I'm done."

"And here was me thinking my beauty regime was intense."

"I'm serious. They won't let him in otherwise. They'll think he's a homeless person." Abandoning the poster-staring competition, Donna goes back to making her coffee, stirring it like she's whisking egg whites. "Hey, do you think the boss will bring that woman? What was her name?"

"Jess."

"Yeah. Things didn't seem great between them. So, do you think he'll bring her?"

"I don't know." Could I endure another hour of her company? I'd rather stick pins in my eyes than have to watch her wandering hands. But there could be a way to ride it out, an option that Donna has unknowingly pointed out.

Just how much havoc would it wreak if I were to bring Shawn Bowling as my plus-one?

There's only one way to find out.

THIRTY
ALEX

It's late, and Ian and I are locking up the shop for the night.

"God, what a day." Ian sighs as he double-checks that the door is secure.

"You can say that again."

"Do you know what the worst thing is?"

I shake my head.

"We're stupid enough to come in on Monday and do it all again." Ian laughs as he stuffs the keys into his battered briefcase.

We fall into a gentle stroll. The day has taken its toll on our bodies as well as our minds.

"Hey, do you mind if I ask you a personal question?"

Hugging my body, I reply, "You can ask. I might not answer."

Ian shoots me a look, but he reads my smirk and continues. "I just wanted to check you're okay."

The car park suddenly seems too far away.

"Yeah, why wouldn't I be?"

"We've just noticed a change in you lately. You don't seem yourself."

No shit, I want to retort, but I nod and play along. "We?"

"All of us."

"Did Donna put you up to this?"

"No, but she's worried about you. We all are. The place isn't the same without your sarcasm."

Ian grins, and my annoyance melts. They care about me. We've all worked together for so long, and so much has changed in the last few weeks that I don't feel like myself anymore, so no wonder they've all noticed.

"I'm fine, honestly. Just have some stuff going on, but nothing I can't handle." Throwing him a smile, I hope it'll be enough to make him drop the subject.

"I've no doubt about that, but just remember—" He stops and turns. "—we're here if you need us. I know you might not want to talk to the new boss— none of us know him enough yet—but we are here, all of us, if you need anything."

"Thanks. I appreciate it."

We reach the small car park I use every day, the vehicles looking sad and lost under the blanket of grey clouds, the fading light having dimmed the evening skyline.

"You need to be careful parking in there." Ian nods toward the few vehicles. "My car got bumped last week."

"Shit. Did they leave a note?"

"No. Just drove off. Bastards. It's going to cost me a respray. I've been parking on Town Street ever since. You might want to consider it." He looks over in the direction of Town Street as if I'm unfamiliar with the road names, even though I know this town like the back of my hand.

"Will do, and I'm sorry about your car."

"Thanks. I'll see you tomorrow at the meal." Ian waves as he spins on his heels.

My car is in the same bay I park it in every day. My back aches, and hunger thunders through my stomach as I fish my keys out of my bag and unlock the door.

"Alex?"

At the sound of my name, I spin around and am faced with Jess, her smile wide like that of a Disney shark who's trying to convince the little fish that he's a friend.

"You're back." It's the only thing I can think of to say, my mind whirling with what she's doing here and why she's cornered me in the car park this late.

"Yeah. Came up ready for the function tomorrow."

My heart sinks.

"I was just here to meet Cade from work," she tells me, the breeze flipping loose hair.

"He's not here," I tell her. "He hasn't been in the office all day." Why doesn't she know this?

"I know. Silly me. I should've checked where he'd be. I just called him now, and he told me to meet him here. Look," she says, taking a step closer, "I'm glad I ran into you, because I wanted to ask you something."

This is starting to feel like some sort of interrogation.

"I just wanted to ask if you have a problem with Cade."

"A problem?"

"Yeah. I don't mean to intrude, but, well, I noticed at the bar last week you were very hostile toward him, which I find strange with you having only just started working with him."

"Is this the psychologist speaking?" There's a snap to my voice like a little dog nipping at someone's ankles, but I'm annoyed that she's ambushed me alone, and I don't have time for her playing fucking detective.

"It's hard to switch off sometimes. I notice things that others wouldn't. I'm just worried he's done something to you or said something. He can be…."

"What?"

"Well, he can get a little hot-headed. I just thought

you might have had a run-in with him over your work or an issue at the office."

I glare at her before opening my car door. "No."

"Because if there's an issue, I can speak to him, help smooth things over." She smiles, and I want to wring her neck. How dare she?

"There's nothing you can do or say that would change anything," I growl.

"I don't understand."

"And that's the point. You don't need to understand. Just because you're a psychologist doesn't mean you have to understand everything."

"I was only trying to help," she retorts.

"Yeah, well, I don't need your help." I slide into my car and am about to close the door when she puts her hand on it, stopping it from closing.

Her concern drops like a mask that's fallen from her face. "It doesn't take a psychologist to see that you're one messed-up woman," she hisses.

"Let go of my fucking door—*now*."

"You stay away from Cade, do you hear?" She glares at me.

"Fuck off." I pull the door from her grasp and close it, then fumble with the ignition.

My breathing is sharp and shallow as I fire up the car and pull out of the bay without checking my blind spot. Who the fuck does she think she is? I should tell Cade, but the thought of calling him when I'm this angry doesn't appeal. I have enough going on with him

without getting tangled in whatever shit they're
dealing with.

But I'm angry now, and even more so at the
thought of having to face her tomorrow night. This
little charade has only sealed my decision that I cannot
attend this meal alone, even if the alternative scares
the life out of me.

THIRTY-ONE
ALEX

Shawn shoves his legs into his jeans. He's hunched over the side of my bed and is already reaching into his pockets for a smoke.

"I'm thinking of leaving," I blurt, tucking the duvet under my knees.

"Leaving where?"

"My job."

"Really?" He runs his hand through his hair.

"I don't like the new boss." Not technically a lie, as I don't like him — I am in fucking love with him.

"No shit. The man is clearly out of his depth." Shawn heaves his T-shirt over his head, strategically missing the unlit cigarette now dangling from his mouth. "From what you've said, the guy sounds like a complete arsehole."

"I don't suppose you have room for a sales negotiator at your place?"

He swivels his head, his body twisting against his stance.

"Not at the moment," he replies, adjusting himself. "If anything, I'm overstaffed. I have some staff who left a few years ago to have kids and have come back on part-time hours. They're not as committed as they were, not willing to put the extra hours in, and I could do with getting shot of them. Besides," he continues, "I don't think it would work."

"Why not?"

"I would be your boss. It's not very professional when you're fucking your superior. It gets messy."

I shove my hands under the covers. He's right. And I don't want to work for him. I can't think of anything worse, but I wanted to see what his reaction would be.

"Well, if you hear of anything on the grapevine," I mumble.

"I have to shoot. I have some work to see to." Shawn fiddles with his phone.

"At eight thirty on a Friday night?"

"The toils of running your own business, I'm afraid."

"I might be calling you tomorrow night."

"Why?" His brow furrows.

"I'm going to a function."

"What kind of function?"

"Cade has organised a meal for all the staff and

their partners to celebrate the official takeover of the shop."

"You're kidding."

"No."

"Fuck me, the guy must have money to burn. What a waste of time." Shawn snorts.

"I don't want to go." Jess's face still leers at me through my car window.

Shawn leaves shortly after, and I should get up and go lock the door, but I'm rooted to the bed. All I can think about is what would happen if I brought Shawn to the function. How badly would it end? He might not even come. He's shown no interest in a relationship, for which I'm grateful, but I can't arrive at this function alone. Not when Jess will be there.

THIRTY-TWO
ALEX

It's one hour before I'm supposed to be at the restaurant, and I'm trying on outfit number seven, which consists of jeans and an old T-shirt in an attempt to rebel against the formal dress code. But it's impossible to dress for an event I don't want to attend. I'm not a big drinker, but I've downed a vodka and Coke in the hope it'll shield me in alcoholic armour. But all it's done is remind me that I am my mother's daughter.

Thoughts of Cade and what he'll look like tonight dance before me like a spiteful court jester. He'll be dressed to impress, some expensive suit, probably tailor-made. It'll hug his perfect body and highlight his muscular frame. He'll smell divine, his most expensive cologne wafting in my face, taunting me like a choco-late cake does a diabetic. And she'll be there, hanging off his arm like some fucking trophy with her shiny hair and thin lips, and she'll smirk at me, knowing that she's the one he's going home with tonight, the one he will probably fuck just for the sake of it.

And I'll have to endure all of it alone.

I pour myself another vodka and Coke into the empty glass, and then I pick up my phone. What I'm doing is catastrophic. I'm not only sabotaging my night but everyone else's.

The screen blurs as I type a text out to Shawn.

Are you busy?

I wait for his reply. Do I really want to do this?

But then I imagine her touching Cade's face, smiling at him like she owns him.

My phone pings with Shawn's reply, and it's game on.

THIRTY-THREE
CADE

PLACING A BOTTLE OF RED WINE AND A BOTTLE OF white in the centre of the table, I check the time even though I just checked it thirty seconds ago.

"I hope you've put this all down as business expenses," Jess says as she reaches for a glass.

"I didn't ask you here to do an inventory," I reply.

"Then why did you invite me?"

I know the answer she wants, but I can't give it to her, so, I tell her the truth.

"You know why," I say with a sneer. "Your last entrance caused a stir and left them asking questions. I can't have them asking more." Or wondering about the man behind the suit, so Jess is here to keep their minds away from the truth and the reason behind this little soiree.

"And here was me thinking you'd missed me and wanted to forget this ridiculous idea of a break."

She's worn her best blue dress, knee-length and conservative, and her eyes are shaded with pearlescent powder. Something stabs under my ribs. I don't want to hurt her, but I don't have a choice.

"I don't know why you're bothering with this. I really don't." Jess shakes her head.

"It's good to get to know people."

"You won't get to know them in a place like this." She tuts, scanning the elegant backdrop and soft lighting of Kiki's restaurant. "People put on their airs and graces. You don't know what goes on behind closed doors."

"You seem to think you do, so why don't you do what you do best and put on your psychologist's head?"

"Can't I just be here as your girlfriend?"

I'm saved by the arrival of the first guests, and Jess turns into the perfect hostess, making sure everyone has a drink and is happy with where they're sitting. It's interesting to see them with their partners and how some of them turn into completely different people.

Donna's husband, Ed, is a burly man and looks like he's been prised from in front of the telly and shoved into an uncomfortable suit as if she's polished him and wheeled him out for the night. Michael's wife is a small woman with a Lego haircut who looks like she doesn't get out much. Sonya has brought her sister, who is a carbon copy of her, and Ian his husband, Mel, who he's been married to for five years.

There's an eclectic mix of people around the table, which will make for an interesting evening. With their partners in tow, I might learn some new things about the people I'm working with.

Lexie is the only person missing, and I'm not the only one who has noticed this.

"Where the hell is she?" Donna mutters, looking at the time on her phone and leaning into Ed.

"Who?"

"Alex," Donna hisses. "She said she was coming."

"Is she bringing anyone?" Sonya asks.

"She said she was, but I don't know who."

"She got any siblings?" Sonya enquires, and I have to stop myself from answering.

"No, only child," Donna replies as she starts to chew on some bread from the small plate next to her. "But she said she was bringing a guy."

"Really?" Sonya smiles. "I didn't know she was seeing anyone."

"She's been seeing him for a while now, but I'm not sure if it's serious," Donna states. "You know Alex." She raises an eyebrow. "She doesn't give anything away. They could be married with a couple of kids for all we know."

Bile tickles the back of my throat, burning my eyes and my heart.

"Help yourselves to drinks, guys," I say as the

wine is passed around the table. "There's non-alcoholic for those of you who're driving."

Never one to drink on the job, I pour myself a glass, regardless that this is a work function, and take a slug, wishing it was something stronger to take away the acidic tang Donna's comment has left in my mouth.

Married.

Kids.

We'd talked about it back then and spent hours laughing about what we would name our kids and whether we'd get a dog or cat or both.

They were our plans, our dreams—no one else's.

I'm not sure I can sit around this table and stare at a man who has stolen them from me.

And where the hell is she?

It's when I'm passing the menus around the table that she arrives.

She walks through the main door, her hair a dark, silky mass fanning around her face. She's in black, the sleekest of figure-hugging dresses. It's dazzling. Her high heels place her head and shoulders above the rest of the women in the room. She's quite simply breath-taking, and I'm completely lost in her.

"She's here at last." Donna's voice hauls me back into the room.

Jess's icy glare cools the air.

"Yeah, but look who she's with," Sonya adds loudly enough for the rest of the table to hear.

We all glance past Lexie to see Shawn Bowling standing behind her.

There's a loud ringing in my ears like a fire alarm blaring in the background. I want to grab everyone and tell them to get out, but I soon realise that no one else can hear the alarm—only me.

"No, she can't have brought him," Donna hisses, sounding like her teeth are loose.

"What the hell?" Michael pipes up.

The whole table is watching now, riveted by the arrival of Lexie and Shawn.

"There has to be some mistake." Donna shakes her head, but when Alex turns to face the bar and Shawn places his hand on her lower back, the table groans.

My fists ball. My teeth grind.

"Oh my God! He's her plus-one?" Sonya asks.

"No wonder she wouldn't tell us who he was," Donna says with tears in her eyes.

"Who is that man?" Jess asks, confused as to the drama unfolding around the table.

Not trusting myself to answer, I focus on my breathing. I could count to ten, to fifty, to a million—it still won't be enough to calm the anger that has erupted inside me. How dare he? How fucking dare he?

"Shawn Bowling." Donna leans in toward Jess.

"He's the son of our biggest competitor," Michael explains.

"And the biggest slimeball on the face of the earth," Donna adds.

"I see," Jess says gleefully, her hand resting on her wineglass.

"He's not a man, he's a snake," Sonya tells Jess. "I don't know what Alex is doing with him and why she thought it would be a good idea to bring him here. I'm not sure if I can sit at the same table as him."

"Hey, come on now." I find my voice and push my anger down into my toes. "I'm sure the evening will be fine."

I stand up at the head of the table as if it were the helm of a ship heading right into a storm.

THIRTY-FOUR
ALEX

"Sorry we're late," I slur. "Taxi was late." Not sure whether my wobble is from the pre-drinks or the height of my heels, I bathe in the heat of the glares coming from around the table.

But none of them burn as hot as the look in Cade's eyes. Rage. Unadulterated rage, and I almost feel guilty for putting him through this, but then my gaze slides to Jess by his side, her grin slick and wide, and all my regret goes out the window.

"Better late than never," Ian says, trying to prise the table from their bewildered state.

"I'm sure you don't need me to introduce you all to Shawn." I waft my hand in his direction.

"No introduction necessary," Sonya says with a sneer.

"Is this the guy you've been seeing?" Donna says.

She's clearly upset, hurt even, that I would lower myself to such a level, but I couldn't give a shit.

"Fucking." I hold my finger up. "Let's get that clear from the start. This is purely sex, nothing more."

"Well, this evening just got very interesting." Jess smirks from beside Cade like a parrot perched on his shoulder.

"Alex, a word please." Cade nods toward the bar.

"Oh no, the big boss wants a word. You're in trouble now." Shawn sniggers, and I can't help but laugh, which only fuels the anger on Cade's face.

He stalks over to the bar.

"You'd better do what the big boss says," Shawn taunts.

"Shut up," I tell him.

He looks at the wine bottles in the centre of the table. "No beer?" he asks.

"No," Ian replies.

"What kind of party is this?" Shawn groans.

I leave him to the pack as I follow Cade to the bar.

"What the fuck are you doing?" he says as soon as I'm in earshot.

"You said to bring a plus-one. He's a plus-one."

"Yeah, and everyone at that table fucking hates him. Why the fuck would you bring him here?"

"You brought your bitch, so I brought mine." I slap his arm playfully, but his face sobers me instantly. Shit. I grab hold of the bar, the room suddenly shifting. What part of this did I think was a good idea?

"This isn't some fucking game," Cade says.

"Isn't it?" I shoot back. "You might want to tell your shrink that."

"Jess? What's she got to do with this?"

"Why don't you ask her?" My head hurts. Why the hell did I drink so much?

"Hey, do they have any beer in this place?" Shawn says as he sidles up next to me.

I feel the crack of his hand on my ass. It stings, the noise ringing in my ears, anger tingling along with my behind.

"Your ass looks fucking hot in that dress, babe."

My eyes shoot to Cade, and I think I'm going to be sick.

Cade lunges at him, his face contorted, his anger wild and feral as he grabs the corners of Shawn's jacket. "If you touch her again, I'll tear both your fucking arms off," he warns.

I'm about to step in, but my words are caught in the back of my throat, which feels tight, my chest constricting. I place my hand on my neck. It's hot. My skin is burning.

Fuck.

THIRTY-FIVE
CADE

My jaw is about to crack. I want to hurt this man so badly, but I hold back, contain my anger, just like Jess taught me. Shawn is grinning at me, holding his hands up and telling me to calm down, but his voice fades into the background as if he's an annoying disc jockey from the radio.

Lexie has gone very quiet.

I register the way she looks and freeze.

Her eyes are wide, her neck red and blotchy as she clutches at her throat.

Donna arrives. "Alex? Alex, are you okay?"

Lexie is now gripping the side of the bar with both hands, her eyes locked in front of her as she struggles to breathe.

"Is she choking? I think she's choking," Donna shouts.

"She hasn't eaten anything," I say.

"She can't breathe!"

"Get back." I shove Shawn out of the way, my eyes falling on the bar. There's a half-eaten dish on the side, some sort of salad that looks as if it's been abandoned by a busy waiter. Half-munched leaves scatter the plate along with a dressing drizzled on the side and topped with nuts.

"Fuck." I grab Lexie by the arms as she falls to the floor. I steady her landing and bend down next to her. "I got this. Stay calm for me, okay?" I tell her as I pull her bag from her shoulder and begin to riffle through it.

"What's going on?" Donna shrieks. "What are you doing?"

"Shall I call an ambulance?" Sonya has arrived and has her phone out, ready to dial.

"Yes, call an ambulance," I say as I frantically search through Lexie's bag until I find her EpiPen. I'd done my homework when Lexie had first told me of her allergy. I'd known it was serious, but I'd always hated how Jacquelin had used her allergy to control her, to cage her, to make her so afraid of living. Even so, I'd watched many YouTube videos on how to administer the adrenaline, and I also know I don't have any time to waste.

I pull the cap off, then make sure I'm holding it the right way before plunging the needle into her thigh. She wraps her hands around mine as I hold it against her leg, counting in my head. I touch her neck. It's burning, the rash having spread up from her chest onto her face. Her eyes look wild like a hunted animal, and her breathing is raspy, like the air is caught in the back of her throat and won't expel.

I realise the reaction won't stop instantaneously, but I'd like a sign that things are improving. I glance at my watch, monitoring the time as Donna continues screeching in my ear.

"What's wrong with her? What are you doing?"

"The paramedics are on their way," Sonya says.

Lexie's face is now red, her eyes rolling back in her head, and she's still struggling to breathe. This is the longest five minutes I've ever endured.

"We need to get her into the recovery position," I bark.

Sonya is beside me and helps to keep everyone else back as I roll Lexie onto her side.

"Is she going to die?" Donna cries, tears rolling down her cheeks.

"Not if I can help it," I tell her.

"What's wrong with her?" Donna wails.

"Anaphylactic shock," Sonya tells her. "We had a boy at my school who was allergic to strawberries. He had to wear this funny little badge that told visitors what he was allergic to and where his medication was."

"What's she allergic to? What's she eaten?" Donna looks searchingly around the room.

"Nuts," I answer. "And she hasn't eaten them. They're on the bar. She must've touched the bar."

When I'm happy Lexie's in the right position, I pick her bag back up. With huge relief, I find another EpiPen in the side compartment and repeat the process, thrusting the pen into her other leg.

"Why didn't we know about any of this?" Donna looks around at everyone else.

Ian shakes his head. Michael shrugs.

"Wait, how did you know?" Donna asks as I check that Lexie's still breathing.

"I'm her employer. It's in her file," I lie. "Can you hear me?" I ask Lexie.

"We have a file?"

"Is everything okay?" The head waiter arrives, looking aghast at the confusion and that a diner is now in the recovery position on the floor. He quickly assesses what's going on. "Shall I call an ambulance?" he asks.

"It's on its way," I reply, looking at Sonya for confirmation.

She shakes her head, the phone clamped to her ear. "It's going to be ten minutes. They've said that if the EpiPen has been administered, she should start to come around soon, and it might be quicker to drive her there ourselves. We aren't far from the hospital."

Lexie stirs. She's coming out of it, the realisation dawning on her, the fear and the emotion of what's just happened rising to the surface of her inflamed skin.

"It's okay," I tell her. "I'm here. Everything is going to be okay."

Alex

I hear his voice. He's here. He's with me.

I put my hand out. It lands on his leg. He takes my hand in his, and his face appears.

"It's okay. I'm here. Everything is going to be okay."

His eyes and his voice are all I need.

With Cade's help, I push myself up to sitting. Faces surround me. Donna, Michael, Sonya, Ian. All of them are pale and drawn. The tops of my legs throb, a stinging pain in each thigh. Cade grips my hand as the fear of what's just happened dawns on me.

Tears start to roll down my cheeks.

"Hey, it's okay. It's over." He pulls me close, wrapping his arms around me, blocking out the audience.

It's just me and Cade. I'm safe. I'm where I need to be. Here, in his arms. I cocoon myself in his body and place my head against his chest.

His hand smooths over my hair and strokes the side of my face. "I will never let anything happen to you," he whispers, kissing the top of my head, and I'm back where I belong.

THIRTY-SIX
CADE

WHEN I LOOK AT HER FRIGHTENED FACE, I FORGET where I am. I forget about everyone except Lexie. "I will never let anything happen to you." And I kiss the top of her head, sealing my words.

She's weak, limp in my arms. I want to stay like this, holding her close, but I have to get her to the hospital.

I reach into my pocket and pull out my car keys, then place my arms under Lexie and scoop her up. She clings to me, her head against my shoulder. She smells like she used to, a sweet warmth like a fresh cinnamon bun straight from the oven. I stop myself from kissing her hair again.

"What are you doing?" Donna's voice intrudes on this moment.

"I'm taking her to the hospital. She needs to be checked over."

"I'll come," Jess announces from the side of the table, grabbing her bag and her jacket off the back of her chair.

I glare at her. I'd forgotten she was even here.

"You'll need someone to sit in the back with her whilst you drive," she states before I have a chance to tell her she isn't needed.

"I'll come," Donna says. "I can sit with her." But then Ed clears his throat, and she looks torn between her friend and her husband.

"It's fine, Donna. I'll go," Jess says.

"What about the meal?" Michael asks, clutching his drink to his chest.

"It's all paid for," I tell him. "You guys carry on." I turn and come face to face with Shawn.

"You seem to have things under control," he says.

I glare at him, hoping to bore a hole in the side of his head.

"And I don't really do hospitals," he adds, just in case I'm about to request his company.

"Just go home, Shawn," I tell him. "And do me a favour—don't ever fucking touch her again." I turn to leave.

"Don't forget her bag." Donna presses Lexie's bag into Jess's hand as the two women follow me.

Restaurant staff get the doors as I bundle Lexie out into the car park. I find my car and click the doors open. I want to put her in the front so I can see her, but I'm aware of Jess behind me.

"Can I do anything to help?" Donna asks as I put Lexie in the back seat.

I clip the seatbelt over her, noting that her eyelids are heavy, her head lolling. My hands brush against her skin, my heart racing. I move to the side, and Jess climbs in next to her.

"No, thanks," I tell Donna. "Just go back in and try to enjoy the rest of the night. I'll let you know how she is."

"Make sure you do," she says before she bows her head and looks at Lexie through Jess's open door.

"You take care. No checking yourself out when you've had enough. Make sure they look at you properly," Donna tells Lexie before turning to Jess. "Please look after her."

"We will," Jess assures her, then pulls the car door shut.

The drive to the hospital is painful. I'm acutely aware of Jess in the car, and she now seems to be the one wound up. Like a snake coiled in a basket, she's biding her time before the lid comes off and she unleashes herself. But for the moment, all I can do is look in the rear-view mirror and see Lexie's face, her head resting against the window, her eyes looking tired and her body deflated.

The hospital isn't busy. It feels awkward, the three of us arriving. Jess is like a spare part, her only purpose to hold Lexie's bag. I carry Lexie, her legs still too weak. Jess holds her bag as I give the receptionist details of why we're here.

I place Lexie down on one of the chairs and sit beside her with my arm around her, pulling her close, her head leaning on my shoulder. Jess glares, but I don't care. It's hitting me now—the reaction, what it could've meant if she'd not had her meds, if I hadn't found them in time, or if I'd not been there and known what to do.

I lost her once.

I can't lose her again.

Jess paces the floor like an animal stalking its prey, ready to pounce when the opportunity arises.

"Can I get anyone a drink?" she says, spotting a vending machine on the other side of the room.

"Coffee would be good," I reply.

A coffee is the last thing I want, but I want Jess to go. I need to be alone with Lexie.

Jess picks up her bag and walks over to the machine.

I cup Lexie's chin. I've wanted to get her alone, but now that we're here, I don't know what to say.

"How are you doing?" I ask.

"Just groggy," she replies.

"I always thought you'd grown out of the allergy," I tell her. "I looked it up, read about kids growing out of all sorts of allergies, and because you'd gone so many years without having a reaction, I often wondered if that had been the case." My voice is slow but purposeful.

Lexie just blinks.

"I'm sorry," I tell her.

"What for?" Her words are mumbled like she has a mouth full of cotton wool.

"Everything."

Jess returns with two cups of tepid brown water. She places mine on the floor, avoiding eye contact. I leave it where it is.

"Cade," Lexie murmurs.

Her body has slumped, and her head now rests on my lap as Jess's eyes burn into the back of her head. I lean in close, as her voice is faint.

"I need the toilet."

"Okay. Can you walk?" I grab both her hands and slide out from underneath her. She grips my hands and stands on shaky legs like a foal taking its first steps.

"I'm fine," Lexie insists.

"Like fuck you are," I tell her. "You can't go alone. You might fall. There's a disabled toilet over there," I point out.

"I can take her." Jess steps forward, and I feel Lexie tense.

"It's fine. I'll take her."

"But…," Jess begins, her face screwing up at the thought of Lexie going to the toilet in front of me, her boss, the man she's apparently known for only a few weeks.

"It's fine. It's nothing I haven't seen before," I tell her.

"What do you mean?" Jess is like a jack-in-the-box—all wound up and ready to pop.

Taking a deep breath, I take the bull by the horns.

"Exactly what I just said." I steer Lexie over to the toilet before Jess blows her lid.

We bundle in and lock the door, leaving Jess seething outside. I'm being cruel, but I don't have the patience to deal with her right now. She isn't my priority.

Lexie is.

Always has been.

Always will be.

With one hand on the wall for support, she grabs hold of the rail by the side of the toilet and tries to wriggle out of her underwear.

I step forward and hold her by the waist.

She looks up at me, her eyes watery, and I almost cave.

There's nothing erotic about this moment. It's not about my craving for her, the need to taste her, to touch her. It's about her needing me and me being here, doing whatever she needs me to do.

She gulps and slides her knickers down. I help lower her so she can relieve herself, and I pass her the toilet paper, then step away to give her some privacy and myself a moment to hold back the fear that has come cascading out of nowhere.

I could've lost her.

"Cade." Lexie's small voice trails over my shoulder as I turn to face her.

I help her stand. She pulls her underwear back up, and then I tug her dress down and smooth it over her legs, making sure she's covered and decent.

"Thank you," she says, holding on to my forearms.

"You don't need to thank me."

"Yes, I do."

I place her arm over mine and move to the side. "Ready?"

"Cade?" She looks at me. "You need to tell her who I am. She deserves to know."

"I will."

"When they call me, you stay with her and explain. You can't leave her out there wondering what the hell is going on. It's not fair."

I nod. I don't want to leave her, but she's right. I can't let Jess stew any longer.

We return from the toilet, and I half expect Jess to have gone, but she's sitting in a chair with her head in her hands.

Lexie is slightly stronger on her legs than she was before. We make it back to the seating area, and we wait.

It's several more painfully silent minutes before Lexie's name is called by a giant nurse who emerges from one of the many doors, brandishing a clipboard and a pen.

"I'll come with you," I tell Lexie, not ready yet to be alone with Jess. But Lexie shakes her head.

"Stay here and watch my bag. I'll get them to call you if I need you."

I sigh as I walk her to the nurse and pass her over into the woman's strong arms.

"Easy does it," she says as she takes Lexie from me.

I can't watch as the nurse leads her through the doors, so I return to the chairs and pick up Lexie's bag, placing it on the empty chair where she was just sitting.

I'm empty and alone.

Jess waits until they're both through the door before she speaks.

"So, are you going to tell me what's going on, or shall I tell you?" She places her coffee on the floor like she can't be trusted to hold it whilst we have this conversation.

My head dips, and I run both hands through my hair, my skin feeling tight and my scalp electric. I haven't got the energy for this now, but Lexie is right. Jess needs an explanation.

"Alex is Lexie, isn't she?"

I look at her for the first time tonight. "Yes, she is."

It's Jess's turn to look at the floor. She shakes her head, a small laugh emanating from her mouth before she speaks.

"I knew it," she sighs. "The first time I met her, I knew there was something. God, I've been so stupid."

I want to say something, but it's almost like she isn't even talking to me.

"The apartment, the long hours up here. I contemplated the possibility that you were having an affair but never —"

"We're not having an affair."

"I know you aren't," Jess snaps back, annoyed that I think she's got it all wrong. "She still hates you. Anyone can see that," she tells me with great satisfaction. "I take it she doesn't know what you're doing up here?"

"No."

"Well, that's it, then." Jess sighs.

"What is?"

"I'm not part of this, and whether she wants you or not, I can't be the runner-up prize."

"Jess, wait." But I don't know what I want her to wait for. I should be telling her it isn't true, but it is, and she knows it. She's always been the runner-up.

"I can't compete with her. And I won't even try." She takes a step back. "I've been kidding myself from the start, even before you took the job up here. I know you don't want me the way I want you."

"Jess," I begin, but she doesn't let me finish.

"Please don't lie to me anymore. I know what happened between us, Cade, and you don't need a degree in psychology to work it out. I helped you, so you felt beholden to me. I provided a haven for you to talk. You latched on to that and felt I was the one who could save you from your past. It's my fault, really. I knew what you needed me for. I was your security blanket to deal with the world. It's never been love—not for you. I thought you might learn to love me, that you might see me as something more, but you never have. I've grown to love you more, whereas you've grown to need me less. Tell me I'm wrong, Cade."

Swallowing the large lump that has developed in my throat, I let the silence answer for me.

She inhales deeply and holds it before exhaling and pulling her bag onto her shoulder. "I'm going to call a taxi and find a hotel."

"Jess," I begin.

"Don't argue," she says sternly. "It's for the best."

"Jess," I say as she turns and starts to walk away. "Jess."

She turns back.

"I can't help loving her. And if I'm honest, I've never even tried to stop. I'm sorry."

"So am I." Jess nods before walking away.

I bury my face in my hands and push my hair back. I should feel something right now—loss, hurt, anger—but I don't. Every feeling I have is for Lexie. The worry, the pain, the fear—everything inside me is for her.

THIRTY-SEVEN
CADE

"Cade Westwood?"

I open my eyes to see the strong nurse staring at me. Her blue scrubs look like pyjamas but with a row of pens lining her top pocket. I'd closed my eyes for a second in the hope of calming my brain, but the over-sized clock on the wall tells me that was twelve minutes ago.

"Yes."

"Hi. You brought a patient in—Alexandria Knowles?"

"Yes. Yes, I did. Is she okay?" Dread washes over me as I try to read the nurse's face. Surely they wouldn't send a nurse out into the waiting room to tell me something bad.

"She's fine. Nothing to worry about," she assures me, "but if you'll follow me, the doctor would like to speak to you."

"Sure."

I grab Lexie's bag and stand up, then follow the nurse through the same door she took Lexie through earlier. The resin floor squeaks under my shoes. The corridor is lined with numerous doors, any of which Lexie could be behind.

At the end of the corridor, we make a right and find ourselves in a square waiting area where two small blue fabric chairs sit outside a group of three rooms.

"Just this way." The nurse beckons as she opens the middle door and shows me into a small room. There's a sink and a thin workstation, but the majority of the room is taken up by the primitive hospital bed resting against the left wall.

Lexie is on the bed. Her face is red, like she's wearing badly applied make-up, and her dress doesn't match the surroundings. She stands out against the starkness of the room, a jewel set in a rusting ring.

"Hey." I smile as I approach her.

She stares at me, her eyes still a little glazed. I fight the urge to wrap my arms around her and pull her close so the outside world can't reach her.

"Mr Westwood?" the doctor guesses as I look at the man perched on the wheeled stool. He looks far too young to be a doctor. His bronzed skin and Australian accent make me think of surfing and barbeques and that maybe he's not a doctor at all and has just wandered in here for want of something better to do.

"Yes." I tear my focus away from Lexie.

"You brought her in?" he asks, surveying me as if I'm also under observation.

"Yes."

"Have a seat." The doctor gestures at a blue plastic chair.

I sit down, and he continues.

"You're her boss. Is that right?" He scrunches his eyes at his computer screen.

I don't like the way he's talking about her like she isn't in the room.

"Yes, we were on a work night out."

"I'm sure you're aware she's had an allergic reaction. But you were quick with the antihistamine. You knew about her allergy." The doctor looks at me like a chat show host, waiting for my response.

"Yes, I make sure I know all my employees' medical details."

"I wish there were more conscientious employers out there like you."

"I see it as just basic health and safety," I tell him, my hands twitching in my lap, wanting nothing more than to hold Lexie.

"You're lucky to have such a great boss, Miss Knowles." The doctor turns to look at her.

She lifts her head, looking to him and back at me.

"I'm sure you don't need me to tell you that he saved your life tonight."

"It was nothing the paramedics wouldn't have done," I cut in.

"Actually, Mr Westwood—" The doctor inflates his chest, his eyes narrowing. "—the paramedics wouldn't have got there quick enough. It was your fast reaction and knowledge of what to do and where to find the medication that saved her. She'll have to make your coffee on demand from now on." He smiles, trying to melt the uncomfortable silence that's frosted over the surface of the room.

"So, what happens now?" I ask.

"We need to keep her in," he says, his voice dropping as his gaze returns to his computer. "I've explained all this to Miss Knowles, but just so you know what's happening, the reaction was a severe one, and there's a risk of a biphasic reaction." He glances up from his notes. "A bit like the aftershock from an earthquake."

I nod my understanding.

"We're going to take her up to one of the observation wards to keep an eye on her and put her on a glucocorticoid and antihistamine drip just to help reduce the hives and help with her breathing. When we're happy there's no chance of a second reaction, then she'll be discharged with a prescription to replace her antihistamine."

She looks so tired. The last thing she'll want is to stay here tonight.

"All right, Miss Knowles." The doctor takes in a deep breath and continues to type away on his computer before spinning around on his stool and turning his attention to her properly. "I want you to hang on here, and someone will be down to take you up to the ward, okay?"

Lexie manages a faint smile and a nod.

"It shouldn't be too long." He stands up and looks Lexie over one more time before nodding at me and leaving the small room through a blue curtain hanging at the back of the cubicle.

I stand up, already feeling caged in this small space.

"Are you okay?" I ask. I want to touch her. I want to stroke her hair and run my hands down her arms, but that window of opportunity has gone. I'm in limbo now, not knowing on which side of the fence I lie: Childhood Sweetheart or the Boss.

"I've been better." She smiles wanly, swivelling herself around so she's sitting on the edge of the bed. Her feet dangle off the side, making her look like a small child. "I just want to go home."

"I know, but you heard what he said, and I'm sure they'll let you go as soon as possible. They don't tend to keep people in longer than necessary."

"I just wish I wasn't dressed like this. I feel stupid."

"I can get you a change of clothes," I offer, although I don't want to leave her. Her skin is still red in patches, her eyes glistening.

"Would you mind?" she asks.

"Not at all."

"My keys are in my bag." She reaches out, and I pass her the bag. "Is Jess still in the waiting room?"

"No, she's gone."

"Gone? Gone where?"

"Home, I think."

"You think?"

"I'm not entirely sure. We had words, and she left. She won't be coming back."

She stops rummaging through her bag. "You broke up?"

I look away.

"Why? What happened?"

I inhale and rub my hands down the side of my trousers. "She knows who you are. That you're Lexie."

"How? Did you tell her?" She grips the bag as if she's about to launch it at me.

"I told her lots of things. I told her about your allergy. I'm not sure how or even why it came up. Some things just used to come out, I don't really know why, but I do remember telling her about your allergy. And then there's the fact that I knew about it tonight and knew where to find your EpiPen. I suppose it doesn't take a psychologist to work out who you are."

"So, you're telling me she's left you just because

your old girlfriend from when you were seventeen happens to be working for you? I'm sorry, that's ridiculous."

"That's the thing, though," I begin, pushing my hands into my pockets. "You aren't just some girlfriend from my teens. You're the only person who I've truly loved, and she knows that. She said she couldn't compete with you."

A tall guy opens the door and grins at Lexie. "Hey, are we ready to head upstairs?" He looks to be in his fifties and is dressed in scrubs, but they're a different shade of blue to the pair the doctor had been wearing. He's sporting a bandana and looks like he's chewing gum as he clutches the handles of an empty wheelchair.

Lexie pulls her keys from her bag and hands them to me, like she'd known where they were all along, before sliding off the bed. She wobbles.

"Hang on, there, miss," he says as we both lurch forward to help her.

I get there first, slipping my hands under her arms as I hold her up.

"You need to take it steady," I tell her as the man wheels the chair over.

It only just fits in the small space. After helping her into the chair, he backs her up and out of the room.

"Do you need my address?" she asks me before the porter turns her around.

"No, it's in the system. I'll find it."

I know exactly where she lives. It's one of the first things I looked up when I realised who she was.

"Just some jogging bottoms and a hoodie will be fine. Oh, and some trainers."

"Sure." I grip her house key.

"I'll text you what ward they take me to so you can find me when you get back."

"Okay." I'm walking behind them now as the guy wheels her down the corridor, heading for a lift. "I won't be long," I call as she's turned around to face me.

The porter opens the lift doors with a key that's around his neck on a lanyard.

"Don't be," she says, and then she's wheeled into the lift and swallowed by the doors.

My driving is erratic, my hands sliding over the leather wheel, the car jerking with every turn as if I've been let loose on a racing track. I didn't want to leave her. She didn't want me to leave either, but she looked so uncomfortable in that tiny dress.

My head is a mess. I can still hear her trying to gasp for breath, can still see every angry red hive growing over her skin and the fear in her eyes clearly showing that she'd thought she was going to die.

I put the radio on, blinking away the tears starting to blur my vision.

I knew they would come.
Jess has finally left me.
But that isn't the reason I'm crying.

THIRTY-EIGHT
ALEX

Goose bumps erupt over my legs as I pull on my dress with my free hand, the other immobilised by the large cannula the nurse has pushed into the back of my skin. I'm not cold, as the ward is warm, but the bed is hard, the sheets starched, and I'm alone.

"Would you like the curtain closed all the way?" a nurse asks. She's been hovering around me for a while, checking the IV hanging next to my bed feeding me a constant supply of drugs.

"No, thank you." I want to be able to see Cade as soon as he gets back. I'm still a little fuzzy, like I've been in a wind tunnel for the last hour, and now that the fans have been turned off, I've been left to acclimatise.

Will he have reached my house yet? Will he snoop around?

I hope he finds the grey hoodie with the star on the front. It's my favourite and just what I need right now.

The evening has not manifested in the way I'd anticipated. I knew what I was unleashing by bringing Shawn to the restaurant, but the look on Cade's face had been painful. He was angry, wounded, and afraid all rolled into one, and I immediately knew I'd hurt him. Again. And who was I really trying to hurt tonight? Jess? Myself?

And I'd been so wrapped up in Cade and Shawn and what everyone was thinking about me that I'd forgotten lesson number one of eating out. New restaurant, new food, new menu—check, check, check. My mum's voice rings in my head, her scolding tone questioning how I could've been so stupid, that I could've killed myself. I haven't spoken to her in months, which isn't unusual, as our relationship was irreparably damaged after Cade and Mark left.

I've tried to forgive her, and for some things, I have. The drinking, wrapping me in cotton wool, the stress she was under as a young single parent.

But some things are unforgivable.

The pain in my chest intensifies. I tell myself it's the reaction, that my airways are recovering from the overtime they've just put in.

Fear rattles through me. If Cade hadn't been there, if he hadn't remembered what to do, if he hadn't recognised it for what it was, I could be dead.

He saved my life.

A tear slips down my cheek.

"Hi."

The voice startles me. Jess is standing by the curtain. Her long coat hangs as if from a wire coat hanger, her hair swept from her face as though she climbed four flights of stairs to get here.

"Hey," I mumble.

What's she doing here? Cade said she'd left. I study her face for signs of war paint. Is she here to fight for her man? Or is she brandishing a white flag?

"I'm sorry for coming to see you like this. I know you need to rest, but I have to talk to you."

"Okay," I say, noticing her slumped shoulders and her smudged mascara.

"I saw Cade leave just now, so I thought this would be a good time, and I managed to blag my way up to see you."

"Why don't you sit down." I nod at the plastic chair at the side of the bed. I want her on the same level as me, not standing over me like some preacher.

"Has he told you I've ended it with him?"

I nod slowly, pressing my cracked lips together.

"I realised, after your attack, who you are."

"He said."

"This is going to sound very messed-up, but I know all about you and what went on between you when you were teenagers."

I gulp.

"You see, Cade and I met through his job. We got

along well, and things moved quickly, but it wasn't long into our relationship that I noticed he had issues."

"Issues?" I ask as if I don't know what she's talking about, even though I know only too well what Cade's issues are—or were. But I'm balking at what she's just said. *"Cade and I met through his job."* She must've bought a house through him, and that's how they met, which means Cade hadn't been lying when I asked him if he was fucking his therapist.

Jess inhales, choosing her words carefully. "He had trouble sleeping. And when he did sleep, he would be woken up by the most horrendous nightmares, his skin soaked with sweat, his body shaking violently. As a psychologist, it was hard not to analyse him, to not intervene, and I wanted to help. I begged him to let me help him, and, eventually, he agreed. It's not like working with a patient. You can't counsel someone who you're emotionally attached to, but I did get him to talk about what had happened to him, what he'd gone through." She glances up at me, holding my gaze. "What you both went through."

I don't like the way she's looking at me, like she's got me under the microscope and has already compiled a report on me. "So, you managed to fix him, then."

"No, not at all." Jess shakes her head. "Far from it. But I like to think I helped. And that's what the problem has been all along. I helped him, so he formed an attachment to me, saw me as his security blanket, the one person who understood what he'd been through."

"You weren't there."

"No, I wasn't. But you were."

A silence drips into the room like the liquid in my IV.

"Have you ever considered talking to anyone about what happened?"

"No." The hives on my neck flare over my skin. "Are you offering?"

"I don't think that would be wise, do you?" Her eyes narrow.

I slide my hand over my arm, the goose bumps back.

"But I suggest you talk to him."

"Why are you telling me this? You've just broken up with him. You should be at his place, shredding up his clothes."

"Not my style. I know enough about human reactions to know that although it'll make me feel better for ten minutes, it won't help me in the long run. And —" She pulls on the scant air in the room. "—I don't blame him. He didn't come here intentionally seeking you out. It was a chance meeting, and I can't compete with feelings he had years ago. I also can't blame him for still loving you."

"What?"

"He loves you, Alex. He's always loved you. He won't stop loving you. When you weren't in his life, he could deal with it, but now you're here, back in his life, he can't hide from it any longer."

Her words are hard to swallow. He still loves me. He's always loved me.

"I still don't know why you're here telling me this."

"Because before I go, I need to know if you feel the same about him. I saw the look on his face when you showed up with that guy tonight. I've never seen him so angry, so hurt. If you don't feel the same about him, he's going to be left broken, and I love him too much to let him spend the rest of his life looking for something he can't have. I know I would be the runner-up, but he'll need me more than ever. So I have to know if you're going to be there for him like I have been."

I stare at Jess, my mouth open. I don't know what to say to this woman who I barely know and who is analysing my life in such a clinical way. I don't want to discuss Cade with myself, let alone her.

"It's complicated," I begin, trying to hammer my resolve in like a stubborn tent peg.

She nods hypnotically, and I see just how good at her job she is—the kind tone, the soft eyes, the lull to her voice that works like a tin opener, removing the top of your skull and letting her have a good rummage around.

"All I'm saying is that you need to talk to him, because he's not the same person he was all those years ago."

"I know that," I tell her whilst trying not to scowl.

"There are things you don't know," Jess continues, her eyes narrowing, her face hardening. "Things he needs to tell you."

"Well, that's up to him."

What the hell is she talking about, and why has she gone all mystical on me? I wait for the cliché line that he's not the man I think he is, but she doesn't say anything else, just stares at me with an intensity I can almost feel bristling against my skin.

"Just know this," she says at last. "I'm not going anywhere until I know he's happy, and right now, he isn't."

Did I expect anything less from her? She loves him. Anybody would do the same for the person they love. My vision blurs, the tiredness returning like a fog rolling in off the hills.

Jess stands up, pats down her coat, and regards me with her cold gaze. "And if you hurt him, I swear to God…." She doesn't finish, just shakes her head and walks out of the cubicle.

"Shit," I say to the curtain as it sways slightly in her wake.

THIRTY-NINE
CADE

Lexie's house appears before me, a small semidetached on a newly built estate. Only a few weeks in and this job has clearly already gotten under my skin, as I mentally compile the brochure for her house: neat brickwork, character bay windows, and a secluded cul-de-sac.

The smell of Lexie hits me as soon as I walk over the threshold. Her coats are hung in the small hallway, and I have to stop myself from burying my face in them and inhaling her scent.

There's no time to linger, so I head straight upstairs and find her room.

I flick the light on, illuminating the small bedroom. It's tastefully decorated in neutral colours. I hadn't expected anything less, but it's tidier than I thought it would be. Lexie's room was always a mess, with clothes strewn over the floor and the bed never made. But this room is organised, nothing out of place.

Guilt stings me as I riffle through her drawers and rummage through her life. I imagine her in this room, looking through these very drawers, throwing stuff to the side as she hunts for the right top or pair of trousers.

Eventually, I find some leggings and a hoodie. I close the drawer and am about to leave when I remember the trainers. They're probably in the hallway. I'll get them on the way out, I decide, then stop. Lexie won't wear trainers without socks, which is also something I've never done myself since the day she expressed her distaste for it. She'll need trainer socks or something. I go back to the drawers and begin to look for them.

Nothing.

There are two bedside cabinets on either side of the bed. Sitting on the edge of the mattress, I open the first drawer and find knickers. There are loads of pairs in all different colours and styles. I shift the pile about, pushing aside the thought of Lexie only wearing these tiny garments, her long legs splayed before me, her smooth skin taunting me.

Fuck. I need to concentrate.

There are no socks. I grab a pair of knickers and move on to the next drawer, which is bras.

Shit. Now I have Lexie in my head, her breasts pushed together in a black bra, running her hands over her chest as she asks me if I want to take it off or should she do it.

I shake my head, quickly closing the drawer, then move around to the other cabinet.

The top drawer is a tangle of earphones, solitary earrings, face creams, and body lotions. A fruity smell fills my nose as I push my hand into the drawer and find a paperback book, the bookmark bent and only a third of the way in. There's also a notebook with nothing written in it and a bottle of red nail varnish.

I'm about to shut the drawer when I spot a velvet bag. My breath leaves me like I've just been winded, the memory of this bag and what it contains so fresh, it may as well have been yesterday.

I remember passing her the velvet bag sixteen years ago and her eyes lighting up.

Then

"What is it?" she asks, her grin widening as she perches on her unmade bed.

"Open it and see."

She'll know what it is, but I'm certain she's never used one. I'd had to go into town to buy it, tried to hide my embarrassment as I'd walked into the shop and found what I'd been looking for, the young woman on the cash register eyeing me with a knowing smile.

Lexie opens the bag and pulls out the pink vibrator.

"Oh my God!" Her hand flies to her mouth, but to my relief, she's still smiling. "Where'd you get this?"

"I had to go into town. I was so embarrassed. But it'll be worth it."

"You think?"

"Well, I can't say I know myself, but from what I've heard, they're meant to be good. Shall we try it?"

Lexie's hand returns to her mouth as her eyes flash, her giggle only heightening my need to rip her clothes off her and take her right there on the bed.

"Okay, but I've no idea what to do with it."

"It's okay. I'll help. I'm sure we can work it out between us."

Lexie nods before pulling her T-shirt over her head and slipping out of her jeans. She lies back on her bed with her arms by her sides.

"I'm going to laugh," she says, a giggle escaping her lips. "It's going to tickle, and I'm gonna laugh and spoil it."

"You could never spoil anything. Besides, your laugh turns me on."

"Oh really?" She arches her eyebrow. "I'll remember that the next time we're laughing at something."

"And when you do, you'll remember this, and your laugh will turn into heavy breathing and you'll beg me to fuck you," I say in my best porn-star-style voice.

I dodge the pillow Lexie hurls at me, her smile lighting up her face as she tells me to shut up.

She's still giggling when I run my hands up her legs and

climb on top of her. I kiss her, gently, softly, before moving my mouth down her neck and onto her chest.

"We won't be needing this on," I tell her as she arches her back, instinctively knowing where I'm heading and letting me unfasten her bra. After pulling it out from under her, I drop it on the floor. My mouth roams her hard nipples, pinching slightly with my teeth as she pulls at my hair, her giggles already subsiding until I turn on the vibrator. Her face creases at the buzzing noise, her legs jolting as I run the tip of it up the inside of her leg.

"Oh my God," she laughs, rubbing at her leg as it leaves its tiny little imprints.

"Just relax."

"It tickles," she giggles.

"A nice tickle?"

"I guess," she replies.

"Hold still," I tell her, moving up her legs, the vibrator making my fingers tingle.

She settles back and takes a breath before closing her eyes and giving in to me.

I continue trailing the vibrator up her legs, gently skimming it over her skin, her breathing coming in pants as I near her underwear. When I slide the tip of the vibrator over her knickers, she gasps, her back arching, her legs wriggling.

I work it over the material until she's writhing beneath me, her giggles now extinct and replaced with heavy breathing. As I slide her underwear down, Lexie lifts herself to ease their removal, and I place the vibrator against her skin. She bucks beneath me, her hand flying to mine.

"Are you okay?" I ask.

"Yeah, it's just intense." She exhales heavily, her cheeks flushed, her eyes bright. "Here," she instructs. We both hold the vibrator as she guides me to where she wants it, her hand gripping mine, her body squirming as she moves to her rhythm. I'm so fucking hard just watching her.

"Oh my God," she moans.

My hand flies up to her mouth. Our parents are two floors below, and we've always managed to remain quiet, but I've never seen Lexie like this. It's like she doesn't care if the whole world hears her.

"You gotta keep quiet, Lexie. Not a sound."

This only seems to turn her on more as she groans against the palm of my hand.

Sensing her growing climax, I push my hand against her mouth, then whisper in her ear, "Not without me."

With my hand still on her mouth, I let go of the vibrator, Lexie having taken control. I pull off my sweats and boxers and slide into her with ease—she's so wet, so hungry. Keeping my hand over her mouth, I reclaim the vibrator.

It doesn't take me long. Watching her has been enough, and I know she won't be able to hold out much longer either.

I thrust into her again and again as her groans escape my palm. I build up a rhythm, fucking her as she grips the vibrator with one hand and holds fast to the headboard with the other.

"I swear we will find someplace to do this again where you can scream as loud as you want," I tell her.

It's when she bites my hand that we come. It's thick and

fast and raw and worth all the embarrassment of going into that goddamn shop.

THERE'S NO WAY I CAN IGNORE THIS, SO I OPEN THE velvet bag. It's not the same vibrator, which figures; we'd used it so many times. But the fact that she still keeps it in the same bag I bought her sends a shiver of something through me.

Her new vibrator lies flat in my palm. My gaze lands on her bed, and I imagine her, legs spread, working herself. I never fulfilled my promise of using it somewhere where we could be alone and not have to be quiet. I never got to hear her scream my name.

Quickly, I put the vibrator back in the bag and shake the image away before I completely lose myself. Shoving it back in the drawer, I bury it beneath the rest of the stuff.

To my relief, the bottom drawer is full of socks.

Time to get back to Lexie. I've been away from her for far too long.

FORTY
CADE

FIGHTING MY WAY INTO A PARKING SPACE, I CHECK both mirrors and breathe a sigh of relief when the car fits into the tiny gap. I curse the inconsiderate drivers who've left me minimal room on either side as I clamber out of the driver's seat with Lexie's clothes clutched tightly to my chest.

Once I've paid for parking, I stomp over to the main entrance, wishing I'd put her clothes in a bag. As the double doors slide open, releasing the sterile smell of the hospital, I don't see Jess until it's almost too late.

"Cade," she says as she moves out of the way of the door whilst eyeing the clothes clutched to my chest.

"I thought you'd left." It sounds rude, but my agitation at having been gone from Lexie for too long has started to fray my edges.

"Not quite." Jess glances back into the hospital.

"Have you spoken to Lexie?"

She rolls her eyes. "I just wanted to see how she was."

"And you waited for me to leave to go speak to her? Since when were you so concerned about her?"

"It's not her I'm concerned about."

"What've you said to her?"

"Only what needed to be said."

"Fucking hell, Jess, she could've died tonight. She needs to rest."

"And we've been together too long for me to just walk out of your life without a backup plan."

"A backup plan." I squint. "Is that some kind of psychologist talk?"

She folds her arms as a woman in a dressing gown shuffles toward the doors, a vape in one hand and mobile in the other. Jess and I part, letting the woman through.

"Have you considered what might happen if she doesn't want you?" she says once the woman is on the other side of the doors.

"I don't see how this is any of your—" I begin, but Jess cuts me off.

"Don't you dare after all we've been through. You may not love me, Cade, but I love you, more than anyone I've ever loved. And you can't expect me to walk away not knowing you're okay."

My shoulders drop, and the smell of Lexie's clothes drifts up my nose.

"I appreciate your concern, and I understand how you must be feeling, but I don't think a hospital doorway is the place to be having this conversation."

Jess glances behind her. "I know I should walk away and leave you to your own demise, but I can't. Love does that to you. Makes you drop your guard and make stupid decisions." She glances again at the clothes bundled in my arms. "I think we're both victims of that." She steps forward, pushing her hair behind her ear. "You know where I am if you need me."

I wait for the doors to close before I pull my phone out to check the text to see which ward Lexie is on.

FORTY-ONE
ALEX

My stomach flips when Cade steps onto the ward, his arms laden with my stuff. He searches the beds, though most of them have their curtains closed.

He finds me and strides over.

"Hey, how are you doing?" His face softens, his eyes searching me for evidence of a further reaction.

"I'm okay. Glad you're back with the clothes. I feel like such an idiot sat here in a stupid dress."

Cade places the clothes on the end of the bed, still assessing me, then looks down at the clothes.

"I'm not sure how I'm going to do this." I hold up my arm that has been punctured with a cannula and is now attached to the IV stand.

Cade's eyes run down my left arm and then down my body. "Well, we can do the leggings." He turns and closes the curtain, then pulls the leggings from the pile of clothes and bobs down at the side of the bed, the IV drip behind him. "Shall I help?"

I nod, the past hitting me like a gust of air. I'm sixteen again, and Cade is by my bed, looking after me when I'd been sick with tonsillitis. He'd brought me soup, tucked me in, and stayed with me whilst I'd lain there feeling sorry for myself.

The touch of his hands on my bare leg sends a shiver through my core. He lifts my legs slightly, then pulls them around so I'm now sitting on the edge of the bed. He kneels. I gulp. He runs his hands up my legs, the goose bumps firing up.

"You're freezing," he whispers, the heat from his hands smouldering into my skin.

"It's cold," I lie.

He grabs the leggings. "Can you stand?"

"Yes. I'm just a bit wobbly."

Taking my foot in his hand, he unfastens the strap of my sandal and loosens the shoe from my foot. Slowly, he repeats the process with my other foot, stroking my sole as he removes the sandals and places them under the bed.

"Put your hands on my shoulders as you stand."

"Okay." I do as he says, the IV drip dangling from my hand as I push myself from the bed. The heat from his skin through his shirt almost throbs, warming my hands and melting my body.

He rolls up one leg of the leggings, and I point my foot into the hole. We repeat this with the other foot until they're on over my ankles. The distraction of having to focus on my feet helps with our proximity, but then he begins to pull the leggings up. His fingers graze my skin, climbing higher as he tugs them up. I bite my lip, air rushing under my dress as he reaches the hem.

His hands slow but not due to hesitation—he's not asking my permission or balking at the sudden intimacy. No, he's savouring this just as much as I am.

He tugs the leggings, the hem resisting as my dress rides up, revealing my underwear. I'd chosen the tiniest pair of knickers, the front panel made up of intricate lace leaving nothing to the imagination. In his kneeling position, Cade's face is inches from my waist, his breath kissing between my legs.

My fingers dig into his shoulders as he grips the leggings, his hands moving over my backside, caressing my cheeks as he pulls them up and over my exposed body. He stands up, but his hands remain on the waistband.

"I'm not sure if we can take this dress off," he says at last.

He's so close, his body so warm. I'd forgotten how safe I feel here.

Tearing my eyes from his chest, I examine the IV. There's no way I'm going to get the arm of my dress off with it attached.

"I can leave the dress on." The room sways as my

eyes move from the cannula back to Cade. I hold on to his shoulders as he tightens his grip on my waist.

"Are you okay?"

"Just a bit dizzy."

"Let's get you back in bed."

He manoeuvres me onto the bed and then pulls the hoodie from the pile of clothes. I lean forward, smiling as I notice he chose the grey one with the star on the front. After sliding my right arm into the hoodie, Cade straightens it out as he drapes the remaining arm over my back and around my shoulders, leaving my left arm free for the IV.

"You'll be pleased to know I found socks." He holds up the pair of socks like it's show and tell.

"Thank you."

He sits on the end of the bed and slowly puts each sock on my foot, deliberately taking his time.

"You've done this before." I smile.

"I have. With you." He searches my face.

"I haven't forgotten the tonsillitis."

"You were really ill."

"I wasn't as ill as I made out."

Cade raises his eyebrow.

"I just enjoyed you being my personal slave, so I dragged it out as long as I could."

"I seem to remember being your personal slave even when you were well." He smirks.

"Your memory serves you well." I laugh, but then

Cade's face drops. I pull on the hoodie, trying to wrap it around me.

"What happened to us, Lexie?" he asks, his eyes sad.

"You know what happened."

I may as well have slapped him. His face hardens, and his eyes narrow. I'm back to being a bitch, and I don't know why. Is it because he's getting close again, and I don't want him to get hurt? Because he will. I'm not allowed to be happy. Everyone who gets close to me gets hurt somehow, and I don't want that to happen again. He's been through enough.

And I'm wandering again down darkened corridors of the only part of mine and Cade's story I've tried to forget.

The split between my mum and Mark had come as no surprise. Their arguments became more frequent, the house a smouldering den of unspoken words, a hotbed of frayed tempers. All the while, Cade and I delved deeper into each other, becoming so entwined that our parents' mutual hatred seemed unable to penetrate the bubble we'd placed ourselves in. Until the day it all came crashing down, and my mum announced that it was over and Cade and Mark were moving out.

We'd prepared ourselves. We weren't stupid. We'd seen the cracks appear and knew the break was inevitable. And we'd told ourselves it'd be fine. We would survive. Our love knew no bounds. We had phones and social media, and we'd continue walking to school. We had it all planned out.

What we hadn't planned for was how far away Mark and Cade moved.

Cade left school after sixth form and got a job as a labourer on a building site so he could save up for when I finished sixth form and could also get a full-time job. Then we would live together, be together, just like we were meant to. Until then, we would survive on this dream.

The buses were infrequent, and between his job and my dog leash, it was almost impossible to see each other. So, we made do with phone calls and text messages, becoming imaginative with ways to pleasure ourselves when so far apart.

But it wasn't the same. I missed the smell of his hair, the smoothness of his hands, the way he would push his hand into mine and circle his thumb on its back. I missed his jokes, the sarcasm that laced every conversation and made me laugh. I missed the feel of his body pressed against mine whilst we tried to be quiet in my tiny single bed.

I missed him so much that my stomach twisted at the sight of a glass of water.

I cried every morning I came down into the empty kitchen.

I couldn't eat breakfast when there was no one there to eat it with me.

So when I got the chance to see him, I didn't hesitate.

Flashes replay. The cold fingers of that day reach out, touching my brain, prying to be let in after I've spent sixteen years shutting them out.

Then

His text message comes through one Wednesday afternoon whilst I'm in biology and supposed to be listening to Mr. Khan drone on about the behaviour of cells.

> I can get a lift over to yours. Can we meet?

Ignoring the possibility of getting caught with my phone on during a lesson, I reply instantly.

> YES.

His reply is instant.

> I can come to your house. Be there in forty minutes.

I can't type quick enough, yet I manage to respond.

> I'll be there.

For the first time in my life, I skip class, complaining to Mr. Khan about cramps. Feeling bad at how embarrassed he looks, I don't have time to dwell on it as he sends me home. I practically run, knowing my mum will be out at work and we'll have the house to ourselves.

THE NEXT PART COMES IN FLASHES. I DON'T RECALL the scene as a whole. My brain has tried to dismember it, maybe to make it more palatable. But even so, I remember enough to know what I saw.

Then

I push the front door open, feeling so many things.

    The anticipation of seeing Cade again.

    The illicit excitement of having skipped school.

    I walk down the hall where shoes are lined up under the coat stand, the sickly smell of lavender floating from incense sticks my mum has displayed on top of the radiator cover. The house feels strange, as if it knows I'm not supposed to be here. Whipping my phone out, I check my messages.

    No messages.

    I type one out.

> I'm home. Let me know when you get here and I'll let you in.

    I hit the Send button.

    I hear the unmistakable chime of Cade's phone, but it comes from my kitchen.

He's already here.

It's quiet.

Too quiet.

Then I notice my mum's work shoes in the hall, her bag abandoned next to them.

My heart sinks to my stomach and squirms.

Taking two steps forward, I push open the kitchen door.

I CAN'T GET RID OF IT, NO MATTER HOW HARD I'VE tried. If I could, I would scrub my brain with bleach and rinse my eyes with disinfectant until they burned.

I've had to live with the memory all these years.

How has Cade endured it?

Because his memory of that day must be far worse than mine.

FORTY-TWO
CADE

W ITHIN THE REDNESS OF THE FADING RASH, I NOTE
the colour change in Lexie's face at the mention of that
day, her cheeks hollowing as a haunted look spreads
its ugly self over her. And even having aged, grown
into her features, and become the woman I'm looking
at now, her face is the same stark white as the day she
walked into her kitchen. The day our lives were oblit-
erated into Before and After. The day that tested me
beyond all resolve and hardened my outer edges that
were already made from stone.

Then

*The forty-minute car journey had only taken twenty-five
minutes due to a shortcut my new friend had known about.
He'd dropped me at the end of Lexie's street, explaining again
why he couldn't pick me up and take me back home again. I*

shrugged it off and told him it didn't matter, that I didn't care about getting home.

I'll walk the entire way back if I have to.

Scanning the street that had become so familiar on our walks to school, the backdrop to some of the happiest memories I have, I edge closer to the house, scraping the gravel with my trainers and glancing at the time on my phone. She won't be long. Loitering like some stalker, I hide in the shadow of a large rhododendron bush owned by one of the neighbouring houses. If I'm spotted, it could land Lexie in a whole heap of trouble, which I've already caused by getting her to skip class.

"Cade?"

Almost putting my hands in the air in surrender, I turn at the sound of my name and the familiarity of the voice.

Jacquelin stares at me. "What are you doing here?"

There's a lazy quality to her speech, and I almost miss the taxi pulling away from the kerb.

"I've just been out for lunch with some friends," Jacquelin continues. "I didn't expect to see you again." She eyes me suspiciously.

"I left something at the house," I quickly reply, my backup excuse already formulated on the drive over.

She glances behind me and down the road. "Did your dad drop you?"

"No. A friend was heading this way, so he said he'd drop me off."

Her gaze rolls up and down my body. "Well, you'd better come in, then." She turns and heads up the path to the house.

I hesitate before following her.

We enter the house together, Jacquelin stumbling slightly, placing her hand on the wall of the hallway to steady herself as she shakes her shoes off.

"That's better," she says, having shrunk two inches. She turns and smiles.

Something beds down in my stomach, the feeling I get before a fight erupts, like the rolling clouds before a storm.

"Do you fancy a drink?" she asks, staggering into the kitchen.

Something is unfolding here, but I can't get a grip on what. All I can think about is keeping Lexie away and out of trouble. It'll be too obvious now if I flip open my phone and call or text her to warn her we've been rumbled, that her mum's home and in rather a sorry state. And why is she offering me a drink like we're old chums? Her feud had been with my dad. But even so, there's an unwritten protocol somewhere that I'm on his side and always will be.

"No, thank you. I'll just grab what I need and head off."

"You can't come all this way without a drink. And I'd like to talk to you." She grins, her mouth sliding drunkenly like an elastic band.

We head into the kitchen, the temperature dropping, my body aching as I picture Lexie leaning over the counter, making me breakfast whilst I make the drinks, both of us laughing about something completely trivial.

Jacquelin pulls a green bottle out of the cupboard and begins clinking glasses as she pours two large slugs, taking one for herself and handing me the other. I take it if only to placate her. Why is she offering me neat gin in the middle of the afternoon? She doesn't bat an eyelid, though, as she downs her measure in one gulp.

"I'm glad you're here," she begins, her words falling from her mouth. "I've been wanting to talk to you for a while now."

My back is against the worktop, the glass in my hand my only weapon. I can't gauge her mood, and I'm unsure of her agenda. It's hard to tell when she's so obviously drunk.

"I said a lot of things to your dad the last time you were here. Horrible things in the heat of the moment. And I've had a lot of time to think since you both left." Jacquelin pauses to pour herself another drink, which she throws back quickly before continuing, her next statement landing like a slug to my jaw.

"I knew what was going on between you and my daughter."

Her eyes sharpen.

I flinch.

Fuck.

"Your dad had no idea. Men never do. But I knew. I could tell by the way she looked at you, the way you looked at her."

For a second, there's a tiny spark of hope. Is she going to offer to help us see each other? Has she noticed how miserable Lexie has been since we were separated? Is she giving us her blessing to continue seeing each other? Will she offer the house as a safe haven for us to meet, regardless of what happened between her and my dad?

But then she smiles, and I've lived with her for long enough to know what that smile means. The real Jacquelin is here under the cloud of alcohol, and she's only just beginning to show her true self.

"My daughter was fifteen years old when you came to live with us, and you were, what… seventeen?"

She edges her way toward me, closing the gap between us and any chance of me getting out of this kitchen.

Her eyes narrow as if aiming at her target before she launches her attack. "That means Lexie was underage when you began to groom her."

The kitchen tilts under my feet.

"Now just hang on," I interrupt, slamming the glass down on the counter behind me. "Lexie was sixteen when we —"

"Let me finish," Jacquelin demands with a soberness that's appeared from nowhere. "Because you n eed to hear what I'm about to say." Her face is grey, and there's a fire behind her eyes, as if the alcohol has stoked it.

I don't want to hear a single thing that comes out of her mouth, but I have no choice as she continues to spew her vile venom.

"You seduced my underage daughter right under my nose, and for that, I should've reported you to the police."

My mouth opens, ready to interject, to tell her we did nothing illegal, but Jacquelin places a cold, clammy finger on my lips. I bat her hand away, her eyes lighting up at my reaction.

"I should've reported you, but I was too upset with what was going on with your dad."

She moves closer. My back pushes into the counter, the heels of my trainers wedged up against the plinths.

"I should've told your football buddies. I'm sure they would've been interested in knowing what kind of guy they were hanging around with. And then there was your school. I'm positive they would've been interested in what you did to my fifteen-year-old daughter. And then there's social media. How I stopped myself from posting something on my Facebook page, I'll never know. But I could. That's what I'm trying to say here, Cade. I could."

Her last two words are delivered with the sharpness of a blade, and I can almost feel them slicing into my skin. My shoulders shake, and my breath chokes me as I try to hold my fists at bay. I've taken down larger threats than this before. One punch, and she'd be on the floor, and I'd be out the door.

But I've never hit a woman.

And I'm not about to.

I'd only be adding assault to her list of accusations along with grooming her underage daughter. But it doesn't stop the anger brewing like a pressure cooker that I'm sure is going to blow any minute.

"What do you want?" I snarl. How long will it be before Lexie gets here?

"And that's what it comes down to, isn't it? What I want." Jacqueline exhales, the acidity of her alcoholic breath stinging my eyes. "You see, I've watched Lexie over the last few months, and she's heartbroken. She's not eating, not sleeping. The girl's a mess." Tears now join the anger, the emotional cocktail becoming lethal. "And I find myself a little jealous. It should be me. I should be mourning the loss of a loved one, but I'm not. It wasn't love between your dad and me. I'm not sure what it was, to be honest, but I know I'm not heartbroken. He hasn't left me craving for something like Lexie is. I've never had that—with anyone, not just your dad. I look at Lexie now and watch her suffering like a sick animal, and I find myself wanting to feel that, to want someone so badly that you can't imagine putting food in your mouth or taking your next breath. And it's not fair. I should be able to feel that. I should know what it's like."

"I'm not sure I can help you with that." I grip the edge of the worktop behind my back, the anger beginning to morph into a primeval fear at what her next step might be.

"Well, that's where you're wrong." Jacquelin steps forward and presses herself against me.

Instinctively, I push her away, but she's insistent.

"I can call the local paper at the touch of a button. I'm sure you're still playing football with the lads and that they would love to know what kind of guy you really are. Grooming an underage girl for sex. You never get rid of an accusation like that. It'll stick to you like mud for the rest of your life. I can do it, and I will. Do not doubt that I can ruin your life before it's even begun."

Nausea washes over me like a sudden downpour. I'm drenched in it. My skin is hot, my whole body shaking, the rage replaced with good old-fashioned fear because I know she's right. I would never clear my name. I would never be believed, and I'd be labelled a predator.

Raising herself on her tiptoes, she pushes her mouth against mine. I turn my head, but she presses her hand to the side of my face, her threat still hanging in the air.

She might as well have a gun to my head.

"It'll be much more enjoyable if you just go with the flow," she says as she reaches down and unzips my trousers.

Bile rises in the back of my throat. She's tiny. This frail, drunken woman has me cornered, and I'm frozen to the spot as she wields a knife of words at my throat. But her threat nips at my skin. I can see the shit she could smear, the mud she could drag my name through. The headlines. The shame. The hurt on my dad's face. With the power of social media, she could ruin me and my name for the rest of my life.

She pushes her hands inside my jeans.

Blood floods my mouth as I bite into my lip and clench my eyes shut.

"Not much going on down here." Jacquelin giggles as she squeezes me in her hand. "Maybe you just need warming up a bit."

She grabs hold of my hand and thrusts it up under her skirt. I try to pull away, tears threatening as my stomach vaults at the thought of what's happening here. I want to push her away, to throw her to the ground, but what will she add to her fanciful list of demeanours—ABH? Beating up a woman? She has all the cards, and she knows it. I'm fucking helpless. And all the while, all I can think of is Lexie. What will this do to her? I'm being blackmailed and raped all at the same time, and there isn't a fucking thing I can do about it.

But I can't let this happen. There has to be a way out of this.

It's then that the text message arrives on my phone, the notification reverberating off the kitchen cabinets. I freeze, but

Jacquelin is oblivious, lost in her own little twisted game like a greedy child doing their worst.

I hear the kitchen door.

I open my eyes.

Alex

Then

It takes a second for my brain to catch up with my eyes.

Cade.

My mum.

And there's a second where I misread it. Cade. My Cade. My mum. Their hands. Her mouth. But the shock allows me to read the rest of the scene.

Cade is pushed up against the worktop, his face ashen, fear coating his skin, sorrow behind his eyes, tears streaming down his face, the gin bottle on the side.

I know Cade. Trust him. Believe in him.

And I know my mum.

Deafening, damning, dreadful silence flows through the air until my lungs explode.

The screaming is different this time. My screams pierce the air. I'm the one who grabs my mum and throws her to the floor. I'm the one who trashes the kitchen, throws the gin bottle, my anger so feral, so unfamiliar, I've no idea how to tame it.

I hear my name, feel his hands around me, pulling me back, his words trying to reach me.

But she's tainted it all.

My hands are not my own.

My cries don't belong to me.

Everything changes.

I change.

Before and After.

FORTY-THREE
ALEX

THE CLATTER OF A TROLLEY ON THE OTHER SIDE OF the curtain makes me jump. Cade doesn't seem to notice it. He's on the chair, his arms resting on his knees, his body hunched over.

"You know what happened. I told you. Right after, when I'd managed to calm you down, I told you exactly what you'd walked in on."

"I know." I pick at my nails.

"Then why do I feel like I did something wrong? You pushed me away. You didn't want anything to do with me. Why?"

My throat constricts, my mouth dry and claggy. "Because it was all my fault."

"What?"

"You were assaulted in my house by my mother because of her jealousy and her issues. It was always just me who handled her, and I was fine with that. But then you came along, and she saw a way to control me, another way to get to me. And it worked. She won. She would always win. And I just had to accept that. I shouldn't have got involved with you. I knew she'd do something like this, and I couldn't risk her doing anything else. I had to end it before she completely destroyed you. It was the only way to keep you safe from her."

"I called you so many times," he says after several seconds of laboured silence. "I was so worried about you."

"I know. And I'm sorry I didn't reply. But I had to sever all contact. It was the hardest thing I've ever done. But it had to be that way. We weren't old enough to run away and survive on our own. I was dependent on her, and she knew that too. And as much as I hated her, I couldn't leave her either. She didn't have anyone else, and that was part of the problem. She was my mum. She'd been my whole life. And I knew there could be no future for you and me. How could there be when she'd done that to you? There's no way you'd be able to be in the same room as her, something even I found difficult."

"I thought she'd locked you up, took away your phone, and kept you inside."

"No. She slept it off and woke up fifteen hours later as if the whole thing had never happened, just like she always did."

And I got up, went to school, did my homework, ate my dinner, and went to sleep every day without fail, without emotion or feeling. That day turned me into stone. I kept my guard up through the rest of high school and then into university.

As I got older, I had more power. When she got drunk, I just walked out of the house and left her. I'd go to a friend's house or a café and sit and wait it out until I thought it was safe to go back. She learned to put herself to bed, and I left the broken ornaments for her to clean up. I think that was when she realised I wouldn't be there forever. So, she started dating again —all manner of men, regardless of their character. I literally didn't know what or who I'd be coming home to.

"As soon as I could afford it, I found a place to rent with a friend and moved out. And all the while, I tried to forget you, to blank it all out, pretend you didn't exist, because that was the only way I could cope."

Cade closes his eyes as if he can feel my pain as well as the hurt of having been shut out for so long.

"Do you still see her?" he asks.

"A phone call here and there, Christmas and my birthday. That's about it. I'm not entirely sure where she is. She met a guy named Kian about five years ago, and they bought a camper van and decided to tour the coast of Scotland together. Maybe it was what she needed."

"I've thought about you every day."

"You shouldn't have."

"But I have. I have continued to do so for the past sixteen years. I'll never stop thinking about you because I'm incapable of it."

I shake my head. "You have to. We both need to stop this nonsense."

"Why? What are you so afraid of?"

"Hurting you."

"Jacquelin was the one who hurt me, hurt us both, and she's not in charge of your life anymore, Lexie. You are."

"You can't possibly think this would work, knowing what we know, having seen what we've seen. It'll always be there, lingering in the background, and it'll rear its head at the first disagreement. How would I know you weren't thinking about that day? How would I know you weren't blaming me for what happened?"

"Because I've never blamed you. Because it wasn't your fault. Lexie, you have to stop blaming yourself."

"I don't deserve to be happy. I don't deserve to feel love like I did before."

"Why not? Why would you deny yourself this?"

"Because I'm just like her. I saw it that day in the kitchen. I saw my rage, felt the anger, and I knew it had been there all along. I always vowed I'd never end up like her, yet there I was throwing things, scream-ing," I cry. "I remember hitting you on your chest, thumping you, trying to push you away. I know what I did to you, and I couldn't risk being that person again."

"You can't judge yourself on one incident."

"Once was enough. How could I be trusted?"

"Has it happened since?"

Pressing the sleeve of my hoodie to my face, I glance at him. "What do you mean?"

"Have you hurt anyone since that day? Have you lashed out at someone in anger?"

"I'm angry all the time. I feel it every day."

"But have you hurt someone because of it?"

I shake my head. "But only because I haven't allowed myself to care about anyone enough."

"What about Shawn?" Cade's face hardens.

"What about him?"

"Do you care about him?"

"God, no. I hate him."

"Then why?"

"Why am I fucking him?"

Cade's jaw tenses, his eyes misting over. It wouldn't have been out of place to see steam coming from his nose.

"I feel nothing when I'm with Shawn, and that's all I'll allow myself. Nothing." I draw his eyes back to mine. "My mother was a monster. It makes sense that I'm one, too, so I deserve to be with someone like Shawn Bowling, a slimy, dirty monster."

A male voice slips through the tiny gap in the curtains. "How are we doing in here?"

"Okay," I reply sheepishly, my eyes darting from Cade to the curtain.

The man pushes the curtain aside and steps into the cubicle.

"Just here to check on your IV," he tells me whilst averting his eyes. His light blue scrubs are almost too bright, his dark skin a stark contrast. His friendly face and happy emoji pin badge are out of place here where monsters are lurking under the bed.

"How are you feeling?" he asks. "Any chest pains still?"

"A little," I confess.

"The best thing you could do now is rest." He glances at Cade.

"Is there anywhere to get a decent coffee?" Cade asks, taking the hint.

"There's a coffee shop in the main dining area, along with a bookshop and some other little shops. Just follow the signs for C block."

"Thanks." Cade nods, rising from the chair. "Can I get you anything?"

I shake my head. Cade moves behind the nurse.

"How long will you be?" I ask before he disappears.

"Not long." He pushes through the gap in the curtain, and I wonder if he'll be back at all.

Cade

When I return, she's asleep, her arm attached to the IV dangling out of the bed, the hoodie having slipped off her. Putting down my coffee, I carefully place her arm over her chest, making sure the IV isn't restricted, then pull the hoodie over her body.

Her chest rises and falls, her eyelids still. She's the picture of peace. I gulp and push past the pain that erupts at how she sees herself, how she's been living for the last sixteen years, hating a version of herself that doesn't exist.

Cade

Shuffling feet wake me. Having fallen asleep sitting in the chair with my head and arms resting on the side of Lexie's hospital bed, the small of my back protests as I sit up.

The nurse in the blue scrubs is back, checking Lexie's IV. "We don't normally let people stay on the ward past 9:00 p.m., but since you've been asleep, you've been pretty quiet. However, it's definitely time you went home."

"Sorry. It's been a long day."

"And it'll be an even longer night if you don't go home and get some proper sleep." His eyes don't leave the IV bag as he fiddles with the tube leading to the back of Lexie's hand.

"What if she wakes?"

The nurse follows my gaze. Lexie is sound asleep, her head resting on one side.

"She's exhausted. I reckon she'll be out of it for a while, and I'm on duty this evening, so she's in capable hands if she does wake."

My face must tell him how unconvinced I am, as he follows this up with "I'm not like the other nurses." His eyebrow arches. "Some of them can be a little stern, you know, tough love and all that, but not me. That's not my style."

"And what about tomorrow?"

"You can be right back in that chair at 9:00 a.m., all fresh-faced."

Pushing back the chair, I study Lexie closely, making sure the scrape of the legs hasn't roused her.

"If she does wake up—" I begin, but the nurse doesn't let me finish.

"Don't worry, I'll tell her I kicked you out, kicking and screaming, and that you'll be back first thing in the morning, bearing get-well gifts."

This inspires a tiny smirk as I gather my phone and car keys and back up toward the curtain.

"I recommend leaving now whilst I'm still here. Then you won't have left her alone."

"Thank you." I nod, parting the curtain and slipping away.

The hospital corridors are steeped in an eerie silence, the lights flickering as if they're trying to keep the building alive. I contemplate sleeping in my car so I can be back here as soon as humanly possible in the morning, but the nurse is right—I need a shower, a change of clothes, and now, a gift.

Turmoil coils in my gut.

She could've died tonight.

I could have lost her for good.

The revelation about why she pushed me away all those years ago has left me empty. She thinks she's like Jacqueline, a product of her mother and not worthy of love. I'd always believed it was because she thought I was tainted, damaged goods she didn't want to have to repair, or that she'd never be able to get past what she saw, the image haunting her for the rest of her life.

But I was wrong. It's none of these things.

As I head back to my apartment, it's clear I have another job here. The thought of Lexie living the rest of her life believing this version of herself fills me with utter despair. It took a trained psychologist to heal my wounds. What will it take to heal Lexie? I'm no psychologist, but I know that if anyone is going to reach her, it can only be me, and tonight has marked the start of her opening up, being forced to talk to me like we used to, trust me like she used to.

It's not going to be easy, but then again, nothing worth fighting for ever is.

And on top of this, I can't forget why I'm here in the first place.

FORTY-FOUR

ALEX

IT TAKES SEVERAL SECONDS FOR MY EYES TO ADJUST to the dim glow, the white curtains cocooning me, and the astringent smell of antiseptic. My tongue feels thick, my mouth dry, my body almost groaning against the unnatural position I fell asleep in.

"Hi there," the male nurse chirps from beside the bed, squeezing the almost empty IV bag, which convinces me I haven't slept for too long, as it's the same nurse who told Cade to go get a coffee.

Cade.

My eyes dart to the empty chair.

"Is he still getting coffee?"

"He got the coffee, but you were asleep by the time he got back."

"So, where is he now? What time is it?"

"It's twenty past five. He fell asleep, and I kicked him out around midnight and told him to go home and get some rest. Don't worry, though. He'll be back first thing, hopefully with a gift."

"A gift?"

"Yeah, I told him to get you a gift, something nice." He winks, his eyes dazzling against his dark skin. "Hospitalization is a great excuse to get a gift out of your partner."

"He's not my partner," I say.

"Oh, I'm sorry. I just presumed."

"It's okay. He's actually my boss."

"Wow." He whistles through his front teeth. "Clearly, I'm in the wrong job. My boss is a middle-aged woman with an inverted bob and an addiction to Mint Imperials, which only seem to make her breath worse."

Seemingly satisfied with the drip, he picks up my chart and starts to make notes. "She wouldn't bat an eyelid if I was ill let alone stay with me in the hospital."

"He was with me when I had my reaction, and…." I trail off, noting the nurse's sly smile and the way he seems to be looking at the chart but not really reading it. "We have history," I admit.

"I knew it." He drops the chart and sticks his pen behind his ear. "I could tell. You guys just have a vibe."

"A vibe?"

"Yeah, like an energy. I can sense these things."

"You're very perceptive."

"It comes with the job." He grins. "It's not all about the scrubs and the stethoscopes, you know."

"I guess not."

Hugging the chart to his chest, his eyes narrow. "And I'm sensing sadness. Is it a sad history?"

"It's a messy history."

"Okay." His mouth turns down as he considers this. "Messy is okay. You can work with messy. Just means things need tidying up."

"It's a bit more than that."

"The bigger the mess just means the longer it'll take to tidy it up. That doesn't mean you shouldn't bother at all." His words float around the cubicle and then get caught in the curtain surrounding us. "Anyway, enough of my rambling. Your IV is nearly done. My shift finishes in ten minutes, so when it's empty, someone will come take it out, and you'll have your arm back."

"Thanks. And what time—"

Again, he doesn't let me finish but pre-empts my question. "Your boss will be in the building as soon as the doors open at nine, but I suspect he's probably already in the car park. Do you need anything before I leave? I promised him I'd look after you, and I don't want to break a promise."

"Could you just pass me my bag? I think it's on the floor."

"Sure thing." He grabs my bag and hands it to me.

"Thanks."

"I won't be on duty by the time he gets here, so be sure to tell him I did a good job."

"Of course I will, and you have done a good job."

"I'm glad to hear it."

He disappears through the curtain, pulling it tight behind him and closing me in with an almost empty IV bag and an even emptier bag. With no EpiPens, my bag feels lighter than it normally does. I shake out the minimal contents. One red lipstick, my house key, and my phone, which has a dead battery. Why is my life not as organised as my bag?

Maybe the nurse is right, and I just need to tidy things up between me and Cade. But where to begin? And what will we find under the mess?

FORTY-FIVE
ALEX

THE WAY HE BURSTS THROUGH THE DOUBLE DOORS makes me wonder how many sets of doors he's already had to blast his way through to be the first on the ward. It's strange, this feeling flowing through my veins and mingling with the drugs they've been pumping me with for the last several hours. I haven't felt like this in a long time, and it's taken me a while to recognise that I'm excited to see him, relieved and overwhelmed he's here.

I hadn't managed to go back to sleep after the nice nurse left, as my mind had been left to wander, and a female nurse took over the removal of my IV. As soon as the sunlight began to filter through the large windows, the ward began to wake up, my fellow patients pulling back their curtains that had been closed when I arrived here last night.

It's a small ward with just one large woman in a

bed opposite me and an older man in the bed in the far corner, and although he opened his curtains, he'd swiftly fallen back asleep after eating his breakfast of toast and marmalade, his light snore adding a rhythm to the ward.

Cade doesn't seem to notice our new audience as he approaches my bed, his casual sweatpants and T-shirt contrasting his tight shoulders and worried expression.

"Hey." I smile as he steps into the cubicle, automatically drawing the curtain around us.

"I didn't leave you," he begins. "I got asked to leave when you were asleep."

"It's okay. The nurse told me."

"He did?"

"Yeah, and he also said you'd be bringing a gift." For a second, I think I've caught him out. His sweatpants hug his hips, his T-shirt tight around his body, no jumper, no hoodie, no man-bag to stash something in, and the only object in his hand is his phone. But a smile creeps across his face as he places his hand in his pocket and pulls out a bar of Cadbury's Dairy Milk.

"Please tell me it's still your favourite."

I beam. "It is."

He perches on the edge of the bed and hands me the chocolate. "Your IV is done," he points out.

"I have my arm back, thank goodness." I shake my arm to confirm this.

"Shame. I was hoping to have to feed you the

chocolate." I can tell by the sharpness on his face that he's thinking the same as me — that this is weird. This is now awkward.

"What happens now?" I ask, brushing my fingers over the wrapper of the chocolate bar.

"That depends." He leans back, placing his arm over my legs.

"On what?"

"On you, Lexie. What you want. What you don't want."

"I don't want this to be awkward," I admit.

"Is that how it feels?"

"A little. But I know when we arrive at work on Monday, it's going to be a whole load of awkward. I'm glad my battery is dead on my phone, because I dread to think how many messages I have off Donna."

"I don't want you to think about Monday, or the office, or work, or Donna." His voice lowers, his eyes searching mine. "I want you to think about you and only you and what you want and whether I can be the one to give it to you."

The rush of air that leaves me almost deflates my chest.

"I lost you sixteen years ago, and I wasn't old enough or strong enough to fight for you back then, but I am now. I'll do whatever I have to do, whatever it takes. I won't lose you again."

As I grab his hand, a tear rolls down my cheek. Cade wipes it away with his thumb.

"I'm not sure I can do this. What if I hurt you? What if it brings back all the bad things?"

"You would be hurting me more by denying us the chance to see if this is right. I know it is. It's always been right, but you seem to need convincing. So, let me convince you that this is where we're supposed to be."

I swallow. "We need to do this slowly. You've just left Jess, I'm in the hospital, and then there's work, and—"

Cade squashes my words with his thumb, then pulls my head against his chest and holds it there.

"Tell me what you hear," he says.

My eyes close, and I listen to the beat of his heart beneath the cotton of his T-shirt, feel the heat from his skin, the warmth radiating from him.

"Your heart," I whisper.

Reaching for my hand, he places it on his chest and holds it there next to my head. "You're the only reason it beats. The only reason."

We are broken apart by the arrival of the female nurse, who flaps the curtains back like she's sorting out her washing and wants to know if I've had any breakfast.

It's after lunch that I am allowed to go home, a young doctor discharging me with a new prescription for replacement EpiPens that we pick up at the hospital pharmacy before leaving in Cade's car that smells like a car showroom and looks like it's never been driven.

I want it to feel seamless, for it to be just like it was sixteen years ago when we were making our way to school, the companionable silences mixed with mean-ingful chatter and playful banter, but there's an edge to us like we've both been sharpened. And maybe that's where I'm going wrong—wanting it to be like it was sixteen years ago, but it's not going to be like that ever again. Despite what happened, we are older now, wiser, full-fledged adults. We will never be teenagers again.

How can I convince myself we can move forward? I don't know how to be with this adult Cade. I don't know how to put what I saw behind me and move on like he seems to have done. And what if we rekindle things and the memories come hurtling back? What if I think about that day whilst we're kissing? What if the image assaults me as we're being intimate, and I end up pushing him away?

How do I let it go?

FORTY-SIX
CADE

After we reach her house, I make her a cup of tea and a sandwich. She's sitting on the sofa, encased in her hoodie, feet tucked under her legs. I've taken the small chair by the kitchen door to be on hand in case she needs anything else.

"How did Jess help you?" she asks in between bites.

Pressing my lips together, I think carefully before answering. "She pushed me to talk about it, asked questions, made me revisit that day and what happened."

"Was it easier because you were involved with her?" She swallows hard, as if the sandwich has left a bitter aftertaste.

"Easier in some ways because she was on hand, so when I had a nightmare or was having a particularly bad day, she would be there to help and talk me through things. It's not like when you see a professional and you've got a date and time slot. And she wanted to help me. It wasn't just a job earning her money. She was invested in helping me."

An acidic taste coats the back of my mouth, the guilt at walking away from her so easily when she's seen me at my lowest and had thrown me a lifeline. I should call her, but I don't want to give her false hope, for her to think I'm clinging onto something that will never be.

There's a buzz from the kitchen, like an egg timer going off or an oven timer, but Lexie doesn't seem to notice it. "Did it work?"

"What do you mean?"

"Did she fix you? Are you better now?"

The timer stops beeping as if I've got to answer her now or I'll lose out on the big prize. "I don't think it's as simple as being fixed. She taught me how to process my anger, how to channel it in other ways, and for it not to consume me. She made me see that it wasn't my fault what happened and for it not to rule the rest of my life or shape the person I was becoming. And it wasn't just that day we talked about."

I press the back of my hand, and my knuckles crack against the silence. "We talked about losing my mum and how angry it made me right up until I met you."

Lexie stares at me, the steam from her mug swirling across her face.

"You helped me, Lexie. I don't think you realise how much you helped me, but you did. You were someone I could relate to, someone I could talk to, and someone who would listen, and you never judged me. You never gave me puppy eyes and patted me on the back and said, 'Poor you, it'll be okay.' You never lied to me by saying that everything would be fine and I just needed time. You always knew what to say and, more importantly, what not to say. After I met you, I knew I could be happy again. You made me happy, Lexie."

She's abandoned the sandwich now and clutches her cup of tea, holding the mug with her hands shoved inside the sleeves of her hoodie like makeshift oven gloves.

"That's what I'm afraid of," she says, her mug starting to shake.

I slide off the chair and kneel before her, taking the mug from her hands and placing it on the coffee table. "What are you afraid of?"

"What if I don't make you happy anymore? What if I'm not good for you? What if I undo all the hard work Jess has done? What if I break you again?" She presses the sleeves of her hoodie onto her eyes, hiding from me, and a pain swells in my chest.

"You never broke me, Lexie. You just pushed me away, and I know why you did that, and I understand it. But you weren't the one who broke me."

Seconds pass, and I pull a tissue from my pocket

and hand it to her. She dabs at her eyes, sniffs, and pushes her hair behind her ear.

"Do you want me to leave?" I ask.

She grabs hold of my wrist. "No. I want you to stay."

Taking her hand off my wrist, I hold it gently. "Do you want me?"

"Yes. I just don't know how to do this. I don't know how we go forward. I'm so scared by it all. Scared of losing you, of hurting you, of this not working out—because if it doesn't, then I know I'll never be happy ever again.

"Then we take it slow. We do this at your pace, and we do what feels right."

"What if it takes forever?"

"I've waited this long. I will wait an eternity for you, Lexie."

She lets her head drop against my chest, and I hold her so tightly. There's no way I'm ever letting her go again.

As the afternoon wears on, Lexie becomes exhausted. She manages a bath as I pace up and down the landing, worrying she's fallen asleep in there. Then I carry her up to bed after she falls asleep on the sofa whilst trying to watch a film.

Her eyelids flutter as I pull her clothes from her whilst she's lying on the bed.

"Are you trying to seduce me, Cade?" she murmurs, her eyes still closed.

"Not tonight," I tell her, tucking the sheet around her and stroking the side of her face. "I want you wide awake when I take you, Lexie. Wide. Awake."

"Hm." Her lips spread, and I wonder if she's recalling what it's like to have me inside her.

If she is, she's in for an awakening, as that was the teenage Cade, an inexperienced and fumbling fool. I've grown in many ways, and Lexie is about to find out exactly how and where. But not yet. Not when she's recovering.

I need her at full strength and awake enough to be screaming my name.

"Do you want me to stay with you tonight?" I ask.

She tugs at the sheet, pulling it up under her chin. "No. I just need to sleep. You'll only miss me snoring and drooling. Go get a shower. I'll see you tomorrow for work." Her words are heavy, laden with slumber.

I don't want to leave her, but she's right. I need to shower and change.

"I don't think work is a good idea."

"Tomorrow." She rolls over, her hair spreading out behind her like a dark veil.

"I'll call you in the morning to see how you are."

Her response is heavy breathing.

Leaning over, I kiss her lightly on her forehead, then leave the room.

After searching through her house keys, I lock up for the night, pocketing her spare key in case there's an emergency. My phone is vibrating in my pocket, and not for the first time today. I know who's calling. I haven't been ready to speak to her, but I can't put it off any longer.

Reminding myself just how much Jess has done for me over the past few years, I try to keep my tone in check. "Hey."

"Hi." She sounds a million miles away. "How is she?"

I don't like the way she refers to Lexie as "she," like she can't bring herself to say her name or Lexie isn't worthy of a title.

"Lexie's okay, thank you." Swallowing hard, I follow this up out of courtesy. "Are you okay?"

"I've been better." A cold silence leaks down the handset. "Look, I just called to make sure things were okay with you two."

"Meaning?"

"I meant what I said, Cade. I can't walk away knowing you might be hurting. If she rejects you, then you'll need someone, and who better to take care of you than me, the only person who knows what you're going through."

Reject me? Fuck. This has to be the psychologist talking.

"Lexie hasn't pushed me away, if that's what you mean."

There's another pregnant pause, and I try not to imagine what Jess must look like as she fights to ask the questions she doesn't want to hear the answers to.

"So, are you guys together?"

"We're taking things slow."

"I see." She's biding her time now, waiting to drop the bombshell. Tick, tick, tick. "And does she know?"

Boom.

"No."

"You haven't told her?"

There's no holding back now. "She's still recovering. Now is not the time."

"She deserves to know."

"She does, and she will."

"How do you think she'll feel when she finds out?"

I sigh. "I don't know. I'm not a mind-reader."

"You have to tell her."

"I know, Jess, and I will."

"When?"

"When the time is right. I can't jeopardise things."

"It's not just about you anymore, Cade. You can't keep this from her. It isn't fair."

Grinding my teeth, I reply, "I realise that. And thank you for your concern. I will deal with it. You have my word. Now, if you don't mind, it's been a long day." Pain squeezes my chest. I'm being a bastard, I know I am, but I'm as tired as Lexie is.

"I can't stop caring, Cade. I won't. You of all people must appreciate that."

"Goodnight." I cut the call and stare at the inky black sky.

The infuriating thing is that she's right. Everything she said is true. But how can I tell Lexie the truth? I don't want to scare her away again. I don't want her running from me when I've only just got her back.

FORTY-SEVEN
ALEX

It's Monday morning, and I'm already on the edge of losing it.

Cade stayed with me yesterday whilst I took a bath and then fought sleep on the sofa, exhaustion taking hold by late afternoon. He'd carried me to bed and asked me whether I wanted him to stay.

Of course I'd wanted him to stay with me, but the old feeling of relying on him was creeping back. I've gone sixteen years without him, sixteen years of learning how to fend for myself, fight my own corner, and keep the insanity at bay. And now he's back, and I'm already indebted to him for my life. How the fuck did that happen? How did I lose control so quickly? So, I told him to go home. And I am still uncertain about what the future looks like for Cade and me.

As I scrape myself from under the duvet, my

phone rings. Cade's name appears on the screen as if he knows he's already in my head.

"Hey."

One word. One fucking word, and I'm melting.

"Good morning."

"How did you sleep?"

"Great, thanks. A little too well, if I'm honest." I glance at my clock, then rise from the bed and head to my closet, calculating what part of my morning routine I can skip so I won't be late.

"And how are you feeling?"

"Fine. Still a little groggy, but nothing a cup of coffee won't put right."

There's a pause as I select my white shirt and knee-length skirt.

"Maybe you should take the day off."

"No, I'm fine, honestly. I'll just be bored at home."

"You need to rest. You should take the day off."

Trying to button a shirt one-handed is not working, so I abandon the task and move into the bathroom. "And I've just said I'm fine. I want to be at work."

"Listen to me. It's too soon. You need a day off." His tone is sharp, and it pinches at my skin.

"If this is going to work between us, you can't just start telling me what to do. I've gone the last sixteen years making my own decisions. You can't expect to walk back into my life and take it over."

"I'm not telling you as your boyfriend. I'm telling

you as your employer that I think you need a day to rest."

Hearing him say "boyfriend" does something funny to my insides. It feels odd, out of place, something kids call each other. Is this what we decided? It all feels so surreal, and I'm not sure if this is the after-effects of the anaphylactic shock or the fact that Cade is in my life again.

"This is exactly why this is not going to work, because you're not just my boyfriend, you're also my boss."

"Lexie, let's just take a minute."

"How do you even think this will work?"

"Because it will."

"You seem so sure."

"That's because I am sure."

"We're not even twenty-four hours into this, and already we're arguing. We're supposed to be taking things slow, but how can we when we see each other every day?"

For a second, I think he's gone, the static on the line my only companion.

"It won't be for much longer."

Now it's my turn to be silent for a moment.

"What do you mean?"

"What I said. It won't be like this for much longer."

"I don't understand."

"I have to be in the office in less than thirty

minutes, and you do as well if you still want to come in, so I don't have time to explain now, but I will, I promise."

"Explain what?"

"This is difficult, and I don't want to do it over the phone or rush it. You have to trust me."

"Are you leaving? Are you handing in your notice? Is this because of me?" I rush out.

"Lexie, please. We'll talk about this tonight."

"Maybe we shouldn't talk about this at all. Maybe we just need to stop this fucking charade of a shitshow and call it quits now, because things are clearly not working here. You've gone all cryptic on me, and you don't trust me enough to tell me what's going on."

"It's because I trust you that I'm going to explain tonight, but I can't do it over the phone when we're both due at work."

"What if I can't wait until tonight?"

"Lunchtime, then. I'll take you out for lunch, and we can talk."

"Fine."

I hang up the phone in a blazing fury at how quickly things have escalated. What the hell is he playing at? What did he mean when he said it won't be a problem? He must be leaving, but why? Why would he sell the business? Or maybe he isn't selling but bringing someone else in to run the day-to-day stuff, or promoting Ian to office manager? Is he going back to one of his other branches?

My head spins as I try to make myself presentable. Any doubts about going to work are bulldozed by the prospect of what he has to tell me at lunchtime and how explosive his revelation is going to be. Will it spell the end of us when we've only just got back together? All I know at this point is, it's going to be a hell of a long morning.

***

OUR CRYPTIC CONVERSATION FOLLOWS ME TO WORK, where I pull into the car park to find someone in my regular space. Then I remember Ian telling me to avoid this area and suggesting I park on Town Street. Taking his advice, I swing my car around, earning myself a blaring car horn from an angry Vauxhall Corsa.

Town Street is busy, but I find a spot in between a red Golf and a silver Audi. My reverse parking skills aren't the best, but I manage to squeeze my car in after holding up the traffic in both directions for a long five minutes.

Arriving at the shop, I wonder how many people I've manage to piss off already today in such a small amount of time. And I know I'll have to fend off Donna and her one thousand questions, but I hadn't really prepared myself for the barrage she fires off as soon as I'm over the threshold.

How am I feeling?

Why haven't I answered any of her text messages and phone calls?

Why hadn't she known about my nut allergy?

When did they let me out of the hospital?

Did Cade stay with me?

What happened to Jess?

What the hell is going on between me and Cade?

That last one is the hardest to answer, as I don't fully know what's going on. Trying to dodge her questions, I find my desk at the back of the shop with Donna hot on my tail. Ian is on the phone and missing all the gossip as Cade steps out from behind his office door.

"Donna, do you have an update on the Queensbury property?"

She glares at him, well aware he's dismissing her. "I'll just grab it for you." She shimmies off to the front of the shop as Cade steps forward.

Lowering his head, he examines me, his eyes roaming over every part of me as if he's looking for a tiny cut or graze to justify sending me home.

"I tried to talk to Donna this morning about giving you some time."

"It worked. She gave me half a second before she started with the interrogation."

"Are you sure you should be here?"

"I've already told you—" I begin, but Cade cuts me off.

"Okay. Just as long as you know I'm here if you need me."

And that's the problem right there. I do need him, and I don't want to because it only leads to hurt, despair, and agony. I can't go through what I did before. I won't survive it a second time. I was younger then, my whole life still ahead of me, but now, things are different. I'm different. Fear trails down my spine at the thought of what he's going to tell me at lunchtime. He must be leaving. It can't be anything else. He's going to walk away, and I'm going to lose him all over again.

"Thanks," I grumble, sliding out of my jacket and hanging it on the back of my chair.

He stalks away, and I think he's gone, but then he quickly returns to place a cup of coffee on my desk, and I think I'm going to cry. Why does he do these things? How does he always know?

Sitting down, I start with a to-do list, dread building in my stomach over the fact that calling Mrs Wells is part of that list.

First off, I call the Larsons—a lovely young couple who viewed Mrs Wells's house on Friday. Then I call Mrs Wells, eager to get her out of the way. Thankfully, she doesn't answer, and it goes straight to voicemail, so I leave a short message. Moving on to my next job, I try to keep my thoughts from the man who is behind the closed door of his office and what the hell he's going to tell me at lunchtime.

After twenty minutes, several gulps of coffee, and striking three jobs off my list, I start to feel a little more grounded—until the door opens, and Mrs Wells arrives.

She's wearing a long coat and a cheap pair of women's trainers, and her wiry hair is as crazed as the look in her eyes. Striding past Ian, who straightens in his chair, and Donna, who is hovering next to Ian's desk whilst waiting for some paperwork, she makes a beeline for me.

"You." Her bony finger extends in my direction. "I want a word with you."

"Can *I* help you, Mrs Wells?" Donna begins, but I raise my hand.

"Thanks, but I got this, Donna." My lip curls. I'm ready for the old cow. Ever since she complained about me, I've been super polite and passive-aggressive to her complaints about her house not selling. But she's here now in the flesh, and my earlier anger is rekindling. I'm spoiling for a showdown.

"I'm sick and tired of your lies and your stupidity. Friday you told me the Larsons wanted to put an offer in. I've waited all weekend, not knowing what's going on, only for you to leave a voicemail not ten minutes ago telling me they've changed their minds and won't be putting an offer in." Her voice cracks with every syllable.

"They liked the house after the viewing but had a few reservations. I told them to sleep on it, and this morning they decided there was too much work that needed to be done, and they didn't have the budget for it."

"You talked them out of it."

"It goes against my job as a sales negotiator to talk people out of sales."

"You've had it in for me and my house ever since I complained to the manager about you. You don't want to sell my house."

"Believe me, Mrs Wells, there's nothing I want more than to sell your house and get it off my books."

"The insolence," she spits. "Always the wisecracks. You think you can get away with talking to me like this?"

"And how about the way you talk to me?"

"I beg your pardon?"

"Mrs Wells, why don't we—" Ian begins, but the door to Cade's office opens, and he strides onto the shop floor.

"Is there a problem here?" He dominates the space, his presence sucking the air out of the room.

"Yes, your staff are the problem. This woman is sabotaging the sale of my property, not to mention how rude and obnoxious she is."

"That makes two of us, then." My blood is simmering. I hate this woman with her stupid house and her fucking wire-wool hair. But most of all, I hate the way my heart bursts when Cade moves to stand next to me, the rush of adrenaline that lines my veins when his words pierce the air.

I hate the fact that I'm relieved he's here.

"I want her off my property." Mrs Wells stabs the air with her finger.

"Gladly," I declare as I scoop up her paperwork and throw it at her.

Silence accompanies the fluttering of paper.

Donna stares at me.

Ian stands awkwardly in the corner as I glare at Mrs Wells.

"Are you just going to stand there and let your staff behave this way?" Mrs Wells barks at Cade, but she doesn't let him answer before she continues. "I've never been spoken to the way I have by her. She's like an animal. She should be locked up."

"I think it's time you left." Cade's voice is low and threatening.

"I beg your pardon?"

"It's clear we aren't going to be able to sell your property. You might want to consider using a different estate agent." He steps forward, his huge frame ushering her from the shop, her head twitching as she faffs with her bag.

"But I-I…," she stammers, but she's at the door now, which Cade has opened for her. He's an immovable force, a barrier between the shop and the outside world.

"Goodbye, Mrs Wells." He guides her through the

open door and closes it firmly as soon as her feet are on the pavement.

Ian and Donna stare as Cade walks toward me. The atmosphere is thick, the heat in the air stirring the turbulence that circles me and him.

"My office."

He glares, but I stand my ground.

"No." I place my hands on my desk.

"Lexie," he warns, but I'm too riled up.

"Don't fucking 'Lexie' me."

Donna gasps from the corner.

"Don't look at me like that, and don't come any closer," I warn.

He stops.

I step out from behind my desk, my anger only just getting started. "I can't be here anymore," I tell him. "I can't do this."

"Lexie," Cade repeats.

"Mrs Wells can go fuck herself, and you can fucking join her because I'm sick of all this shit." I flip the stack of paperwork balanced on my desk, and the whole pile falls to the floor. "You think we can just pick up where we left off? We can't. I'm not that person anymore. This is the real me, and if you can't see it, then you're as blind as that fucking bitch who just walked out the door." Not sure whether I'm shaking or the floor beneath me is, I grab hold of the side of the desk.

Cade takes a step forward, his head down like he's approaching a feral dog. "Lexie," he utters.

It's enough to make me see red. I pull my arm back and launch it toward my computer screen just as he catches it midair, inches from the glass.

The silence is back.

"Leave us," Cade says to Ian and Donna without dropping my hand or looking back at them.

Ian doesn't argue, just grabs his jacket and makes his way to the door.

Donna hesitates. "Are you going to be okay?" she asks, hovering by her desk, not sure if she should leave me in Cade's hands.

"We'll be fine," he tells her, his eyes not leaving mine.

Donna grabs her bag and shuffles out the door, which Ian is holding open for her.

Once the door is closed, Cade drops my hand. My fingers tingle at their release. He strides over to the door and locks it, turns the Closed sign, then pulls the blind down, shielding us from the outside.

He walks back over to me.

"You want a fight, then give me your best shot," he says, taking his jacket off and slinging it over my desk before unbuttoning the cuffs on his shirt.

I glare at him.

"Come on. This is what you've been spoiling for all morning. You want to punch something, then go ahead. If it'll make you feel better, be my guest." He rolls his sleeves up, tucking the material in to reveal his firm, tattooed arms.

"Fuck you," I spit.

"Gladly," he goads.

"You really want to go there?"

"Are you telling me you don't? Haven't you been wondering what it would be like after all this time? I've been picturing it for sixteen years. Don't tell me you haven't been doing the same."

"We can't." My head shakes as if trying to stop his words from entering my brain where they'll take root and grow.

"Why not?"

"Because it won't be the same. It can never be the same."

"Why?"

"You know why."

"Because of what happened in your kitchen? Lexie, you need to let it go. I have; otherwise, I would never have slept with anyone ever again, and I wasn't about to give your mum that power. She doesn't deserve it."

"But how can you just forget?"

"You don't forget. You replace it with new memories."

I shake my head. "I'm not like you. You've had help."

"What do you think I'm doing now, Lexie?"

"It's been too long. You don't know me anymore, just like I don't know you, and that's the problem. This is never going to work."

"You're scared. I get it. But you gotta stop pushing me away, Lexie."

"Stop calling me Lexie. I hate it. I hate it, and I hate you." Tears stream down my face, my body shaking as my words slip out weakly.

"You don't hate me. You hate a lot of things, but you don't hate me."

"I hate you and Jess and how she's fixed you. I hate how fucking perfect you are and how you always know what to do and what to say. I hate the way you look at me, the way you make me feel. I hate that I can't get you out of my head and the fact that no one will ever match up to you. I'm fucking doomed, all because of you. I'm the daughter of a monster. I hate who she was, and more than anything, I hate what she did to you. And now you're back, and I owe you my life, and I want you so badly that it hurts, but I'm scared it won't last. You and I were not destined to be together; otherwise, we would've never been torn apart."

I bolt for the door. He catches me and spins me around, his arms closing over my body and restraining my arms by my sides. I continue to push. We stumble over to the wall, Cade's back hitting it with a thud. He holds me tighter as I squirm in his arms.

"Listen to me, Lexie," he growls in my ear, his voice calm and commanding. "Stop fighting it. You're going to self-destruct if you keep battling the inevitable. I am here. Get used to it, as I'm not going anywhere. So, let me help you. I can take it all away. Only I can ease your pain. You know I can. I've done it before, and I can do it again. You need to trust me."

His words burrow under my skin and ripple through my nerves like an electrical current on high voltage. My body is stiff as I try to shield myself from him, but it's useless.

His breath brushes the side of my face, and I let myself wonder what it would be like to feel his touch again—not the boy I knew and loved, but Cade the Man.

My shoulders drop.

His right hand slides over my stomach.

"That's it, Lexie. Let me help you." His hand continues down my skirt, smooth and purposeful until he reaches the hem. "You want this. I know you too well. If I'm wrong, then tell me to stop, and I will."

My mouth clamps shut as my body relaxes. There's no fight left in me. I don't have the strength. My head rests against his chest, my eyes close, and I know this will be my undoing.

"That's it. Good girl." His hand roams over my thigh, stoking the heat brewing inside me before dipping between my legs. I bite my lip as he tugs my underwear to one side, the rush of air to my exposed skin only adding to my need.

It's nothing like what I remember. His fingers are more purposeful as he parts me and circles my clit. Pleasure shoots through me that is so powerful, I can't help but gasp, air leaving my lungs like it's been bulldozed out of me.

"You've forgotten, haven't you?" He continues to massage me as my hips begin to writhe against his hand.

"No."

"I think you have, so I'm going to have to remind you of what it feels like—what *I* feel like."

When his fingers dip inside me, my legs buckle, and we slide to the floor, Cade keeping hold of me with his other arm. Pushing my bottom against his crotch, I can feel how hard he is, how aroused, but he continues to pay attention to me and only me.

He thrusts his fingers deep inside me as his thumb continues to circle my clit, sending waves of pure bliss through my entire body.

"You remember now, don't you."

"I've never forgotten." My voice is husky against my deep breaths, my head swimming in a pool of pleasure as I grind against his hand.

"No one will have made you feel the way I can. No one knows your body like I do. No one will have touched you like I do, and no one will make you come the way I can."

Fuck. I'm on the brink of delirium, his fingers, his words, his presence all working me into a state of unbridled glory, yet I don't want to do it this way.

It takes all my effort to pull his hand away. I turn to face him on my hands and knees, my body on fire and throbbing for him.

For a split second, there's confusion on his face. I lick my lips, my panting having dried them out.

"Not without you," I tell him, and the sly grin that spreads across his face nearly sends me over the edge.

Gripping my chin in one hand, he kisses me whilst unfastening his belt with the other one. My eyes drop, my lips leaving his, and I stare as he pulls himself from the confines of his pants.

Fuck.

He's grown in more ways than one.

"Can you take it, Lexie?"

I nod, uncertainty pooling in my stomach.

"Then turn around," he tells me.

I do as I'm told.

He pushes my skirt up over my bottom, sliding his hand over my smooth skin and squeezing my cheeks before I feel him enter me from behind, his hands now gripping my waist.

"Oh my God," I gasp as he fills me.

Slow at first, he starts to fuck me with long, hard thrusts that make me cry out.

God, I've missed this. I never thought it could be

better than what we had, but he's stronger, bigger, firmer.

He twists my hair in his hand and pulls me up so my back is against his chest. Keeping hold of my hair, he works my clit with his other hand.

"Fuck!" I cry as the ecstasy mounts. I was close before, but this is something else.

"Face me, Lexie," he tells me. "I want to see you when you come."

He withdraws quickly, and I spin around and straddle him, desperate to get him back inside me. Why have I been fighting this? Why have I been so afraid of this? It's nothing like when we were younger. This is primal, desperate, and so fucking hot.

Linking my fingers behind his neck, I gaze into the eyes I've longed to be looking at for the past sixteen years.

It's too much.

It's all too much.

He thrusts into me, once, twice, three times—and then I lose count with the way he's pounding away at me ferociously as if ensuring I'll remember what every inch of him feels like. And then I shatter, my whole body shuddering against his, his cock thickening inside me as I feel the warmth of his release. We cling to each other, our breathing mirrored, our bodies depleted.

Holding each other tight, we stay like this, my inner core still shaking, my legs feeling like I've run a marathon. Then I feel the wetness pooling around the base of his cock.

"Shit." Glancing down between us, Cade leans over and grabs the jacket he threw over my desk, pulls it toward us, and fishes a packet of tissues out of the pocket.

Carefully, he lowers me back onto the floor, lifting my legs as he slides himself out of me, then places a tissue against me and gently begins to clean me up before bending down and kissing my clit so softly, it brings tears to my eyes. He nips at my bud, and a tremor runs through my already exhausted core.

"How do you feel now?" he whispers, his breath tickling my inner thighs.

"Fucked."

He pulls his head back, a grin lighting his devious face. "That was the idea." Gazing at me, he wipes himself. "And what were you thinking about when I was fucking you, Lexie?"

Meeting his stare, I reply, "You."

"That's right. Me. It'll always be me who claims your thoughts, your body, and your pleasure. Me and only me."

"It's always been you."

Leaning over me, he runs his hand down my cheek. "And it'll stay that way until we take our dying breaths." He brushes his lips against mine, and a new rush of desire awakens as his tongue dips into my mouth. Releasing my head, he slides his hand down between my legs, and I yelp when his fingers dip inside me.

"So fucking wet still, Lexie. What am I going to do with you?"

"We have sixteen years to make up."

"And we will make them up," he tells me as his fingers sink deeper. "Every last hour, minute, and second, we will spend making up all the time we've lost together. I'll make sure of it."

A groan escapes me, his fingers picking up speed as his thumb circles my clit.

"This is just the start, a taste of what's to come when we're confined to the shop floor. Just wait until I get you in my bedroom, where I can tie you to my bed and use your body for as long as I want. I will make you come over and over again until you've forgotten every single day I wasn't with you."

I grind my hips against his hand. I'm unsure of what's doing the most damage, his relentless fingers or his words.

"Do you want me to fuck you again?"

"Yes," I whimper.

"Yes, what?"

"Yes, please. Now. Please. Now." I rake my fingers down his spine, and he moves back.

Grabbing my ankles, he spreads my legs and fucks me hard until my eyes water and the ceiling starts to spin.

"Oh my God." I can't reach him now, so I grip the

backs of my thighs, helping to spread my legs wider. He pounds against me, every thrust filling me so completely that I think I'm going to cry.

"Say it, Lexie. I won't let you come until you scream my name. We don't need to be quiet anymore, no need for me to smother your cries. So, let it out."

I groan, but it's more in annoyance at how he's toying with me. And he knows this.

"How long can you last?" he asks. "I can do this for hours. I can keep you here like this for as long as it takes, but if you want to come, you need to say my name."

He withdraws completely, leaving me wild and furious, and I know he's going to win. He always wins. Cade the Winner.

"For God's sake, Cade, just fuck me already."

"What was that? I didn't quite hear you?"

Placing the tip of his cock at my entrance, he stares at me, and then a smile laces his mouth that I suddenly want to bite. The burning throbs between my legs, and I place my hand against my clit, which Cade bats away. "Oh no you don't. Not until I say. Not until I tell you. Not until you say my name."

"I'll scream your name when you fuck me like you said you would."

"You're so fucking greedy, Lexie. So demanding. How can I refuse you when you're spread out for me and so close to coming?"

On his last word, he pushes his cock all the way in, and I cave. "Cade!"

As soon as his name leaves my lips, his thumb finds my clit. Light erupts around me, the room spins, and my body shatters into a thousand tiny pieces as my orgasm rips through me.

Lying on the hard shop floor, I wonder if I'm dead and this is heaven, Cade in between my open legs, my body devoured and depleted.

"If you expect me to work now, you're sadly mistaken," I tell him.

"I hope you're fit for nothing." He grabs another tissue from the packet and cleans me up again as I press my legs together to abate the heat that remains.

"I don't even think I can stand."

"Then don't." He stands up, fastens his trousers, then scoops me up and places me in my chair before retrieving my underwear.

I stand up, too, and he pulls my knickers up, kissing my pubic bone before pulling back and smoothing my skirt back down.

I flop back in the chair, my legs still weak.

"It goes against all my instinct to put your clothes back on you."

"We can't open the shop if I'm not dressed."

"I couldn't give a flying fuck about the shop right now."

Neither could I, but the thought of Donna and Ian niggles me.

"What if Donna and Ian are outside? What if they heard us?" It's like being a teenager all over again and worrying if my mum and Mark had heard us.

"I hope the whole town heard us."

"Oh, God." Smothering my face with my hands, I let my head dip forward.

"Hey, I know I'm good, but a god? Do you want to put me on that pedestal?"

Dropping my hands, I bat the side of his arm. "You know that's not what I meant. I have to face both of them."

"Don't worry about it. You're thinking too much about this."

"This?" I ask. "And what is this exactly?"

Cade squats in front of me, trailing his fingers up the side of my arm. "This is where we remind ourselves of what we had, how fucking good it was, and how we belong together."

Biting my lip, I gaze at him. "I thought it would be awkward."

"And was it?"

"No." It's as if he's still inside me, like he's left a part of himself rooted in my core. "It was a lot of things, but awkward wasn't one of them."

"And I haven't even started yet." His eyes glaze as if all the delicious things he's going to do to me are flashing before him.

I want to slide off the chair and let him do them, everything, all of it, every last goddamn thing he can think of, because he's right—we belong together, and I need to stop fighting the inevitable.

Rolling his sleeves back down, he glances at his watch.

"Got to be somewhere?"

"I have a viewing in fifteen minutes." He grimaces.

"Back to the real world." I smirk, but he just stares at me.

"You are my world, Lexie." Holding out his hand, he pulls me up before he edges toward the door.

"Cade."

He stops and turns.

"Promise me this is it. You and me. This is us forever. I can't lose you again. I can't go through that pain. It has to be all or nothing."

He strides back over and pulls me into his chest, cradling my head. His heart thunders in my ear. Sinking into his warmth, I place my hand on his chest.

"You are my all. You are my everything, and it would take an apocalypse to tear me from you. From now on, wherever you go, I go. Together."

"I never stopped loving you." The fabric of his shirt is soft against my lips.

He pulls back and cups my head in his hands. "I will spend the rest of our days showing you just how much I love you."

The phone rings.

I tut, tearing myself from Cade's arms.

"Answer that, and I'll go let the rabble back in."

Summoning my most professional phone voice, I pick up the phone whilst watching Cade walk over to the door.

He's perfect. Every inch of him. He's my safe place. My home. My heart.

And he's mine.

All mine.

FORTY-EIGHT
ALEX

"I'm only going to ask you if you're okay. Are you?" Donna asks when Cade has left.

I'm perched at my desk, trying to remember how to do my job. "I'm fine. Really."

Her scowl remains. "And you and Cade?"

"You said one question."

"I never specified the number of questions. Come on, Alex. You can't expect me just to sit back and ignore everything that's happened over the last few days. I worry about you."

"Seriously?"

"We've worked together for a long time. I spend more time with you than I do my husband, which sometimes is a blessing, and you can't say that if this was reversed, you wouldn't be worrying about me."

She's got me there, and she knows it.

"Besides, you make great coffee, and I'd hate to be left with just Ian for company."

"Hey, I'm fine. Why are you talking like I'm going somewhere?"

"Just with the fight between you and Cade and then you showing up with Shawn Bowling, I thought you were leaving us and going over to the dark side." She twists the hair elastic she wears around her wrist in case of emergencies.

"Things have been pretty weird lately—well, ever since Cade arrived—but I can assure you, we've sorted things out, and hopefully, things will settle down a bit now."

Her stare almost pins me to the back of my chair.

"And I'm not leaving."

"And you and Cade?" she repeats.

"Cade and I are… a thing."

The hair elastic snaps against her skin. "I knew it. I knew something was going on between you two. Ian owes me twenty quid now."

"What?"

"We had a bet on that something was going on with you two. He reckoned I was just trying to create some drama, but I knew I was right. I saw it the first day he arrived. I've never seen you look like that before. It was as if someone had turned you inside out."

The image turns my stomach, as does the fact that they've been making bets on my life, but I'm still too focused on the euphoric high of Cade and two orgasms to let this bite me. "I'm glad my life has been providing you guys with some entertainment."

"Hey, don't take offence. Nothing ever happens around here anyway, so you've been a huge scoop." Twisting the hair elastic back on her wrist, Donna shifts her weight from one foot to the other. "So… are you going to spill the beans?"

In response, I raise my eyebrow.

"Where and when did you meet? What's the history here?"

Giving in, I provide her with enough to let her sleep tonight. "We were high school sweethearts. Then we broke up due to Cade moving away. It was tough. I missed him."

"So, how long…?" Her brow furrows, trying to do the math.

"Sixteen years. We hadn't seen each other in sixteen years."

"And then he walked through our door, just like that, and you were none the wiser. Did he know you worked here?"

"No. He was as shocked as I was."

"It's like stuff from a movie. So romantic."

"Yeah, well. This isn't a movie, and we both have work to do."

"Say, how's it going to work with you and Cade working together?"

Glancing at the clock, I remember that he has

something to tell me at lunchtime that will supposedly solve that little conundrum.

"I don't know. I guess we'll figure it out."

"Donna, Mr Carson is on the line for you," Ian hollers from the front of the shop.

She rolls her eyes.

"He wants to know why you haven't spoken to his solicitor this week," he adds.

"Because his solicitor is in the Canary Islands, sunning her beautiful backside, which is where I should be right now." Donna clicks her tongue and slides behind her desk, then picks up her phone and patches the call through.

The vibrating noise from my phone breaks into my thoughts as I glance down at my bag sitting under my desk.

Cade. It has to be.

I rescue my phone from the depths of my bag, then stare at the screen, my stomach rolling in on itself.

The call is from Shawn.

FORTY-NINE

ALEX

Shawn.

In my Cade-filled weekend, I'd forgotten all about him.

Shawn has always known our agreement is nothing more than physical, but it's still something I'm going to have to end, and ending it suggests there has to have been something there in the first place. Why does this feel like a break-up? Why do I feel like I'm going to have to let him down gently? Why do I feel like the bad guy here?

Like pulling a plaster off, I answer his call as I scoot into the small toilet at the back of the shop. "Hey."

"Alex." There's a pause like he knows what's coming before he adds, "Where are you?"

How are you, Alex? Are you feeling better? Are you out of

the hospital? He doesn't ask any of the questions a normal, functioning person would ask even if they didn't really care about the answer. But I've never expected him to be anything more than subhuman scum because that was all I would allow myself to have, all I thought I deserved.

I was wrong.

"I'm in the toilet at work, if you must know, and I'm fine, thanks for asking."

"What?" The line crackles. "Oh, yeah. Are you okay?"

"Yes, fine. What do you want?"

"I need a favour."

"What kind of favour?"

"I'm supposed to be doing a viewing in twenty minutes, and some dickhead van driver has blocked my car in. I can't fucking move."

"Can't you get one of your minions to do the viewing?"

"No. Leon is in the shop on his own, as Carol has gone home sick. There's no one; otherwise, I wouldn't be asking."

"Can't you cancel? If they want the house, they'll rebook."

"Fuck, Alex—no, I can't rebook them."

His voice is high and laced with anger, and I'm puzzled as to why he seems so agitated about this viewing.

"This is important. It's an important viewing.

We've let them down before, and I don't want to mess them around again."

Since when did Shawn Bowling grow a conscience and care about his customers? Maybe it's a big property they've been having trouble selling. Maybe there's big commission to be had.

"Where is it?"

"It's on Mason Way. You are literally five minutes away."

I know Mason Way. The houses are average, nothing to get your pants in a twist about, so why the fuss? The last thing I want to do is waste half an hour of my time showing some people around a house that will earn me no commission, but I have yet to tell Shawn that we can't see each other anymore, that our thing is now not a thing and will never be a thing ever again. If I do this for him, it might soften the blow and allow me to sleep a little easier tonight.

"Okay."

"Alex, you're a fucking lifesaver."

"What's the house number?"

"Thirty-eight, and the key is in a key safe on the wall, code 1617."

"Okay."

"Alex, before you go, just listen to me."

My hand rests on the door handle, my phone clamped to my ear as I note the change in Shawn's voice.

"The people who are viewing the property don't

like to be followed around the house. Just let them in and wait in the kitchen until they're done."

"Are you sure?" How am I supposed to sell the house to them if I can't go around with them and point out the features of the property? Then I remember this is not my account, not my sale, and not my commission. Why should I care if Shawn sells this house or not?

"Yes. Don't engage with them."

"What?"

"Just listen, Alex, and do as I say. They can be a bit funny, and I don't mean comedy-wise. Just let them in and give them some space. Can you do that?"

"Sure."

"Thanks. I'll meet you there as soon as this arsehole moves his fucking van." Shawn ends the call.

What the hell is going on? The only thing I do know is that I've just saved his ass, so when I end things with him, I hope he'll consider this.

I leave the bathroom, grab my jacket off the back of my chair, and head to the front of the shop.

"Bit early for lunch, isn't it?" Donna asks as I pass her desk.

"I wish." My stomach growls at the lack of food, my escapades with Cade having unleashed a raging hunger. "I'm going to do a viewing."

She raises an eyebrow. "Great. Happy selling."

Guilt-ridden relief pinches at my skin that she

doesn't ask which property. I don't want to lie to her, but I don't have time to explain where I'm going or what I'm doing. I can confess later when, hopefully, Shawn will be off my books for good.

FIFTY

ALEX

Mason's Way could be any housing estate in the North of England. The bottom of the road is made up of regular semidetached houses all built circa 1960, but the top end of the road has a smattering of detached properties that have been renovated or extended over the years. The street itself is lined with giant symmetrical sycamore trees that, judging by the size, must predate all the houses.

Number thirty-eight is a detached house in need of a lot of TLC. The red paint on the front door looks like a bad case of eczema, the paint having flaked off onto the porch that has seen better days. The windows appear black, as if there's nothing inside the house, and the garden is an overgrown paradise for all the local wildlife. The For Sale sign is propped up in the garden, something I'm shocked that Shawn hasn't rectified. I wonder how long this house has been on the market and what he isn't doing to sell this house. It could be a big earner with a lick of paint, a good lawn-mower, and a few repairs.

Unsure of what will greet me inside, I unlock the key safe and push the brass key into the lock.

As expected, the interior is as neglected as the exterior, with the smell of dampness adding to the experience. Why has Shawn not met with the vendor and talked about how to present this property? The vendor could be abroad. Sometimes people inherit houses in different countries and have no vested interest in selling the house quickly and are happy to let it sit on the market for as long as it takes to sell. In my line of work, I find it hard to understand why someone would not want to reap the benefits of selling a valuable house.

The kitchen is down the hall at the rear of the property, and I'm surprised to find it in a better state of repair than the rest of the house. The units are old, with dark cherry wood cabinets and black mica work-surfaces coupled with magnolia walls, but it doesn't look as neglected as I'd expected. Resisting the urge to clean the place up a bit, I prop myself against the worktop and pull out my phone, checking the time before the potential buyers are due to arrive. There's a text from Cade.

> I'll be back for lunchtime. Where do you want to eat? I love you.

Even through the font of the screen, those three little words filter through the wall of my heart and embed themselves there.

Is this the beginning?

Is this the start of the life Cade and I should've had all those years ago?

Pressing the handset to my chest, I wonder where he is now and what he would say if he knew I was helping Shawn out.

***

Cade

From my vantage point behind the wheel of my car, I watch Shawn Bowling pacing the ground, his shoes almost smoking at the rate he's stomping.

His car is in a small car park belonging to a Tesco Express he'd stopped at on his way back from who knows where. He'd bought a can of Diet Coke, a bag of Doritos, and a Mars bar, but when he'd returned to his car, a large white van had blocked Shawn's small sports car in, the van driver oblivious.

Needless to say, Shawn is not a happy bunny, and the pavement and his phone appear to be taking the brunt of his anger right now. He's made several calls—

to whom, I'm not sure—but all I can think of as I watch him pace the tarmac is how he had slapped Lexie's bottom on Friday night and how much I want to rip that fucking arm from his body.

And I will.

Maybe not today.

But soon.

FIFTY-ONE
ALEX

AT ELEVEN FIFTEEN, I GO BACK THROUGH THE HALL and wait outside the property. I have the details of the house up on my phone via Shawn's website just in case they ask me any questions. They arrive a few minutes later, and I hope my surprise doesn't show on my face.

When you've done the job as long as I have, you get to know buyers and the type of people who will be interested in the property you're showing them. This is a large house with the potential to be a great family home. I'd expected a young couple, an executive with a passion for a big project, or arty-type people with long hair and thick-rimmed glasses who can see past the dirt and grime and envision their dream house. But the couple I am smiling at does not resemble either of these stereotypes.

She's thin. Way too thin, her face gaunt like she hasn't seen a good meal in at least three years. Her hair is lank, a dirty blonde making her look even paler than she is. And the man is built like a brick shithouse, his leather jacket straining over his huge shoulders, his skinhead so tanned, it appears as if he's been abroad for weeks. They walk separately, as if they aren't really together and don't really want to converse, let alone stand next to each other.

"Hi, I'm Alex from the agency," I begin, extending my hand toward the woman, but she looks straight at the man as he says, "Where's Shawn?"

His voice is like rusty corrugated iron, and I want to slap my hands over my ears, but ignoring my instincts to run a mile, I widen my smile and explain. "Shawn has been caught up with something, so he sent me instead. I'm more than happy to show you around the property."

The man eyes me with what can only be described as curiosity before glancing back at the woman, who hasn't taken her eyes off him.

"You want to show us around the property?"

The way he repeats my words makes me feel as if we're speaking different languages and struggling to understand each other.

"If you like, or you can look around on your own." Remembering what Shawn said, I quickly add, "Whichever you feel more comfortable with."

The man chews on the side of his mouth as if he's stored some old gum there and had forgotten about it until now before turning back to me and laughing.

There's nothing remotely funny about this man's laugh, and I have to force the smile this time to appear as if I'm in on the joke. What the hell has Shawn involved me in? None of this feels right, and I'm starting to wonder what the game is here.

"I think we can find our own way around, Alex."

And with that, the pair almost push past me and make their way into the house, leaving me standing on the broken path.

I don't even bother to follow them, as I don't want to share the same air space as them, and I don't give a damn what they're up to in there. Instead, I call Shawn, but he doesn't answer, and I hope to God he's on his way over here like he said on the phone, as I don't want to have to spend a second longer than I have to with these two goons.

Cade

The van driver finally returns, and Shawn's anger evaporates when he clocks his impressive shoulders and bulging arm muscles.

The driver appears to be apologising, shaking his head, and holding his hands up in the air. Shawn seems to react like it's no big deal as he slinks back to his tiny sports car. I don't need to lipread to know the obscenities Shawn is spewing in the safety of his car as he waits for the van to move so he can drive away.

Shawn is difficult to tail, as his driving is erratic, and he gives no signals to let other drivers know his intentions. But I manage to keep up with him even though I'm hoping his next rendezvous will be quick enough so I can go and meet Lexie for lunch.

My stomach sinks, and not at the thought of food.

It's time to tell her what's been going on, and I'm not sure how she's going to take the news. What if she doesn't understand? What then?

Alex

As quickly as they arrived, the strange couple leaves, brushing past me as I hover in the front garden. There's no way they've been in there long enough to look properly at the house. Just when I think they're about to walk off without saying anything, the man turns around.

"Tell Shawn we missed him, and he'd better be here in person next time." The pair take off down the road, the woman struggling to keep up with the man's giant strides.

Turning, I look at the house as if it might be able to tell me what's going on here.

Shaking my head at no one, I make my way back

inside, wondering if there are any clues they've left behind.

After scouting the house and finding nothing of any interest, I return to the kitchen as the front door opens. A tiny trickle of fear simmers that the strange couple have returned, but then I hear Shawn's voice.

"Alex?"

"In the kitchen."

He appears in the doorway, slightly out of breath as if he's run all the way here.

"Have they been?"

"If you're referring to Tweedledum and Tweedledee, then yes, they've gone."

"Shit. Did they say anything?" He glances around the kitchen as if they might still be here hiding in a cupboard, ready to leap out and shout, "Surprise!"

"Only that they missed you and you'd better be here in person next time."

"Fuck." Pushing his hand through his thinning hair, he takes a step back.

"What the fuck is going on here, Shawn? Who were those people? Because they sure as shit weren't house buyers."

"It's nothing, honestly. Just business—nothing to worry your pretty little head about."

I'm about to bite back when he fires his next question.

"Did you go around the house with them?"

"No. I stayed outside."

"Good."

"I don't know what's going on here, and quite frankly, I don't want to know. But I'm done here." I push off on my feet, aiming for the doorway when Shawn moves to block me.

"What's the rush?"

"What?"

He edges closer. "Do you have somewhere to be? It's been a long weekend, and the house is empty."

The penny drops.

"Absolutely not." I put my hand up in front of him. "I have to get back to work."

"Tonight, then."

I'd almost forgotten my original intention in doing this favour, the two goons having rattled me into distraction. But now I have no choice but to address this and get it over and done with.

"Not tonight and not ever. This has to stop. Now. Today."

He leans back, his arms outstretched in a questioning stance. "What are you saying? I mean, I think I know what you're saying, but I need to be sure I heard you right."

"You knew the deal, Shawn, so don't act all surprised. It's always just been a convenient arrangement between us and nothing more. We never promised each other anything, never asked for anything more, so we've not lost anything here."

"But that's not true, Alex. You were the one who

invited me to your work gathering. You were the one who introduced me to your colleagues. You were the one who put this into a whole new ballpark, and now you're saying you want out?"

"I'm sorry about that, I truly am. I didn't intend for it to appear that way, and I thought you were on the same wavelength as I am that it was just to ruffle some feathers."

"Is that all I am, then? A feather ruffler? Someone you can use for your own gain and then kick to the kerb when it suits?"

"No, no, that's not what this is. Fuck, Shawn, you've always known what this is. We both have." It's when my back hits the worktop that I realise he's been inching forward, slowly boxing me in.

"This is about your new boss, isn't it?"

"No."

"Oh, I think it is. I was there on Saturday night. I saw how he was with you. You've been fucking him, haven't you? I should've known. You dirty little fucking whore."

I go to push past him, but he grabs hold of my wrist and pulls me back toward the worktop as he grasps my other arm. "Oh no you don't."

"Get the fuck off me!" My shout scrapes the back of my throat as my heart pounds in my chest and fear pulls at my insides.

This isn't happening.

This is Shawn.

I've known him for months. I've had him in my bed. I don't need to fear him.

So why am I suddenly so afraid?

"You don't get to walk away from me. You don't get to tell me this is over. *I* say when it's over. *I* tell you when I'm done with you, and I'm not quite finished. Not yet."

Straining my arms against his vicelike grip, I decide to go for the low shot, but as I raise my knee, he anticipates my move and nudges my leg to the side, nearly toppling me before planting a head-butt on me that makes my stomach roll.

The room fractures before my eyes, breaking into tiny little pieces as pain travels across my forehead and down into my face.

"Stupid bitch. Did you think you could get away with a sly kick to the balls?" He presses himself against me.

The worktop digs into my back as I keep trying to wriggle my hands free from his grasp. I try to blink the black splodges away that have appeared in my vision. As I do, he lets go of one of my wrists, and I'm about to charge when he pulls a pocketknife out of his trousers.

Flashing the blade in front of my face, he laughs. "I could cut you right here." He drags the flat of the blade down the side of my cheek. "I'm not sure the new boss man would appreciate his plaything having a great big dirty cut down her face, now would he?"

My throat constricts, air not going in nor coming out. The cold blade pushes against my skin, and I feel the stab of pain.

"Now fucking behave yourself; otherwise, I'll make you look like the fucking Joker."

Letting go of my other wrist, the blade still tight against my cheek, he begins to unfasten his belt, and all I can think about is Cade.

I've gone over and over in my head how all those years ago my mum managed to strip Cade of all his fight, how she managed to get him to heel so easily, so effectively. No blade required, no gun to his head, no blinding head-butt. Just words. Threats. Things she promised she would do that would ruin his life. And I've always come back to the scenario wishing he'd fought more. That he'd taken the risk and pushed her away, knowing we could've dealt with it after.

But here I am, a tiny blade to my face, my head a spinning mess, about to endure exactly what Cade did sixteen years ago.

FIFTY-TWO
CADE

Shawn pulls into Mason's Way, which I know to be a cul-de-sac, so I park my car on the corner and pursue him on foot.

I'm hoping this is going to be the last meeting, the one where I can finish this once and for all. I check the time. It's almost lunchtime, and Lexie will be expecting me to call.

Shawn disappears into one of the detached houses at the top of the street, and I hang back. Déjà vu hits me, and I don't know why, but I feel like I've been here before, stalking the streets, waiting for the right moment.

Then it hits me.

I have been here before. Not this street, but here all the same.

Shaking off the feeling, I put it down to nostalgia and what Lexie and I had done in the shop this morning. Surely it's just old feelings and memories being rekindled. It's only natural that things will come flooding back, just as Lexie said they would.

So why do I have the feeling Jacquelin is lurking around the corner?

Pressing a little further to the property, I remind myself why I'm here and angle my phone to get some good shots of anyone leaving the house—and that's when I spot it on the curve of the road, right in the far corner, and my stomach drops.

Lexie's car.

Alex

So, I fight.

I reach up and grab Shawn's hand, the one that's holding the blade, and angle it toward his face. The whites of his eyes flash as he spits in my face, knowing what I'm trying to do.

As I screw my eyes shut against the thick saliva now stuck to my face, Shawn laughs. "I don't think so," he snarls as we enter an arm wrestle, him trying to push the blade toward my face and me trying to push it toward his.

I blink repeatedly, trying to clear my vision as my hand lands in his hair. I pull. He then throws his body forward, slamming the base of my spine into the worktop, all the air rushing from my lungs. He grabs hold of my free hand with his other one and twists it behind my back, pain searing behind my eyes and burning my shoulder.

"I never pegged you liking the rough stuff. Just shows what I know, doesn't it?"

His breath is like battery acid as it slides down the side of my face along with the remaining saliva. I grind my teeth against the hurt, tears springing at the pain in my back, head, and arms.

I can't give in.

I won't give in.

This can't be how it ends.

If Cade were here now, he'd be begging me to fight back just like I begged him sixteen years ago.

With a feral rage, I open my mouth and bite Shawn's cheek.

Blood gushes into my mouth, and I gag as his scream fills the kitchen. One of his hands shoots up to his face as he wobbles backward, and I brace myself, ready to run, but then he glares at me, a rabid grin elongating his face as blood runs down the side of his cheek, the ugly bite mark stark and fresh.

"I'm done playing now." He takes a step forward, and I know I'm fucking done for.

Cade

I run.

I don't think. Just run.

My phone is in my hand, and I'm dialling her, hoping to God she answers and tells me off for being late and wanting to know where we're going for lunch, but it just rings as I run up a street I could've sworn had not been this long two minutes ago.

The call tone blares in my ear as I push up the broken path and slam into the front door of number thirty-eight. As I run down the hallway, the dial tone gets drowned out by the sound of her phone ringing from the room at the end of the hallway.

This is not my memory, yet it feels like it is. I'd always wondered what Lexie must've thought, must've felt as she'd walked down her hallway, my phone going off in her kitchen, not knowing what awaited her on the other side of the door, how it would change our lives forever.

This time, I'm ready. I'm prepared, and I will not let whatever I find destroy us again.

Alex

We stand there like the bull and the matador, and I'm

not sure who is which, but Shawn sees red as his eyes blaze and his nostrils flare.

There's an unearthly atmosphere swarming us, one I've felt before, sixteen years ago when I stood in a kitchen similar to this one, my life irrevocably changed by the actions of my mother. The parallel is eerie, even down to the haunting ringtone playing in the background as a ghost of suppressed memories claws at my headspace. And it feels so real. All of this. Even though I know this has to be a nightmare.

Then Shawn lunges.

His hands wrap around my throat, pushing what remaining air I have out of my mouth. Digging my nails into the backs of his hands, I claw at his grip, scratching, scraping—anything to try and get him off me. The room tilts. My vision blurs as Shawn's manic eyes blaze into mine.

Black spots swim, Shawn's face swirling and then morphing into my mother's.

I don't want to see either of them. If this is the last thing I'm going to see, it can't be them.

Cade.

Closing my eyes, I think of Cade, of that day sixteen years ago when he was on the receiving end. And I see it differently now.

What would've happened if I hadn't walked into the kitchen when I did?

What else would he have endured?

What scars would my mother have inflicted upon him if I hadn't arrived when I had?

I wasn't the cause. I wasn't to blame.

I saved him.

Cade is right. We have to replace our memories with good ones, and that's what I see now — that it wasn't the day that ruined our lives.

It was the day I saved his.

My legs buckle, my chest burns, and my heart slows as I wonder who will save mine.

FIFTY-THREE

CADE

I burst into the kitchen to find Shawn Bowling squeezing the life out of Lexie.

My Lexie.

"I told you, if you touch her again, I will fucking kill you." The words don't feel like mine as I grab him by the scruff of his neck.

I pull him away from her and land the hardest fucking punch I've ever delivered into the side of his head. He goes down before he even fully registers that I'm here. Kicking him to the side, I reach out to Lexie, who is sliding to the floor, her face ghostly white, her lips blue, and her eyes unfocused as she gasps for air.

"I'm here. You're safe. I'm here." Scooping her up, I try not to look at the redness around her neck or the way she gulps the air. I can't or I will kill him. I will strangle the fucking life out of him until he's died a thousand times over.

But I won't because Lexie needs me more than I need to kill him.

I kick out a chair and place her on it, helping her to catch her breath.

"Cade." It's a whisper, faint and hoarse, but it's there, my name on her lips, the only thing she wants to say with her scant amount of oxygen.

"Shh, don't try to talk. Just breathe. I'm here now. I'm here, and I'm not going anywhere. You're safe now."

I know this part. I can remember how I felt when Lexie walked into her kitchen and saved me from Jacquelin and what she was about to put me through. I loved Lexie. Had always loved her, but in that instant, she was my saviour. She was my rescuer, and my love tripled for her in that blinding instant when she was there when I needed her, just like I'm here now.

Lexie reaches out to me, her hands shaking as the tears start to fall.

Pressing her head into my chest, I hold her, pushing down my anger at the fucking excuse of a man laid out cold on the floor.

As Lexie cries, I place my phone to my ear and wait for an answer.

"Hi, it's Cade. We have a slight situation. I suggest you come and help deal with it. Thirty-eight Mason's Way." I end the call and shove my phone back in my pocket. Then I continue to hold the only person who I've ever truly loved.

Alex

He's real.

There'd been a moment when I thought I'd conjured him like a mirage in the desert when you're dehydrated and start seeing water holes, the brain letting you see what you most desire. But when his arms were around me and his words were patching me back together, I knew he was the real thing, here to save me just like I saved him sixteen years ago.

"I'll take you to the hospital."

"Not the hospital," I say, my voice faint, my words barely making it out. "I've only just come back from there."

"You're hurt."

"Nothing that you can't heal."

"I'm not a doctor."

"I didn't say you were."

Cade takes a tissue from his pocket and dabs at the cut on my cheek. "I'm also not an estate agent."

My mind swims. This doesn't come as a shock. I've always grappled with the idea of Cade as an estate agent, the job never suiting him, never sitting right with what I know about him. I have a thousand questions, but my oxygen-deprived brain can only compute one thing at a time. Why is he here? How did he know? I don't want to ask these questions, though, as I'm frightened this bubble might burst, and he'll vanish into thin air.

"Figures. I always thought you'd be a footballer or a sports coach. What are you, then?"

Regarding me like I'm a precious vase, Cade sighs. "I told you I had something to tell you. I was going to tell you over lunch."

"It's past lunchtime now."

The corner of his mouth curls up. "I guess it is. Better late than never, I suppose." His chest inflates as he grips my hand. "The truth is, I'm not the owner of Malcom and Co., and I never have been."

The room feels slippery again as if it's about to slide out of my reach. What the hell is he talking about? This doesn't make sense.

"If you aren't the new owner, then who is?"

That's when Mathew Bowling walks into the room.

FIFTY-FOUR

ALEX

HE LOOKS OLDER THAN I REMEMBER, HIS SKIN A dark tan, his wrinkles creasing his brow, but he's dressed as sharply as ever in a chequered suit and cream shirt, dated if not smart. He assesses the damage to the kitchen, not even flinching at the sight of his unconscious son on the floor.

"Lexie, I'd like you to meet the new owner of Malcolm and Co."

"You're fucking kidding me."

"Not quite the reception I expected, but considering the circumstances, I won't hold it against you." Mathew Bowling steps over to his son and gives him a little kick.

"He's out cold. I had to hit him," Cade tells him.

"Saves me doing it. You know, it's classed as abuse when a father hits a child. Better that you had to deal it out rather than me."

The coldness of this man sends goose bumps up my arms. "Will someone please tell me what the hell is going on here?"

Mathew glances at me and then at Cade before saying, "She doesn't know anything?"

"No. But she needs to. It's only fair after what your son just did to her."

Mathew holds his hand up. "Spare me the details. I only want to know what I need to know."

"I want the details," I chip in. "I know nothing, and I'm getting annoyed with this cloak-and-dagger thing."

Cade drags up the chair opposite me, then sits down and pulls both my hands into his lap. "Mathew Bowling bought Malcolm and Co. months ago and has been running the shop from behind the scenes and through me."

"What? Why?"

"He needed someone on the ground, someone who could use the position to their advantage to get close to Bowling Sales."

"Okay, maybe I do need the hospital, because you're not making any sense."

"I can put it a little clearer, Miss…?"

"Alex."

"Okay, Alex, this is the deal," Mathew Bowling begins. "I'm old, and I'm not getting any younger. I retired two years ago and put my son in charge of running Bowling Sales. I thought it was in good hands. I've taught him well over the years and wanted to put my feet up in my old age and bow out at the right time. But I couldn't settle, not until I knew he was taking care of the business I'd worked so hard to build up.

"So, imagine my surprise when I learned from my accountant that there was an issue with the books. He shouldn't have been coming to me with this concern, but I'd worked with Clive Davenport for years, and he had my back. There was money coming in, but he couldn't work out where from. There were irregularities in the figures that didn't quite add up. So, I had a little problem and wasn't sure how to proceed. Then Malcolm and Co. went up for sale, and I saw the perfect opportunity to purchase my biggest rival, eliminate them from the game, and kill two birds with one stone. Enter Cade." Mathew flourishes his palm in Cade's direction. "I hired him to pose as the new owner, to be my eyes and ears, my man on the ground. And, by the looks of things, he's done exactly what I've paid him to do."

Cade stands and pulls an envelope out of his jacket pocket, placing it on the table. "My report is in there. Not that you need it."

"Is it as we thought?"

"I'm afraid so."

"What's going on?" I ask.

Cade stares at me, a man I thought I knew and now seem to know nothing about.

"Shawn Bowling has been using the business to run drugs through. He uses the empty properties on his books as drug drops. I'm sure you'll find some money stashed somewhere in this house from the drop-off that took place today. He's also been using the business to launder the money. I'm not sure what cartel he's working for, but from the photos I've taken, it won't be hard to find out. I've spent the last few weeks tailing him at every opportunity, and I have evidence of all his pick-ups and drop-offs. There's enough there to nail him."

"So, you're with the police?" I shake my head, this new version of Cade appearing before my eyes as if he's transformed in front of me like some shapeshifting being—Cade the Man of Action back from beyond.

"Of course not," Mathew jumps in. "I don't want the police to know what my son has been up to or my business dragged through the mud. I've had to keep this under wraps, and that's why I hired Cade here."

"Hired you?" I search him, looking for the signs, the clues I've missed as to the man he is, the person he's become.

"I'm a private investigator."

FIFTY-FIVE
ALEX

"Are you sure you don't want me to take you to the hospital?" Cade asks as we reach his car.

The sunlight had almost burned my eyes when we'd left the house, Mathew Bowling remaining inside to deal with his son as he saw fit.

"No. I told you, I've spent enough of my weekend in there. I don't want to go back." My hand flies up to my neck as Cade examines me. It's sore, and I'm pretty sure it's bruised. But it will heal. Everything will heal. "What do you think will happen?"

"With what?" Cade opens the passenger door for me, having decided to drive me home without finishing the rest of the day.

Which is fine with me. I can't go back to the office with a cut on my face and the bruising around my neck. I've only just pacified Donna — I don't want to get her riled up again. Cade will pick my car up for me later and bring it back to my house.

"Mathew and Shawn."

"I've no idea. It's their business now. My job is done."

I slide into the car and watch as Cade stalks around the front of the car. Cade the Private Investigator, not the estate agent. He has never been an estate agent.

After he climbs in next to me, we sit, him blinking at me as we adjust to the calm of his car.

"Are you okay?"

"Okay?"

"I feel like we've been here before."

I nod. We have, and it was just as hard.

"What did he do to you?"

"It's not what he did, Cade. It's what he could've done if you hadn't shown up," I redirect, as there's no point telling him. "Besides, if I tell you, you'll only march back in there and kill Shawn with your bare hands and get locked up for murder, and I'll lose you all over again. I can't do that. Not again. Not ever."

"It's the only thing stopping me from doing exactly that."

"I just can't help feeling shut out that you couldn't tell me any of this." It's childish of me, I know this. He had a job to do. I wasn't part of that job until now, and I wasn't exactly welcoming when he first arrived.

"I wanted to, but it was too risky. Everyone had to

believe I was the new boss. I thought everything was blown when Jess showed up."

"She knew?" This hurts. It shouldn't. But it does.

"It's how we met." Cade glances out the window. "She hired me because she thought her husband was cheating on her."

"And was he?"

"No. He was just working long hours and drinking himself into an early grave because of the stress of his job."

"So how did you end up with her?"

"Even though he wasn't cheating on her, their marriage was over. There was a reason he wasn't coming home to her, a reason he turned to the bottle and worked every night. Hiring me just gave the marriage the push it needed. She said I'd helped her realise she didn't love him anymore. So, she left him for me."

"I can't pretend I'm happy you kept me in the dark about this or that you've deceived us all for such a long time, but I do understand."

"Really?" He turns to me, reaching out for my hand.

"Don't get me wrong, I'm smarting inside, but I'm too relieved just to be alive right now to be upset about you having pulled the wool over our eyes."

"I was going to tell you today."

"And you have, as promised and right on schedule, if minus the lunch."

"I have a mint in the glove compartment if you're hungry."

Leaning my head back, I laugh, but it hurts my throat. Cade strokes the back of my hand, his finger tracing the red marks where Shawn had gripped my skin. He tenses, sucking the air out of the car.

"They'll fade. It will all fade," I tell him as I smooth my hand over his. "And eventually, it'll disappear, just as long as you're here."

Slipping his hand around my waist, he pulls me onto his lap. Straddling him, I lace my fingers behind his neck, the heat from his skin spreading over my palms.

"I'll be with you when you sleep, when you breathe, when you dream, when you wake. I'll be with you when the sun rises and when it sets. I'll be here when you're sad, happy, and downright moody. I'll be with you when it rains, when it snows, when the sun is too hot to go out, and when the wind is so strong, it'll nearly blow you over. I'll be here every waking moment for the rest of your life because I'm going to live with you, marry you, kiss you, fuck you, make love to you, bathe you, feed you, laugh with you, cry with you, and grow old with you, all of you, every fucking inch of you until they lower me into the ground, because that's the way it's supposed to be. You won't do anything on your own ever again. Not without me."

Biting my lip to hide the wobble, I gaze into his eyes. "What about my mum?"

His face scrunches up. "What about her?"

"We can't go through life avoiding her."

"Lexie, I don't give a shit about your mum. I don't care if you decide you never want to see her again, and I don't care if I have to hide in the cellar if she comes over on Christmas Day. I don't care if I have to face her on our wedding day and plaster the biggest fucking smile on my face and tell her everything is forgotten. I don't give a damn if I have to hand my son or daughter over to her for her to be the doting grandparent. I don't give a flying fuck how hard I have to push my hatred of her down if it means getting to spend the rest of my life with you, which is where I belong." He pushes my hair behind my ear, then wipes at the tears rolling down my cheeks.

"You promise?" My throat feels tight again, but it's nothing to do with the bruising around my neck.

"I promise, Lexie."

Falling forward, I press my lips to his, sealing his words with my mouth so that they can't escape, can't leave the confines of his car.

They're inside me now, trapped in my heart where they will stay forever along with Cade, who I will never be without and who will never be without me.

EPILOGUE
ALEX

Three Months Later

My kitchen feels different, less stark, less clinical. It has nothing to do with the cluster of utensils on the work surface or the splodges of tomato sauce smearing the tiles behind the hob and everything to do with the man who greets me with arms wide open, a chef's apron knotted around his waist, and a dazzling smile.

"Whatever you're cooking smells divine." I hum as my stomach almost claps in appreciation at the aromatic aroma.

After planting a kiss on my forehead, Cade cradles my head, examining my face as if looking for evidence of the kind of day I've had.

"I've missed you," he says once he's convinced I've made it home unscathed.

"We met at lunchtime, which was only four hours ago."

"Four hours too long." Cade smiles, and every knot that's accumulated in my back whilst I've been hunched over my desk today eases.

He releases my head, and I let my bag slide from my shoulder and slump to the floor before shaking out of my jacket and throwing it over the back of one of the chairs of our newly acquired dining table—something I'd never needed when eating alone.

Cade returns to the hob to stir the simmering sauce.

"How was your day? Sold any houses?"

"Jeez, anyone would think you were my boss."

He arches his eyebrow as I quirk my lips, the memory of him being just that still fresh on the fringes of my mind.

"Speaking of bosses," Cade says, "how's Ian doing as the new manager of Malcolm and Co?"

"He's doing great. A natural. I was so relieved when Mathew Bowling offered him the position and wasn't intent on running the business himself."

"You still don't like him?"

"He's not a people person, never has been, and a leopard doesn't change its spots. I'm more than happy for him to operate behind the scenes. Ian is the perfect boss, even if his choice of ties is rather garish."

After discovering the truth about Mathew Bowling

being the real owner of Malcolm and Co., we had to come up with a cover story, as Mathew didn't want his son's dirty dealings to become common knowledge. So, between myself, Cade, and Mathew, we cooked up a story that Cade and I had decided we couldn't work together and be in a relationship, something which felt close to the truth, and so Cade had decided to sell the business to none other than Mathew Bowling.

Although appreciating our decision, Donna and the team had been hit hard by the news. They'd taken a real shine to Cade, not surprisingly, and were worried about what working for a man like Mathew Bowling would be like. Ian had been the least phased by the new turn of events and seemed more concerned about what Cade would do for work now he was relocating to Harton to be with me. But Cade had reassured him by saying he fancied a career change and was thinking about setting up his own business.

"Not another estate agent, I hope?" Ian had asked with a light chuckle.

"Don't worry. There's no danger where that's concerned. I'm thinking of something entirely different," Cade had told him, knowing full well he was going to relocate his PI business up here.

We'd all been worried about the future of Malcolm and Co., whether a new "hot shot" boss would be drafted in or, even worse, Mathew Bowling himself would take hold of the reins. But Mathew made it

clear he was still intent on enjoying his semi-retire-
ment and didn't want a hands-on position in the firm.
We were delighted when he appointed Ian as our new
manager, something which has proven to be the
perfect move.

Bowling Estates remains our biggest competitor,
now being run by a nephew of Mathew's, yet the
people of Harton are oblivious that no matter which
estate agent they choose, they're still lining Mathew
Bowling's pockets.

"I know my reputation in this town," Mathew had
told us. "I'm like Marmite. People either love me or
hate me. The people who hate me are going to want to
put their houses on the market with Malcolm and Co.,
so what better way to secure my empire than to own
my biggest competitor without anyone knowing."

The man has no moral compass. As I said, a
leopard never changes its spots.

"And what about you?" I ask as I sidle up next to
Cade, taking the spoon out of his hand and stirring the
pot. "How's your day been?"

Cade leans back against the counter and folds his
arms over his apron. "I've sorted most of the paperwork out for the relocation of my business, and the
lease ends on my old office space at the end of this
month, so I've booked to view a small office on the
outskirts of the city centre at the weekend. I was
wondering if you'd like to come and look at it
with me."

"Of course I do." Tipping the spoon to my lips, I sample the sauce, a smoky, spicy tang bursting in my mouth. "This is good. Maybe I don't want you setting up your PI business up here. Maybe I want to keep you as my personal chef and slave."

His face darkens with a delicious grin. "I'm already your personal slave."

"Very funny." I place the spoon back in the pan. "I just hope there's enough work for a private investigator in this town."

"This town had its own drug cartel, which is why I was drafted in the first place," Cade reminds me. "You'd be amazed what goes on in these small towns." Cade rescues the spoon and takes over stirring.

"I have your first job for you if you'll take it."

Cade stops stirring. "Yeah?"

I press my lips together, prepping myself. "I've been talking things over with my counsellor, and a few things have come to light."

Shortly after the incident with Shawn, Cade insisted I have some counselling sessions, which I grudgingly agreed to. But having had several sessions over the last few months, I realise that I should have sought help a long time ago. "In last week's session, we talked about Anna."

"Anna?"

"You remember Anna, my best friend in high school when you first moved in with me?"

"Oh. Wet T-shirt Anna. Of course. How could I forget."

I roll my eyes. "Well, after she alerted me to the fact that you were madly in love with me, she was very invested in our relationship and almost as heartbroken as I was when my mum and your dad separated and you guys moved away. But in typical Anna fashion, she didn't let me lose hope with imaginings of a long-distance romance and love knowing no bounds." My heart warms at the recollection of Anna clutching her hands to her heart and swooning, comparing myself and Cade to Meg Ryan and Tom Hanks in *Sleepless in Seattle* and suggesting that in years to come, we finally reunite at the top of the Empire State Building.

"She was just what I needed when I felt like everything was lost, but then the thing in the kitchen happened." I take a breath, steadying myself. "And I couldn't tell her. She knew something was wrong because I was distraught, a complete mess. But I couldn't bring myself to tell her the truth about my mum and what kind of woman she was. I was ashamed, heartbroken, and not thinking clearly. So, I told her that we'd argued and agreed it wasn't working out, so we split up. I had to stop her from hunting you down as she was adamant things could be fixed and that we were meant to be together. And it was hard, having her be so positive whilst I was dying inside, unable to confide in her for fear of what she would think of me, of my mum. So, I pushed her away, just like I did with you."

Anna tried so hard to reach me, exactly like Cade did. She invited me over to her house, and she tried to get me to go shopping with her or to the cinema; she tried to show me that the world still spun even though I'd fallen off it. She offered me a hand, but I never took it. I closed myself down and pushed everyone away because I didn't think I deserved to be happy. I didn't want my mum to hurt anyone else. I didn't think I was worthy of living a life because my life without Cade was not the one I'd envisaged.

Cade places his hand on my arm, his thumb soothing my skin.

"Anna and her family moved away after we finished school. Her dad got some swanky job down south, and we lost touch. She was a good friend. I see that now."

"So, you want me to find her?"

"Yes. I'm ready to tell her what really happened, to explain why I cut myself off from her the way I did. And I think she would want to know that we found each other, that we're happy."

If nothing, Cade has made me realise that I can't hide from my past. I can't let it shape my future like I have been doing for the last sixteen years.

Cade pulls me into his arms, and I inhale. I didn't think anything could smell better than the sauce he's cooking, but I was wrong.

"Of course I'll find her for you." His lips brush the top of my hair.

"Do you think you could find her, say, in around six weeks?"

Cade leans back, his eyes narrowing.

"Why, what's happening in six weeks?"

"Oh, nothing important. Just you and me and a date with the registrar."

"Oh, that." Cade beams.

"You asked me, remember?"

His smile widens, and I know he's remembering the day, four weeks ago, when he brought me to Smyths Toys and literally pulled me by the arm to the outdoor section where a giant trampoline was on display. Ignoring the strange looks of the shoppers, Cade had unzipped the netting and hauled me inside before telling me to lie on my back and close my eyes. And we'd laid there, oblivious to the shop assistant asking us to get off the display model as Cade had told me to picture the night sky, the vast stars above us, his hand in mine as he'd asked me to marry him.

"I won't forget the way those kids were staring at us like we were nuts."

"Or the store manager coming and telling us we would be removed with force if we didn't get off the trampoline." I laugh.

"It was worth it." He pushes my hair from my face. "*We* are worth it."

He's right. I know that now.

"Oh, my dad called today. He wanted to discuss the dress code for the wedding."

We've agreed on a small ceremony with just Ian and his husband, Mel, Donna, and Ed, who will no doubt be wearing his one-and-only suit, and Mark and his new wife, Pippa, who I met a few weeks ago.

I was nervous about seeing Mark after all these years. Cade told me that after the incident with my mum in the kitchen, he'd returned home and told his dad a rather edited version of what had happened. He'd said Jaquelin had been drunk and tried to kiss him. He said he couldn't tell him the whole ugly truth as he knew his dad would have wanted to report her to the police, but Cade couldn't imagine bringing that down around me. Even back then, he was always thinking about me. I added Cade the Protector to his list of accolades.

There'd been no need to be nervous about seeing Mark again. He hasn't changed one bit, and neither have his jokes, something I pointed out to which he said, "Like all good wines, my jokes get better with age."

At which Pippa had remarked, "Unless it's a cheap wine." We'd all laughed, and it'd been such a good feeling.

"I hope you told him there isn't a dress code."

"Dangerous ground with my dad," Cade says. "He might turn up in his budgie smugglers."

I laugh, placing my hand flat on Cade's chest before narrowing my eyes.

"He wouldn't, would he?"

"Relax. I've told him to dig out his best suit." Cade gulps, and I already know what he's going to say. "Any more thoughts on your mum and the wedding?"

My jaw clenches. "I've not changed my mind, if that's what you mean."

"I just hope you've made the right decision about not inviting her. I hope you're doing it for yourself and not because you're thinking about me."

"I've decided for the both of us. This will be the happiest day of our lives, and she doesn't deserve to share that with us. She lost that right the day she placed her hands on you. That's on her."

The topic of my mother has been a recurring one in my counselling sessions. When I told my counsellor how my mum never appeared to remember what she'd done, my counsellor explained that people often use denial as a defence mechanism, and until she recognises what she's done, there will be no way of reaching her.

"I'll tell her after the wedding."

"Are you sure?"

"Yes. She'll probably tell me it's wonderful news and send me some flimsy congratulations card through the post." I shelve all thoughts of my mum. She doesn't belong here. One day, maybe, but not here, not now.

Cade leans back, his eyes moving to the bag I

abandoned on the floor. "Has Ian got you bringing your work home with you?"

I step back, pull out the brochures sticking out of my bag, and place them on the table. Cade peers down at them.

"What are these?" He sifts through the glossy brochures, a range of three- and four-bedroom properties all larger than my two-bed house, which we both reside in, after Cade sold his apartment and his house down south.

"I just thought that maybe after the wedding, we could look at some houses."

He faces me. "We have a house. Your house. We decided to live here. Together."

"I know we did, but it's just as you said, *my* house. I want a house that is *ours*, and with a name like Mrs Westwood, I will need to reside in a larger property. Besides, we might need the extra space should we decide to… expand."

"Expand?" There's a glint in his eye.

"Yeah, expand, like get a dog or a cat."

His face hardens. "The day you bring a cat home is the day I start wearing no socks with my shoes."

"Okay, maybe not a cat, but a pet or…." My voice trails off.

"Or?"

"I'm just thinking about the future," I tell him.

Cade drops the brochures on the table.

"You are my future, Lexie, you and whatever

animal we decide to adopt. And I don't care where we live, just as long as we're together."

I place my hand on the side of his cheek, just to reassure myself that he's real, that he's here in my kitchen, and he's not going anywhere ever again. Because he is my future, and that's all I can see.

ACKNOWLEDGMENTS

I'm so grateful to everyone at Hot Tree Publishing, but special thanks go out to my amazing editor, Kristin Scearce, for her constant support and guidance and Becky Johnson for all the behind-the-scenes mayhem she manages so well.

I am indebted to my content editor, McKinley Hellenes Krantz, who made the first round of edits so enjoyable. She just "got" me, and that is a rare thing.

Huge thanks to my beta readers, Andrea Robinson and Mandy Pederick, whose eagle eyes polished this book to perfection.

A chef's kiss goes out to Claire from Booksmith Design, who interpreted my vision for the front cover beautifully.

I'd like to thank author Kerry Williams, as without her support and encouragement, this book would never have even been submitted to Hot Tree Publishing.

A heartfelt thank-you to all my readers, friends, and family, and a special shoutout to Susan Hogg and Nicola Dudley, who have been in my corner from day one.

As always, my thanks go out to my children, Dexter and Harrison, who live on cereal whilst I'm in a writing frenzy, and my dog, Mo, who is my little writing buddy.

And finally, immeasurable love and thanks to my husband, Ryan, who has never lost faith in me even when I have.

ABOUT THE AUTHOR

Maria Dean is an author from Yorkshire in England, where she lives with her husband, two boys, and her faithful Boston terrier. Her short stories have appeared in various publications and range from fantasy, sci-fi, and the supernatural, but for the long-haul, her heart remains rooted in romance.
www.authormariadean.com

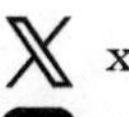 x.com/MariaDeanAuthor
bookbub.com/authors/maria-dean